YOU SHOULD HAVE BEEN NICER TO MY MOM

ALSO BY VINCENT TIRADO

We Came to Welcome You

Burn Down, Rise Up

We Don't Swim Here

YOU SHOULD HAVE BEEN NICER TO MY MOM

A MODERN GOTHIC HORROR

VINCENT TIRADO

wm
WILLIAM MORROW
An Imprint of HarperCollins*Publishers*

HarperCollins books may be purchased for educational, business, or sales promotional use. For information, please email the Special Markets Department at SPsales@harpercollins .com.

hc.com

FIRST EDITION

Designed by Michele Cameron

Library of Congress Cataloging-in-Publication Data has been applied for.

ISBN 978-0-06-338323-4

26 27 28 29 30 LBC 6 5 4 3 2

To my extended family:
You should have been nicer to my mom.

YOU SHOULD HAVE BEEN NICER TO MY MOM

2:04 P.M.

Rain droplets fell like pins against the car window. Small and ineffective at obscuring Xiomara's vision, they traveled down the glass as far as the wind could push them, leaving disconnected trails of water. She stared into the lines and the way they warped the image of any passing foliage, street, or car on the other side of the glass. She wanted to melt into it herself, blur and escape just as quickly.

"Are you listening to me?"

Her father's voice brought her back to reality. He sighed into the cell phone, already knowing the answer to the question.

"Sí, Papi," she lied. Xiomara switched the phone to her other ear, putting space between her and the glass. The rain continued downward. The rideshare driver clicked his signal and turned down another street.

"Mentirosa." Papi chuckled. A quick little sound to let her know he wasn't mad at her. He already knew she didn't want to go there. What kind of person was excited to be surrounded by reminders of the dead? It was not at all an unreasonable assumption. But the truth of the situation was worse. Xiomara didn't want to pretend to be polite and cordial with the very same people who'd done nothing but harass her mom with rumors and lies. She didn't want to hug and give a kiss on the cheek to the same people who would slander her mother's character to anyone who would hear them. Did Papi know this? Of course not—and truthfully, that was by design.

Xiomara didn't want to go anywhere near those people. But Papi insisted. After all, her grandfather Papi Ramon had died, and there was a reading of the will. Xiomara had to go, because it wasn't like Mami could.

She was dead too.

So for just an hour or two, Xiomara would have to grin and bear it. Kiss her aunts and uncles on the cheek and sit still long enough for the lawyer to read out the will.

"Xiomara?" Papi was hesitant.

"I'm still here." She shut her eyes and sank into the leather. She knew this voice all too well. It was the one he put on when he wanted to calmly broach a subject she wasn't comfortable with.

"Are you sure you don't want to me come?"

"No!" Xiomara blurted. The last thing she wanted was for him to deal with the fake concern and well-wishes of her two-faced relatives. Papi was too naive. He would believe it to be genuine, and she didn't want to tell him what they said about his wife when she was still alive. Everything from Mami draining Papi Ramon's wealth for a selfish lifestyle to implying Mami had cheated on Papi. No matter what, Mami had made sure these rumors never made their way back to him—she never wanted him to feel like he'd married into a troubled family. With her gone, it was Xiomara's turn to shield him. Mami never had to ask her to, but Xiomara didn't want to let all those earlier efforts be in vain.

Still, it made Xiomara's blood boil to remember the very first time she realized her extended family couldn't be trusted. She was around five years old, and for one reason or another, her tía Aury was babysitting.

"Are you sure that man is really your father?" Aury had asked.

Xiomara had been very confused by the question, and even more confused by the way her aunt was giggling between her teeth, like she was circling around a really funny joke.

"You can be honest with me. I won't tell anyone!" But then the phone had rung and Aury had busied herself with a conversation.

Later, Xiomara had asked her mother about what Aury meant. She remembered the way Mami's face pinched before she excused herself to get to the house phone. Xiomara wondered what about her made everyone run to phones, but then she heard Mami shouting. It started a whole family-wide fight, with Papi Ramon getting involved as a mediator.

When he asked Aury why she would say something like that to a child, her answer was simple: she didn't. Mami must've made that up just so she'd have an excuse to pick a fight.

"Or maybe Xiomara lied," Aury had said, throwing the young girl under the bus. "Josefina didn't raise her right."

It was the last time Aury was allowed to babysit Xiomara, something she apparently never wanted to do in the first place.

Xiomara cleared her throat now and returned to Papi.

"It's fine. I can handle it. By the time you get here, it'll be over anyway."

"Okay," Papi conceded. "But as soon as it's done, hurry back. There's supposed to be a storm tonight."

Xiomara's eyes skated up to the sky. The hovering clouds indeed looked ready to bring down the heavens.

"I will," she said. "I'll text you as soon as I leave. Love you. Bye." She hung up as soon as she could. If she stayed on the phone any longer, Xiomara was sure that Papi would make up an excuse to come anyway. He wasn't an overbearing father by any means—but when it came to a death in the family, he wanted to make his condolences known, even if it was to the abusive in-laws.

And as much as Xiomara had loved Papi Ramon, she knew that her relatives didn't deserve any sympathy.

The rideshare driver glanced at her through the rearview mirror. He'd been doing that almost since the moment Xiomara climbed into the back seat. If it weren't for the fact the man seemed to have more wrinkles than he had the sense not to stare, she would have thought this was the start of a kidnapping. Or at least the beginning of some toxic masculinity about to rear its ugly head. Instead, the wrinkles just reminded her of Papi Ramon.

"Sorry for your loss . . ." the man said. His thick Dominican accent colored the sentence. "You are one of the Abreus, yes?"

Only technically, she wanted to say. But it didn't matter to them that

Xiomara had her father's last name, Castillo, because she was connected to a greater man.

Xiomara could see in his eyes that he knew exactly who she was—or at least who her family was. It wasn't the first time a stranger knew her family's name before she knew theirs, and it likely wouldn't be the last time. A-B Millennium was a multimillion-dollar corporation that started building its wealth since before Xiomara was born. Its roots began in the Dominican Republic, financing cars and businesses, and then grew enough to create a second base of operations in New York City. It meant that Mami's childhood home was farther north—in Yonkers, rather than the city itself—where the houses were spacious and the family could have a bit of privacy.

Not that the privacy lasted very long. With the creation of the Abreu Scholarship, whose mission was to send young Latinos to college for free, the family became a beacon of hope and a shining example to every immigrant, telling them that no matter where you were from or where you were headed, there was always a way to find success.

I should have never taken those promotional photos when I was a kid. Regret piled on with each moment of recognition.

"Your grandfather was a good man," the driver continued.

I know, she thought. "Thank you."

Soon, the car slowed to a stop. Xiomara exited the car and stood in front of the large two-story home, walls painted dark wine with a faded gold trim around the windows. The overgrown lawn pushed cracks into the pavement, and dandelions took residence in the added space. A broken window was boarded up on the second floor. Xiomara's mouth fell open. This couldn't be it. Not the house she remembered. She was so shaken that she actually looked down at the rideshare app on her phone—it pinged her at Papi Ramon's address. She looked back up at the ramshackle state of the house, shaking her head again. Her grandfather had been a man who valued appearances, always wanting to look his best, and that generally extended to his home.

But Papi Ramon was dead. And before that, he had long been sick. It was only right that his home would match his condition.

Had it truly been that long, though? For the house to look like *this*?

The cold drizzle sapped Xiomara's body heat slowly, and she cursed herself for not wearing a thicker coat. Going to school in California the last couple of years certainly changed her sense of appropriate clothes for chilly weather. She jogged to take refuge under the archway of the front door and lifted a hand to knock—then froze. Something about the house gave her immense pause, the feeling of a field mouse at the entrance of a bear cave. *Or a lion's mouth.* It wasn't just that she was no longer welcome—if she entered, there was no guarantee she would escape.

It had been a while since she had been to see Papi Ramon. Her last visit to this house was after Mami's funeral, and Xiomara just couldn't bear to be around more reminders that she was gone. Which now made it seem like a cruel joke that she had to return, when the only person worth being there for had already been buried. Xiomara glanced at the square bit of plastic perched above the door frame. A circular glass center was fixated on her like an eye.

Right. She had forgotten they'd installed a camera after the break-in all those years ago.

Suddenly, there was movement behind the sidelight. Before Xiomara could brace herself, the door was unlocked and open.

"Xiomara?" A familiar face greeted her first. "Were you just waiting out here?"

Naomi's brows knit together in confusion. Not at her standing outside, but like she didn't know why Xiomara was there at all.

Xiomara tried to hide the prickle of hurt in her chest. "No, I just got here. Am I late?"

The young Haitian-American shook her head. "Compared to everyone else, you're pretty early." Naomi stepped aside, allowing Xiomara entrance into the family home. The slightly older woman's face relaxed into a neutral expression. From the corner of her eye, Xiomara studied her. Naomi was an old friend of the family, one she spent a significant amount of time with from childhood up to her teen years. Yet it had been so long since the two had been together that Xiomara felt she was looking at a different person entirely.

Naomi's dark skin was porcelain smooth, save for the tiny moon-shaped scar behind her ear. The large forehead that she'd had as a child was less pronounced; Xiomara could see she had grown into it.

A spark of guilt ignited with the surprise of seeing Naomi again. A few years ago, Xiomara had gotten a call from Papi Ramon. It was about the break-in that had occurred. His television had been stolen, as well as a handful of old jewelry belonging to Xiomara's grandmother. He wasn't hurt, but Xiomara knew that there was something he wasn't telling her.

"Do you remember Julia?" he had asked. Of course she did. Julia was Papi Ramon's housekeeper. Xiomara liked Julia because although she was a no-nonsense woman who kept the house orderly, she was always kind to the young girl even when Xiomara's own family wasn't. Julia was also Naomi's mother, and the reason the two had become friends in the first place.

"Julia was killed." Papi Ramon tried to hide his sniffling by forcefully clearing his throat. "You should reach out to Naomi. She . . . doesn't have a father, you know, and she shouldn't be alone."

Xiomara's ears were ringing for the rest of that conversation, and she felt a distinct pain in her core. She processed a single detail later—that, mercifully, Julia's death was quick. A single bullet pierced an artery, and she bled out in the hallway on the first floor. It wasn't until an hour later that Xiomara's uncle Rafael had shown up to find her.

Not much else was said. Xiomara remembered hanging up. She remembered looking up plane tickets to fly back for the funeral, only to get a stomach bug the day before boarding the plane. She remembered telling herself she would call Naomi and apologize for not being able to make it.

And now she remembered never making that call. Once the fever broke, Xiomara simply forgot about the recent tragedy and focused on regaining her health.

Since then, Xiomara had wondered about Naomi, but had also thought she had missed her chance to reconnect from that first missed flight. Except Naomi was here now for Papi Ramon's funeral.

If Xiomara thought she had a hard time coming back to her mother's childhood home after her death, she couldn't imagine what it meant for Naomi to be in the same place her own mother had died. Had been *killed*. Maybe that was why Naomi seemed to now be keeping her at arm's length.

It was clear their childhood friendship had all but withered away.

"Is everyone already here?" Xiomara shrugged off the thin coat she wore and folded it awkwardly over her arms. It was less of a question and more of a feeble attempt to resuscitate their relationship.

"Not everyone." Naomi locked the front door. "Just your aunts and, uh, Rafael." The *uh* hit the back of the woman's throat like an *ugh*, but Xiomara couldn't figure out how to ask why she'd reacted like that.

Without another word, Naomi quickly strode away toward the kitchen. The length of the hallway ended at the start of the dining room, where Tía Aury idly sat, doing something on her phone. She was dressed in matching peach blazer and slacks over a sleek beige button-up, a sharp contrast from Xiomara's black jeans, gray shirt, and cardigan. It was like her aunt was running a light-hearted press conference for a country club rather than in a period of mourning.

As Naomi passed by, Aury's eyes darted up once, twice, and then she broke into a toothy grin. Xiomara stiffened, knowing what would come next.

"Xiomaraaa!" Aury's voice boomed loudly. Her chair screeched as she pushed it back and made a beeline to her niece. She wrapped both arms around Xiomara in a half-hearted squeeze, engulfing her in a thick cloud of fruity perfume and planting a kiss right next to her ear.

"How are you?" Aury asked. "Are you looking for a job yet? We could always use more people in Alluria."

Alluria was the women's empowerment skin-care company that Aury had created. Founded by women, for women, it boasted cruelty-free products, partnerships with charities to end domestic violence, and generous maternity leave. A place truly crafted with women in mind, it promised to provide endless opportunities for growth for "average but extraordinary working women."

That was the copy, at least.

It was a noble sentiment . . . that had never made any sense to her. Average but extraordinary? Which one was it? Regardless, Xiomara did not want any part in the company, which was almost certainly a pyramid scheme. She thought back to the way Aury had said it. "*In* Alluria."

Not "at."

Yeah, definitely an MLM scam.

"I'm okay. I've still got a couple of job interviews." Xiomara forced a polite smile, then glanced around the home. "Is anyone else here yet?" On the other side of the hall, Tía Marisa leaned against the wall with a phone pressed against her ear. She waved from afar, with an ecstatic smile that Xiomara could tell was less for her and more for whoever was on the other end of the phone. Aury returned the wave and smile with her own. The moment Marisa turned away, Aury's eyes went sharp. Her voice dropped into a disdainful whisper.

"I hope she doesn't get her heart broken again." Aury's lips pointed to her sister. "She loses her head every time she does. Remember the time her old boyfriend broke up with her after cheating on her and she drove his car into a river?"

Xiomara didn't have to be reminded. The oldest daughter of Papi Ramon was also the messiest. It didn't help that the story—which *she* told in a series of Instagram posts—launched her into influencer infamy. Then a movie was optioned to retell that story, and Marisa got it in her head that she was going to be a movie star . . . until she found out that Sofía Vergara had been cast in her role.

The movie never went into production due to a series of events that caused Marisa to be placed on house arrest with a restraining order set against her. Whatever the reason, Xiomara had learned it was better not to get on her tía's bad side.

"How long has she been dating the new boyfriend?" Xiomara asked.

"With her, who knows? But you know, the longer the relationship, the worse she blows up at the end of it. Just thinking about it makes me need a drink." Aury twisted on her heel and went back to the dining room. "Naomi! Get me a glass of wine. And come get Xiomara's coat."

Xiomara let out a slow breath. The sticky chemical smell of the perfume remained lodged in her throat, along with her own mounting irritation. "No, it's okay. I can handle it!" she shouted for Naomi's benefit.

Where's the lawyer? Papi had told her to get to the house by 2:30 p.m. She assumed this meant the reading of the will was exactly at 2:30, so she arrived a little early. Unless . . .

Xiomara leaned back against the wall once the realization hit her. Two thirty was probably what everyone was told because no one was ever on time. A lot of her family—like her cousins, Yaritza and Henry, were always "fashionably late." So did this mean that the actual start time was 3 p.m.? Had she arrived a whole hour early for no reason?

Goddamnit. This was the downside of avoiding her family for so long: she'd forgotten a lot of their idiosyncrasies when it really counted. Maybe Xiomara could hide in one of the rooms until everyone else arrived. It was a large house to accommodate a large family, so if she really wanted to, she could avoid just about everyone until the reading began.

With an actual plan, Xiomara turned toward both ends of the hall. On one end, Aury sat at the dining room table, right between the storage room and the kitchen. In the other direction, Marisa stood in front of the steps to the second floor, which also happened to be across from Papi Ramon's study. Between the two of them, only one would talk her ear off, but that didn't mean that Xiomara liked Marisa any better. When the woman wasn't attached to a man, she made every other woman her enemy. Xiomara remembered how Marisa made excuses to be alone with her father when Mami was alive. The sheer audacity of the woman made Xiomara want to crack open her skull and see what had gone wrong.

That settled it. The only other place Xiomara could find solace would have to be the library. The memory alone both lifted her spirits and calmed her nerves, birthing a near-instinctive feeling that said, *yes, go to the library*—she would be safe there.

Luckily, it was right across from the front door, just a few feet away from her. The tiny room initially functioned as a coat closet in her mother's days. Then when Mami and all her siblings grew up and moved out, Papi Ramon turned it into a little library—just for Xiomara. Her cousins were never very interested in reading and rarely visited the house as often as she did anyway. It was just a bonus that it was the only way he could get her to stop running around and causing trouble for Julia.

Xiomara wondered if her old books would still be there. Or had Papi Ramon slowly gotten rid of them, the way he'd slowly removed all the coats?

A door squeaked open. To her right, Xiomara spotted Rafael exiting the storage room, rolling cobwebs and dust off his clothes. Like Aury, he glanced at her once, twice, and then smiled with all the warmth of a burning campfire instead of an all-consuming conflagration: cozy and contained and careful not to overwhelm her.

"Hola, Xiomara. ¿Cómo tú tá?"

Approaching him first, Xiomara sank into his hug. Unlike Aury, Rafael wore the lightest touch of cologne that complimented his natural scent. It was an odd comfort but a welcome one considering her sensitive nose was beginning to pick up on how old the house smelled. Like wet moss and fungi.

"Hi, Tío. I'm fine." To her own surprise, she sniffled. She didn't think she was on the verge of tears at all, but being bombarded with so many emotions had the effect of wrenching them from her.

"It's going to be okay." He patted her back. Over his shoulder, Naomi's head poked out of the kitchen. Her eyes fell onto Rafael's back, souring for a moment before disappearing again.

Rafael pulled away. "How's school? Are your grades still okay?"

Xiomara's smile became strained. "I graduated last semester." Not that she expected him to know that. She kept away from him just as much as she did from her aunts. He was mildly better than Aury and Marisa by virtue of having been a little nicer to Xiomara's mother—but when those two tried to tear Mami apart, he hardly ever had come to her defense. Maybe it was because he thought it was all just a catfight. Maybe he thought he was too much of a man to get in between women. Regardless, Xiomara knew that if any of the women in her family started treating her the same as they did her mother, she could rely on no one's help but her own.

So it was best to keep everyone at arm's length.

"That's good to hear." Rafael took in a deep breath.

"Is something wrong?" Xiomara asked.

He shook his head, but as he gave a sweeping look around the hallway, she noticed how wide his eyes were. Like he was doing his best to keep from crying. He cleared his throat forcefully and brought his shoulders up. "It's just been a while. Being here, you know . . ." His words hung in the air. It was clear to Xiomara that Rafael was also not prepared for the emotions they were going to be battling all evening. Aury and Marisa may have quickly moved through the mourning period, but Xiomara and Rafael seemed to still be taking up residence in it.

She could sympathize with him.

She wasn't going to, though.

"Why were you in the storage room?" Xiomara peered around him. The door was already shut, and Rafael hadn't budged since Xiomara approached. If he was hiding something, he wasn't doing a good job of not being suspicious about it.

"Ah, I was just looking for something." He waved her away and turned back into the room. "Something from a few years ago."

"Do you need help—" Xiomara tried to ask, but Rafael had already closed the door behind him. He probably hadn't heard her, she decided. Yet the lack of creaking floorboards clued her in that he hadn't stepped away from the door at all. He simply waited in silence. Xiomara turned away, somehow feeling like she was intruding on his privacy.

Whatever. She wasn't here to dissect every odd movement of her extended family. She was here to find out what Papi Ramon had left her—or hadn't left her—and go home. With any luck, she'd be back in her own childhood bedroom at Papi's house before sunset.

"He's been in there all afternoon," Naomi said, sidling up next to Xiomara.

"All afternoon?" She raised an eyebrow. "He got here that early?"

"Mm-hm. Won't even tell me what he's looking for so I can tell him where to find it."

Xiomara blinked, perplexed by that statement. "Why would you know?"

"Because I'm the home aide . . . ?" Naomi gave her look that said, *no one told you?*

Embarrassment lit Xiomara's cheeks aflame. It was bad enough she'd never gotten around to calling Naomi, but now she was exposing how little she knew about her former friend.

"Oh." She swallowed her guilt. "When did that happen?"

"When Ma died," Naomi said, so nonchalant that Xiomara took an extra moment to process that. She imagined the turn of events that had brought them here. Mami had died, and Xiomara couldn't stand the house, so she'd left behind not just Papi Ramon, but Naomi. Then Naomi's mother was killed, and unlike Xiomara, she didn't have an extended family to lean on. It had been three years since that call should've been made. Naomi would've been freshly eighteen then, and in need of some income to take care of herself. Papi Ramon would've been too kind to turn her down. After all, he was getting too old to be without a home aide, so in a way, they needed each other. It made sense.

Xiomara watched Naomi from the corner of her eye. It had been years, for sure, but somehow Naomi looked just as much the same as a kid as she did now, growing into a version of her mother.

"I'm sorry . . ." Xiomara mumbled. "About your mom."

Naomi's arms tensed for a moment and dropped with a shrug. "Yeah."

Welcome to the Dead Mom Club.

The words were so close to being spoken aloud, but they never made it through Xiomara's lips. It was something that Yaritza had said to her once. Because Yaritza's mother died during childbirth, she seemed like the de facto leader of the club, and welcomed Xiomara with something close to consolation. It only seemed right that Xiomara welcome Naomi into the same club . . . but she also should have done it ages ago.

So instead, she followed Naomi in silence. The younger woman opened the library door first and went in. Xiomara stopped right behind, afraid of what she would find. What if her books were no longer there? Suddenly, Xiomara missed the hours she'd spent reading *Coraline* and *The Phantom Tollbooth* and *Bridge to Terabithia*. She'd run straight to the little library as soon as she crossed the threshold of the front door and wouldn't come out until it was time to go home. In the blink of an eye, the afternoon would have passed and she'd be content.

The memories were magical, and if the books were no longer there, it would only be further proof that her time in Papi Ramon's life had come and gone.

Xiomara took a deep breath and entered.

At first, the dim lighting made it difficult to see the stacks of overflowing boxes huddled against the walls, with a promise to trip anyone who was not attentive enough in their entrance. A pang of hurt shot through Xiomara's heart until her eyes adjusted to the dark. The boxes were all marked *books*. A wave of relief fell over her, and she mentally made plans to get all of them shipped to her new apartment.

"Hey!" Naomi's head peeked up over a tower of boxes in the corner. If she hadn't said a word, Xiomara might not have noticed the little nook at all. "Close the door," she whispered loudly.

The door was closed. "What are you doing?" Xiomara asked. Naomi's head dropped down. Xiomara carefully stepped behind the makeshift cardboard box wall. The light of Naomi's cell phone was the only illumination upon her face as she texted quickly.

"Hiding," she answered. "Every time your aunts see me, they start ordering me around like I work for them."

Xiomara couldn't fault her for staying out of sight, but it begged the question—why was Naomi here? Shouldn't she have gone as soon as the funeral was over?

Unless she's also a recipient in the will. Xiomara wouldn't be surprised if Papi Ramon had left her with *something.* At this point, she was part of the family, even if Aury acted like she was still an employee.

Xiomara crouched next to Naomi, if only to make it seem like she wasn't looking down on her. The home aide sat on a pile of coats, which Xiomara recognized as those of her aunts and uncle. Taking a page out of Naomi's book, Xiomara rolled her coat into a ball and sat on it.

"Where is everyone else?" *Everyone else* meaning Tío Manuel and his two kids, Wanda and Henry. And technically Yaritza should have arrived with her father, Rafael, but it looked like she had yet to make it.

"Not sure," Naomi answered, barely glancing up from her phone. Her thumbs danced across the screen. "Manuel and his kids should be in soon."

"Why didn't Yaritza come with Rafael?"

Naomi brushed a rogue curl away from her forehead. Much of her hair was pulled back into a bun, but the edges were loose and coiled with sweat. Xiomara wondered how hard her aunts were working Naomi.

"I don't know," Naomi responded. "She'll probably be here soon, though."

And if she isn't, her flippant response implied, *it's not my problem.*

Crossing her legs, Xiomara rested against the wall and closed her eyes in quiet reflection. Without Papi Ramon, the house was just a house like any other. It was wood and drywall and concrete, susceptible to infestations like roaches and termites and rodents. Without him, this hardly seemed like the place her mother had grown up. All that was left behind were fond memories found in books and the vermin known as her relatives.

Xiomara felt a twitch. It was on her upper back, right where her neck poured in between the scapulae, the tiniest sensation that could barely be called an itch and would have escaped her attention if not for a distinct feeling, a *hunch,* that something was amiss. If she'd poked and prodded at that little hunch, it might have grown, deep enough to call a rabbit hole and wide enough to swallow her whole.

Not safe, the feeling might have spoken in the same place she'd always felt secure, and she'd wonder why that was no longer the case.

As the situation stood, Xiomara had no reason to think anything of that hunch; she simply scratched the itch.

"Your cell phone's ringing." Naomi nudged her leg. Xiomara hardly felt the vibration of her phone in her pocket. Dread filled her stomach. There could only be one of two people who were calling her at this time—and she'd already spoken to Papi today.

"Hello?"

"H-hey, Xo," Her ex, Marcus, spoke with a smile in his voice that only thinly masked the underlying shaking nerves. "Did you get there okay?"

"Yes, I did." Xiomara pinched the bridge of her nose. "Did you need something, Marcus?"

"I just wanted to make sure you were safe."

Xiomara held back a groan. "I'm safe."

"And, you know, if you needed anything. I'm not too far."

"I'm aware," Xiomara said. Beside her, Naomi hardly perked up at the sound of conversation. If it was Aury, she would've been demanding answers to who Xiomara was talking to—not because she cared, but because Xiomara sounded annoyed and Aury was nothing if not a chismosa—a gossip.

"So . . ." Marcus seemed to be waiting for something.

"So what?" Xiomara turned to the wall.

"How are you?"

Xiomara paused. She considered not answering, if only because the answer itself was complicated.

"My grandfather died, Marcus. How am I supposed to be doing?" She tried to keep the bite out of her voice. Marcus didn't deserve snark. He was sweet, really. Too sweet. The kind of person who was a chronic problem solver. Which could be great, but also meant there was no way to vent to him without him giving unsolicited advice. *No thank you.* She didn't need advice right now—and she definitely didn't need sweet. Xiomara needed *space.* She had told him well enough before she'd flown out for the funeral.

How was she supposed to know that the guy's hometown was Brooklyn?

Maybe if I'd paid attention while dating him, I'd have known. That was just further proof the two were not a good match. Yet she found herself not feeling guilty, but annoyed.

Marcus stumbled through a well-meaning answer but was overshadowed by Marisa's sudden shrieks.

"Ay, where is Naomi? Naomi!" Clacking heels went right by the door and continued down the hall.

Now it was Naomi's turn to hold back a groan.

"When. Will. They. Learn. I. Don't. Work. For. Them?" With each word, she dramatically hit her head against a box. She waited another minute and then slowly rose to her feet. Outside, Marisa was already accusing Naomi of moving her phone charger.

"Aury, did you see where Naomi moved it?" The door hardly muffled her shrill voice. Xiomara watched Naomi wrap a hand around the doorknob. She slowly inhaled and held her breath. On the exhale, her posture straightened and she opened the door.

"Yes, did you need me?" The door clicked shut.

"Xo?" Marcus spoke. "Is everything okay over there?"

No, she wanted to say. *Nothing is ever okay over here.* But if she said that, she would have to elaborate, and the only thing that put her in a worse mood than interacting with her family was talking to someone who thought they could *fix* her family.

"I gotta go." She hung up.

It will just be an hour, she told herself. She could deal with her family for an hour, right? It's not like reading the will could take all night.

2:47 P.M.

Whatever her aunt wanted with Naomi, it meant that Marisa was now away from the staircase. Xiomara peered out cautiously. Perhaps it was the fact she hadn't seen the house in years that gave her trepidation—immense change unsettled her. She learned this when she got an official autism diagnosis. It came late, for sure, spurred by her initial troubles in college, but once she came to terms with it, change became manageable. The first thing she had to do was understand she didn't have to like change—she just had to acknowledge it.

With the obstacle now gone, Xiomara set out to do just that and ascend to the second floor. Her foot nearly broke through the first step. She looked down in shock and found a large split in the wood that she hoped had already been there. A shiny nail stood out to her—Papi Ramon must've had to reinforce the step several times. Clearly, he was not a carpenter. Xiomara skipped over it and climbed the staircase.

Even then, the entire structure creaked loudly under her weight. It didn't use to do that. Xiomara wondered just how much of it was the natural result of her growing up and how much was the house showing its age. The building seemed eager to respond to her, a groan for every step forward. *My, look how big you've grown*, it said. *I remember when you were barely one hundred pounds.* Now she was fifty pounds heavier, and the house could not stop reminding her.

She stopped at the second-floor landing, perplexed at how little time it had taken for her to get there. Didn't it use to take longer? Weren't the steps supposed to be deeper? And why had her shoulders instinctively tensed when she was halfway up? Suddenly, Xiomara recalled another aspect of the library. There'd been many times when she would hear strange noises from above. The sound of something clawing at the floor with a great thud. Papi Ramon would claim that it was only rats—which would be bad enough—but to Xiomara, the clawing sounded like it came from something much larger than a rat. Like a dog.

Or a wolf.

And right then, on the stairs with that memory, she was a deer. Her hair stood on end, an odd sense tingling that she was being watched, and not by anything human. It set off an alarm in her head, and while she jolted in spirit, her body took to freezing. But she was safe as long as she did not look back.

Why?

The question both surprised and scared her; the answer was rooted in childhood fantasies. If she didn't look back, didn't look under her bed, didn't sleep with one limb hanging out from under her bedsheets, the monster would not get her. It was silly, the way this logic worked, yet she tended to not question her gut. After all, trusting her gut had never steered her wrong before. Why would it now?

Except it did *steer me wrong.* Right when she entered the house, unease had hit her like a wall. Sitting in the library, it had intensified. She felt like she should've turned tail and run, but she didn't, and nothing so terrible happened to make her regret it, did it?

Maybe not yet.

Xiomara couldn't help but question every feeling she discovered upon arriving. Ever since she'd pulled up to the house, things had felt . . . *off.* Or rather, the house had always felt off to her, and it was as if her time away had shielded her from that memory.

Well, the memory was back, and it was throwing her world out of whack and making her question so many things.

The only answer she got from her body was a set of tense shoulders and shaky knees. Her memories impressed upon her the need to not turn back. It was truly visceral too: the sensation began at the base of Xiomara's spine and traveling upward, the conviction that something would be waiting for her if she so much as spared a glance.

Don't look, don't look, don't look, her thoughts chanted as if it were normal. It was almost jarring. The fear was familiar—like she was *always* afraid of the stairs and just hadn't remembered until this very moment. She wondered what would happen if she *did* look back. What sort of consequence awaited her if she disobeyed? Audacity forming, Xiomara turned on her heel and gazed down the staircase.

There was nothing. Just a normal, if old and rickety, set of stairs.

She scoffed at her fear. Reality snapped in—she was never afraid of the stairs. What she *had* been afraid of was what she always felt watching her from the stairs—and from much of the house. Xiomara had forever felt *something* lurking in the corners and shadows and bathrooms. Something she couldn't quite parse. Eyes coming from places a person could not always fit.

Eyes that always made her think, *Maybe it wasn't a person.*

Xiomara lingered with *that* thought for a moment, still not moving. She wondered if it was the sound of the pounding rain, or the miasma of animosity toward her family (and Naomi's animosity toward *her*), or Papi Ramon's lingering death, but this house that had always been so welcoming now suddenly felt *other.*

She looked down the hallway. It mirrored the first floor—long, with several doors on each side, four to her left and three to the right. The floral wallpaper peeled intermittently, exposing wooden paneling, like wounds. She traced a finger up and down the torn edges as she trailed down the hall, wondered exactly when it had started to fall apart. She remembered what it had looked like when she pulled up in the Uber, and thought it was like the house itself was sick. Infected. A virus that was once confined to a single moment now spreading itself over the vast length of the house. Or maybe the house had always been this imperfect, and the mask could no longer be maintained.

Xiomara tried to recall the last time she was here, because she couldn't picture the house ever looking like this. Couldn't believe Papi Ramon would *let* the house look like this.

Has it been so long? Xiomara thought.

It's been years, a voice supplied, not quite her own.

Shortly after Mami's funeral, she remembered once again, and it took her a moment to realize she'd already been through this. It was like her memory was on a loop, and yet she let it play out anyway.

She had stayed for a week, and though Papi Ramon insisted that she stay longer, Xiomara had to get back to school. And while that was a legitimate excuse, it wasn't the only one. Xiomara just couldn't stay in the same place her mother had grown up. She couldn't stomach sleeping in the same bed that Mami had slept in. It was bad enough that she saw Mami every time she looked in the mirror. She had seen pictures of her mother when she was younger—Mami was slender with a round face and a mole on her earlobe. And while Xiomara had no mole, the older she got, the more she could see that picture looking back at her, in the curves of her cheeks and the folds of her eyelids.

When Mami was still alive, she would brag to her friends about how similar Xiomara was to her, even in personality. Xiomara was well-behaved, quiet, didn't cause trouble, and above all, always listened to her elders. Maybe that was why Papi Ramon had wanted her to stay longer. She looked and acted so much like Josefina. And Josefina was Papi Ramon's favorite child.

If he could see her now, she was sure he would mistake her for his youngest daughter.

That brought out a bitter laugh, and the echo startled her for just a second—she hadn't realized how quiet it was compared to the stairs. Did anyone else have these same emotions? The same sudden realizations that lent to distant memories they'd thought were long forgotten? Rafael seemed to be having a few. Aury and Marisa appeared entirely detached. And Naomi—well, Xiomara couldn't imagine that the home aide would be struck by nostalgia, having never really left the house at all.

Grief. Xiomara settled on that word for explanation. She was grieving and feeling guilty, and the combination of the two was heightening all the wrong senses, twisting her perception of what used to be against what simply *was*. The truth was she loved her grandfather dearly, and was attempting to justify her absence in the last few years of his life.

The only thing wrong with Papi Ramon's house was that he was gone.

Xiomara stopped in front of his bedroom door. Across from it had been her mom's room. It was strange the way she felt like there was a direct line between the two. A link that kept the other's memories alive. Through Xiomara, Mami could relive her childhood. To Papi Ramon, Xiomara was a lovely reminder of the daughter he favored.

Without either of them, Xiomara was an anchor without a ship, weighed down and unable to stop as she continued down the length of the hallway. As a child, the house had felt so big to her that it might as well have been the size of the whole world, with undiscovered secrets lying in wait. But right now? It felt snug. And with the rest of her extended family coming for the will reading, *snug* didn't mean cozy. It meant suffocating.

Somehow she knew it was only going to get tighter.

She looked away from the doors, to the end of the hall, where a window that seemed to have been glued shut did little to let in the gray light from outside. It hadn't always been glued shut, Xiomara remembered. Her grandmother left it cracked to keep the air from going stale—when had that changed again?

Do you want to fly?

Xiomara shuddered and turned away, rubbing that small spot behind her neck until it was soothed. Her gut told her to head back downstairs, to leave the second floor and return to the library immediately. She frowned at the impulse, not knowing where it came from. None of her memories were so bad that they validated the apprehension she felt, constantly buzzing beneath her skin. Sure, Xiomara was too afraid to venture up the steps alone—*the eyes*—but the rest of her childhood memories were largely positive. She stalked forward, pushing against the unknown phobia of the window while relaying the good memories in her head. Xiomara either played with Naomi in the library, watched cartoons in the dining room, or sat in Papi Ramon's study while he regaled her of the time he'd been a pastor.

Oh, right. He used to be a pastor. How did she forget about *that*? It was back in DR, before Mami was born but sometime after Marisa. He was very poor as a pastor, and so he and Xiomara's grandmother, Mami Inez, struggled. With his last thousand dollars, he decided to create his own business—A-B Millennium—and only flourished from there. It was like God had decided to reward him for all the years he'd spent guiding His sheep. There were entire hours dedicated to Papi's experience as a pastor, while she was still small enough to fit on his lap. Mostly on Sundays, because Xiomara always got in trouble for falling asleep between the pews and Mami was so embarrassed she'd want Papi Ramon to set her straight. But each time, Papi Ramon would only chuckle and bounce his adorable (his words) granddaughter on his knee while she complained about how tedious Sunday school always was.

"What about church is so boring?" he asked.

"All we do is sit and pray." She pouted. "Or stand and pray. Or kneel and pray. Can't you just teach me how to do what you did?"

"Preach?" he teased.

"No! Egg-sersize!"

Xiomara blinked. The memory had hit her like a slap upside the head. Papi Ramon wasn't just a pastor—he was an *exorcist.* A traveling one, if she remembered correctly. What a strange background for a successful businessman. Back then, Xiomara was too young to know anything about demons or that an exorcist had to be appointed by the Vatican.

And she was pretty sure the Vatican had never once approached Papi Ramon for such a thing. For one thing, he was Pentecostal, not Catholic. And no governing body within *that* denomination decided who could and couldn't be exorcists. She'd remember if that were the case, otherwise. Except . . .

Would I?

For she was finding that memory was a tricky thing, and in the hour she had been at home, she'd already been assaulted by odd recollections she had no choice but to consider as facts, while "remembering" things that seemed like they should have been ingrained in her. Xiomara rubbed the back of her head, nearly sent into vertigo by the memory of Papi Ramon doubling over in laughter. He always thought her awkward pronunciation of the word *exorcist* was the cutest thing in the world.

What he didn't find so cute was when she kept going.

"He didn't like talking about demons," Xiomara said out loud as if to her reflection. It moved in time with her as she dug a little deeper to why. Unpleasant thoughts suddenly jumped to the surface. When the topic came up, he couldn't help but shift his eyes around, as if searching for something. He'd try to hide it in that laugh of his, but once Xiomara realized it, she couldn't stop noticing it. And once she did, she would push. Most of the time, Papi Ramon made an excuse to get away, once even practically dumping her off his lap to "take a call."

Except one time . . .

She remembered it, or "remembered" it—whichever it was didn't matter. But in that moment, Papi held a stern facial expression. His eyes went tight and he squared his jaw, and at the time, she thought she was in trouble, like she had asked about something forbidden. Looking back, however, she didn't read annoyance in his expression.

She read absolute terror.

He forced his eyes straight ahead, as if avoiding the gaze of some creature as he leaned over and whispered into her ear. She listened now for those words . . .

And found she couldn't hear anything. What did he say? Why couldn't she remember? Bits and pieces of information slipped in between blinks, but nothing she could latch onto until, suddenly, the tangential answer appeared in her mind: that of her wetting the bed for weeks. Of Josefina getting sick of washing the sheets daily. He'd said something unpleasant—so horrific that it had scarred her as a child. But where was that scar now?

What the hell did Papi Ramon say to me?

"Demons are . . ." She struggled to find the word, find the memory. Her mouth felt like a broken record, skipping back to the start of the sentence but never finishing it. "Demons are . . . demons are . . ." Xiomara watched her reflection in a daze when it finally answered for her.

"Crafty."

"¡Hola, Manito!"

Aury's voice shot through the floorboards, jolting Xiomara out of her thoughts. God, that woman had a set of lungs on her. She lacked both an inside voice and tact, determined to announce arrivals to everyone in a ten-mile radius. Xiomara glanced down the hall and then back to the window. Her reflection seemed to have grown more transparent. Xiomara rubbed her eyes with a vigor that felt motivated by unique fear.

Get away, get away, get away, GETAWAY—she could not fend off the sudden distress until she looked again to confirm that her reflection remained transparent. Of course it did. Window reflections were *always* transparent, unlike mirror reflections. And she wasn't in front of a mirror, was she? Xiomara took in a deep breath and shed the uncertainty that clung like a second skin. A fog rested over her mind as she turned her attention back to the family that arrived.

If Tío Manuel is here, then Henry and Wanda probably are too.

She wasn't any more excited about that prospect than anything else happening in this house today. Xiomara's cousins were respectively nine and five years older than her, and acted as though they lived on another planet altogether. Wanda had adopted her father's Pentecostal holier-than-thou attitude, which made it difficult for anyone to carry on a conversation with her if it wasn't about the Bible. And Henry made brand names a personality trait. If he wasn't decked out in Louis Vuitton, it was Burberry, or Gucci, or some other luxury apparel.

Personally, Xiomara couldn't understand it. When Mami had spoken about Papi Ramon's hardship as a pastor, she'd mentioned that the family had been so impoverished that all of the kids had had to learn to share pairs of shoes. Yet, Manuel was also a pastor, and he was on his way to building a second megachurch. *Maybe their styles in sermons were different.* Not that she'd ever find out—she had no intention of ever stepping into one of Manuel's buildings.

Xiomara descended the steps slowly and carefully.

Once upon a time, she'd read an article that outlined the mark of a wealthy person. It went beyond the usual clues, like clothing and cars, and instead focused on the subtle politics of scent. What was a better symbol of status and leisure than a temporary sensation? After reading that, Xiomara couldn't stop noticing it among her older relatives. Aury liked to pile on sweet fragrances until it burned nostrils, Marisa preferred the smell of vanilla bean (believing it classy), Rafael's cologne was a kind of bergamot blend.

Even Papi, who didn't truly experience upward mobility until he married into the family, had begun wearing Aēsop Rōzu EDP after Mami gifted it to him for their anniversary. Naomi barely smelled like anything other than the soap used to shower and household cleaning products. Scent was a tried-and-true method of distinguishing the upper class from the lower.

And what would Manuel's scent be? Xiomara could guess. For a man who'd become a pastor just like his father had been, while still attending the family business just like his father had, who was his father's first child and therefore had had a special connection with his father—for a man like *that*, Xiomara could only imagine that he'd find his way along to a specific Ralph Lauren brand.

She stopped at the bottom of the steps. Manuel was already developing gray hair and crow's feet, but his wrinkled hands still looked strong and steady. He peeled off his light jacket and handed it to Naomi, who pursed her lips tight in response. Force of habit had made her open the door, and now it was force of habit that shoved her back into the role of housekeeper.

"Hey, Naomi. You're looking good." Henry acknowledged her with a sweep of his eyes. Naomi tightened her grip on their coats as she stepped away, stoic expression souring into revulsion. Her reaction prompted a cheeky laugh from him.

"Hi, Tía." Wanda waddled over to Aury with a kiss. Her ankle-length jean skirt made her strides short and slow. Henry had to match her gait as he followed. What Henry lacked in height, he made up for in broad shoulders. The stocky young man had never been able to hide his playful nature, earning the nickname "Chico" when he was a youth. Now he picked up Aury in one sweeping hug and spun her around, showing off his strength.

"Chico, put me down!" Aury laughed. He did, and then picked up Marisa right after.

"When did he get so strong?" Marisa swatted his arm with just as big a grin.

"Aury, Marisa, ¿cómo están? Where's Rafael?" Manuel asked. Henry's father was stoic as ever, preferring to keep a respectful distance from his siblings. It was like he didn't want their sin rubbing off on him.

Upon hearing his name, Rafael's head poked out of the storage room. "Manito! ¿Qué lo que?"

"I'd be better if you stopped calling me that," Manuel complained, crossing his arms. "I'm older than all of you, you know."

"Yeah, but it doesn't show." The youngest sibling gave him a hard pat on the back, nearly shoving him forward. Rafael was a beanpole compared to him. He stood over his older brother with inches to spare.

"Uh-huh. Is everyone here already?" Manuel searched the rest of the hall with his eyes—and immediately caught sight of Xiomara. She stilled for what seemed like years while the family continued on between them.

"Everyone but Yaritza and the lawyer." Aury sighed. "What was his name? McClaren?"

"You would think lawyers would be more punctual," Marisa complained.

"He's not supposed to be here until three—give him time," Rafael said. "Besides, I don't think he's been here before."

Henry asked, "Didn't he have to visit Papi Ramon at least once? Naomi, you've met him, right?"

Xiomara wasn't sure what Naomi's response was—the voices blurred and melted into the background. Xiomara's feet took her to Manuel, and her arms wrapped around his waist, moving as a puppet led by strings and certainly not affection. It was simply obligation. And when he kissed her on the cheek, she could feel the obligation in that greeting as well. No warmth or kindness; the two might as well have been strangers.

If only.

To twist the knife, when Xiomara breathed, she recognized Papi Ramon's scent easily. Polo EDT—a mature blend of pine, leather, and tobacco.

Papi Ramon's favorite.

It played on his natural smell differently, so it didn't *exactly* smell like Papi Ramon, but it was close enough that Xiomara nearly closed her eyes and imagined she was hugging her grandfather.

"You've gotten so big, Xiomara," he murmured, just loud enough for her to hear. "You look so much like your mother. I hope you're making better decisions than her."

And there it was—the reason she usually kept her distance. She didn't respond. Instead, Xiomara held her breath. If she so much as exhaled, it would be with a string of curses. This was his greatest sin, in Xiomara's opinion: this ludicrous sense of superiority. People made the mistake of believing him to be a humble person of integrity because he didn't flaunt his wealth or gossip behind anyone's back. As a pastor, he had to be above all that. And she supposed he was—on the surface. Manuel was too good for the dirt, so he had to float above the clouds.

That was why it was difficult to breathe around him. He smelled insecurity like a shark smelled blood. Xiomara understood why his ex-wife had left him.

Still engrossed in their own conversations, the family moved into the dining room and sat around the long oval table, each in the chair they always seemed to gravitate toward. Xiomara hung back, falling in step with Naomi.

"Full house," Naomi remarked. Xiomara hummed a quiet "Mm-hm," then said, "I remember thinking the house was so big when I was younger."

Naomi nodded. "You and me both."

Xiomara mentally stalled, wishing she had more to say. There was a familiarity to this moment, a recognition of the pattern. Xiomara and Naomi would be talking, idly chatting among themselves about books or cartoons or about Papi's stories, until the conversation fizzled to nothingness. Xiomara would get the impression that she had to say something—anything—but the longer they passed in silence, the less equipped she felt to disrupt it.

"So, um, about the funeral—your mom's funeral—"

"It's fine." Naomi cut her off. "You were sick. Don't worry about it."

Was Naomi just saying that? Xiomara inspected her expression, taking an almost scientific guide in analysis.

"You're staring," Naomi pointed out.

"Sorry," she said, still not turning away. "It—it's been a while since I've been here, and I just don't know what to do with myself when I'm with them." Xiomara's eyes made a sweeping motion to her relatives. Naomi matched it, pursing her lips and flaring her nose as if she was fighting an impulse. "Stick with me, then." She sighed in defeat. "It'll be like old times."

"I'd like that." Xiomara felt relief loosen her shoulders. It was nice to have at least *one* ally in the house.

"What was that phone call earlier?" Naomi suddenly asked, referring to her talk with Marcus. "You sounded upset."

The question sent a spike of adrenaline through Xiomara's body. Her eyes darted around the rest of the family, who spoke and laughed too loud to have heard Naomi. She probably knew they wouldn't—or at least, they had gotten used to blatantly ignoring the home aide until they needed something from her. Still, it wasn't something Xiomara even wanted a hint of interest in from them.

"Naomi, get me a glass of water." Marisa waved her hand.

Saved by their rudeness.

Marisa's eyes barely met Naomi's, and the younger woman took it in stride, only rolling her own eyes the moment she turned her back. She soon returned with a water bottle in hand . . . only for Marisa to refuse it.

"Ay, no, it's too warm," she said, lips curling in exaggerated disgust.

"There's no ice," Naomi informed her. She kept her tone flat and uninterested during the whole interaction, as if not willing to extend it further than she needed.

"What? Why is there no ice?" Marisa questioned.

"The refrigerator's busted," Naomi answered, with barely a blink. Xiomara frowned, noting the way the home's imperfections packed on. Didn't Papi Ramon love to chew ice? He'd blamed it on old age and kept the ice maker fully operational in preparation for his children to pick up the habit. Marisa passed a look of exasperation to her siblings. "How many times did I tell him to just buy a new fridge?" she asked. "That thing is always busted! There has to be cold water somewhere in the fridge. Maybe it's all the way in the back—go check." And again, Marisa waved Naomi off. She went without complaint, but the grip on the water bottle told Xiomara something else. She followed her into the kitchen and watched her fill a glass with cold tap water instead.

"You can just tell her no," Xiomara offered. Yet Naomi shot a look that said, *no, I can't*, heading back to the dining room before Xiomara could press her as to why. Marisa's outstretched hand practically snatched it from her.

"This isn't tap water, right?"

"No," Naomi lied.

Marisa gulped down half of it and gave the glass back to Naomi. "That's much better."

Naomi disappeared to the kitchen once more. Xiomara had a feeling the home aide would be making herself scarce for the rest of the evening. She wanted to follow her out, but the opportunity was snatched from her by the same demanding aunt.

"Xiomara! It's been so long since I've seen you. Come sit!" Marisa gestured to an empty seat across from her. "How are you? Are you dating anyone yet?"

Xiomara felt herself puff up defensively before she let out a sigh. She sat down on the edge of the seat, not so comfortable that she couldn't jump up at a moment's notice.

Don't react too strongly. The more she did, the more her family would pick at her.

"I'm good. And no, I'm not—I'm not dating anyone." She shook her head, despite thoughts swimming around Marcus and wondering if she had slipped on social media at some point. No—she was sure they didn't know about him. Because if they did, they would immediately descend on the topic like vultures to corpses. Not even bones would be left.

No, Xiomara knew this game too well. Keep to herself and there would be peace. Divulge too much information and it would only be weaponized against her, just like with her mother, made into rumors and ill-informed stories meant to slander her character—all in the name of familial "love" and "concern." Xiomara folded her hands on her lap, refusing to budge even when Marisa's eyes pinched.

"You're so *quiet*. Were you always like this?" Marisa cackled. "By the way, Aury, you should come with me on my trip to Aruba . . ."

The conversation seemed to quickly shift away from Xiomara. She let out a deeper breath, then slipped out of her chair to join Naomi back in the kitchen. The home aide stared out of the window while drinking from the water bottle Marisa had refused.

"Like old times, huh?" Xiomara asked, with a forced laugh as if to make the joke land. Naomi didn't respond until the bottle was half-empty.

She looked absentmindedly to Xiomara and, like an instinct, blurted, "Huh? Yeah."

I will take it, Xiomara thought and leaned against the kitchen counter. As awkward as it initially felt, she welcomed the silence between her and Naomi. At least she could tell it wasn't a pointed passive aggression.

"So . . . why *are* you here? Did Papi Ramon leave you something in the will—"

"Shh!" Naomi waved her hand. "Lower your voice!"

Xiomara's eyes flew open. So he did. But how would Naomi already know? Did even *she* know what was written in the will? How could she, but not Xiomara?

She knew Naomi couldn't—or wouldn't—answer any of those questions. But one felt like it couldn't go unasked. "What did he leave you?"

Naomi peered through the doorway before answering. "I don't know. He said he wanted me here because he was going to leave me something.

In the meantime, I'm letting your family be your family," she said, negative connotation purposefully applied, "just so I can find out what I got. Don't say anything, okay?"

Xiomara felt the air lighten. Every good interaction with Naomi meant she was already shaping up to be a better friend.

"Okay," she said, burying a grim satisfaction next to the pang of short-lived jealousy. "I won't say anything. I promise."

Naomi crushed the empty water bottle in her hand and tossed it in the trash can. "So, what was with that phone call earlier?"

Xiomara's mouth flapped open and closed. An explosion of laughter out in the dining room jolted her, but between her family and Naomi's growing irritation, Xiomara knew who she was much better off with. And if Naomi trusted Xiomara enough to reveal the reason behind her appearance, why couldn't Xiomara divulge a little information about her personal life? It would be the start of mending their friendship.

"His name's Marcus." Xiomara shrugged. "We dated for a bit before I broke up with him. He still wants to get back together."

Naomi raised an eyebrow. "He told you that?"

"No." She shook her head. "You can just kind of . . . tell."

Having come from a family where everyone spoke in conniving half-truths and spread rumors like they were currency, it should have been a refreshing change of pace for Xiomara to meet someone who wore their heart on their sleeve. She never had to guess his feelings, or double-check what he said to make sure it matched with his actions. Marcus was always open and honest with her, the perfect picture of a man without a debilitating sense of toxic masculinity.

And yet she just . . . couldn't ease herself into it. Couldn't relax in a relationship where the other person was so lovely that she felt like thorns in comparison. Maybe her extended family had poisoned her against the idea of happiness.

Maybe it was genetic.

Maybe it was something more. Something constantly lurking, out of sight, but that instincts kept Xiomara aware of.

"What about you?" Xiomara asked. "Dating anyone?"

Naomi scoffed. "Me? With what time? Do you know how much of a handful your grandfather was? I never had a moment of peace. I was so busy!"

Considering the size of the house, Xiomara believed it. Before Papi Ramon's health began to decline, it was probably easier to just focus on cleaning—but soon enough, she'd heard he needed help with grocery shopping and meals. She had just assumed her grandfather hired more staff. They could certainly afford it.

Apparently not.

"And when he wasn't running me ragged, the man was so paranoid, there were days he refused to let me in the house unless I proved who I was." Naomi threw up her hands.

Xiomara's face slackened. This was the first time she heard of these issues. And how could she? She hadn't visited since Mami died. Had he developed Alzheimer's in such a short time?

"And he only got worse after . . ." Naomi's voice trailed off. Her eyes fell to her hands, finding interest in picking her nails.

After Julia died.

Xiomara's stomach clenched for her childhood friend. She should have visited, if not for Papi Ramon, then for Naomi. If she had, maybe his health wouldn't have declined so quickly. It wasn't unheard-of for people to die of a broken heart.

And Papi Ramon's heart was surely already broken after Josefina's death.

After a moment of silence, Naomi cleared her throat. "Anyway, no. I haven't had the time to meet anyone. Not that I want to. Have you seen Henry? Men these days are a mess."

Xiomara snorted. "What's wrong with Henry?"

"Are you kidding?" Naomi raised an eyebrow. "It's pretty obvious."

Well, if she were talking about what was *obvious* about Henry, the first thing Xiomara would think of was his allegiance to name brands. He was fixated on them, glowing whenever someone noticed his new Nike sneakers—which weren't particularly extravagant by themselves, but when you weighed in his personal collection that included the latest designs and limited-edition runs, the ease of money—of *class* and status—spoke for itself.

Okay, so he's a little . . . Superficial? Wasteful? Whatever the adjective, his gluttony seemed like the least awful sin.

"Papi Ramon wasn't so bad," Xiomara said, preferring to defend someone who actually deserved it. Paranoia aside, the man really was a saint compared to everyone else in her family. What other employer would've allowed Julia to bring Naomi to his house every day as a child? And no matter what trouble she'd gotten up to, Xiomara couldn't recall a time when he'd raised his voice. His patience had been boundless, no doubt practiced from the time he'd led a church.

God, she would miss Papi Ramon.

Your grandfather was a good man, her driver this afternoon had said. She agreed.

Naomi, however, fell silent. And what was that look on her face?

"What?" Xiomara asked. Concern prickled across her skin.

Naomi's lips quickly curved upward, a bulwark against sudden tension. "Nothing."

It didn't look like nothing. Before Xiomara could open her mouth, however, there was a loud knock at the front door.

"Naomi!" Marisa called. "Can you get that?"

Naomi gritted her teeth. Xiomara grabbed her arm, stopping her from making her way down the hall.

"Naomi's busy," Xiomara shouted, hoping Marisa would take the hint. But when silence followed and a second knock came, she realized that no one else would pick up the slack. Naomi's shock gave way to expectation. *Well?* the look in her eyes said. *Are* you *going to go get that?*

A third knock came. No one budged.

"Xiomara?" Marisa called.

Xiomara sighed, giving in. "I'll get it." Shame followed her steps to the front door. She didn't bother looking through the peephole to see who it was.

Draped in a fur coat and dark sunglasses, Yaritza leaned a hand against the wall to adjust her kitten heel.

"¿Prima?" Yaritza slid the sunglasses down her nose. The chunky accessory still took up half her face, but nothing could hide the smile stretching from cheek to cheek. "It's been so long! Mwah! How are you?"

Xiomara could feel a layer of wetness on the coat, as though her cousin had waited a minute too long before coming under the archway, and subtly disengaged, all the time wondering what it was with everyone asking after her, as if they hadn't already met once during the funeral. It hadn't even been a week.

Yaritza shed her coat and looked up and down the hallway. "Where's Naomi?" She fiddled with the coat, as if nervous that something would tear it from her.

"Busy." Xiomara held her hands out, taking the coat. "I'll put this away for you."

"You're so nice! We should hang out more." Yaritza pinched her cheek and sauntered to the dining hall. Xiomara's face curdled. Yaritza always did this. Ever since they were kids and she found out she was two years older than Xiomara, she made sure she would never forget it. The hierarchy in the family went in order of age as long as success wasn't too far behind. For example, Marisa was four years older than Aury, but Aury was the one with her own skin-care company. Her success trumped Marisa's age. Whereas Manuel was older than both of them and led a large congregation, so he remained seated on his throne.

Until the moment Xiomara created her own patent or became a doctor, Yaritza would be pinching her cheeks—and looking down her nose at her younger cousin—until the day she died.

Yaritza was lucky that it was her only flaw. Other than the pinches, Xiomara enjoyed her genuinely cheerful disposition just fine.

Better than most of this lot, she thought, glancing toward the dining room.

"Let's get the party started!" Yaritza's voice boomed. If Xiomara didn't know any better, she would almost assume she was Aury's kid, not Rafael's.

Speaking of Rafael, Xiomara watched Yaritza completely stroll past her father. No kiss, no hug, no form of acknowledgment. His eyes glazed over just the same, refusing to give her any attention. Their combined cold shoulder practically chilled the room ten degrees. Marisa and Aury shared a look before turning to Yaritza.

"Yaritza, come sit over here!" Marisa shouted.

"When did you get so big?" Aury chimed in. "I remember when you were *this* small . . ."

Xiomara watched the energy shift from afar. Manuel, Rafael, and Henry huddled together, a mountain of masculinity in the strangest of ways: Henry with his excessive luxury wear, Manuel with his staunch religion-backed patriarchal values, and Rafael seeming to be a moderate, even as it was clear something was going on between him and Yaritza. And this triumvirate was barely talking to one another.

On the other side of the table, Yaritza, Marisa, and Aury were chatting rapidly, switching from English to Spanish and back midsentence. They leaned in together, starting a circle of gossip and "girl talk." Wanda sat awkwardly at the edge of the circle, finding nothing in common to chime in with. Instead, she busied herself with her phone.

Yes, this was the whole of the Abreu family. Manuel and his kids, Wanda and Henry. Rafael with his daughter, Yaritza. And the childless, husbandless aunts, Aury and Marisa. They were very animated for a group of people who should have been in mourning. Even Rafael was no longer plagued with sudden tears. He was surrounded by his own kind, of course.

Deciding she wanted no part in this particular dynamic, Xiomara returned to the library, fingertips digging into her palms. She didn't know what she expected from them. A bit of decorum? Some goddamn sense? Seriously, why was Yaritza still wearing her shades indoors? Why was Marisa treating Naomi like her personal servant? They were acting like this was business as usual, and yet everything Xiomara could feel was that *nothing* was the same.

Perhaps—and a bit more gracious, she realized—the family was simply used to the way death lingered. After all, Yaritza's mother, Carmen, had died in childbirth. Josefina had perished in a car accident six years ago. And then there was Julia's tragic death during a break-in. Maybe the Abreus had simply gotten used to misfortune. Or maybe they were calm because there were no mothers left for death to target.

Regardless, Xiomara's temples pounded as tears stung her eyes. Would this have felt different if Mami were still alive? It was possible, but probably not. It wasn't like her family had been any kinder to Mami when she'd had surgery for a hernia. If Mami were alive, Xiomara was certain Aury and Marisa would cook up new lies to spread about her, while Rafael would be useless, and Manuel would find new ways to pretend she had slighted God. Just imagining it made Xiomara want to light the house aflame.

Why did it have to be her? She had asked this once, asked Mami why she was always picked on in her own family. Surely, they were twice as disgusted by Manuel's superiority complex, just as annoyed by Aury's two-faced nature, or as put off by Marisa's unpredictability. Did Rafael's cowardice not earn his siblings' irritation?

Mami didn't have an answer. "I wish I knew," she'd said.

A soft knock at the door pushed Xiomara out of her head and made her unclench her jaw, which she realized was so tight she'd been grinding her teeth. She rubbed her eyes quickly with the back of her hand.

"Xiomara?" Naomi peeked in. "Mr. McClaren is here."

Finally. Time to get this over with.

And then I can be done with these people forever.

3:15 P.M.

Xiomara looked out the front window. Mr. McClaren arrived in a bright red Chevrolet sedan. With the driveway being already packed with Yaritza's Toyota, Manuel's Honda, and Aury's company car—an all-too-expensive Bentley—he had no choice but to park on the side of the road and quickly jog up to the house as thunder rolled behind him. It was an imposing first impression—or it would have been if Mr. McClaren hadn't been a pale runt of a man. Even before he made it to the front door, Xiomara could see he barely made it to Henry's height. He could even be mistaken for a preteen, dressed in a tweed suit for an eighth-grade dance.

And it fit perfectly.

"So sorry I'm late." He huffed, wedging a briefcase under his arm and pulling off his aviator glasses. The drizzle had already marked them several times over in the short walk toward the door, and Mr. McClaren grabbed a silk handkerchief from his breast pocket to wipe them clean. He only succeeded in causing streaks.

Xiomara and Naomi stepped aside to allow him entrance. He came in with the smell of the rain and not much else.

"First, let me just say I'm so sorry for your loss." He offered a hand first to Naomi, then to Xiomara. They shook quietly. "Second, you should know—"

"Who is this?" Aury shouted from down the hall. Distrust twisted her face and she narrowed her eyes as she looked him up and down. "You're not Papi's lawyer."

The house went silent and thick with tension. Manuel stood up, as if ready to run the strange man out of the house. Mr. McClaren ran a hand through his wet hair, seemingly embarrassed.

"Ah. That was what I wanted to tell you next." He paused for a moment, stealing glances at each of the family. It was clear he'd not expected such a large one. "Your father's lawyer was Roger McClaren, I believe. Unfortunately, he was rushed to the hospital this morning after suffering a stroke."

Manuel's shoulders dropped.

"I am his son, Mark McClaren," Mark said. "I'm also a lawyer—his partner, actually. Normally, we would've rescheduled any and all meetings, but considering this seemed to be a simple reading of the will, I didn't want to cause an unnecessary delay and prolong your mourning period."

From the look on everyone's face, Xiomara knew they couldn't contend with that—though some of them were clearly trying to find *something* to criticize. But the man was so logical and compassionate that it stunned them. Above all, it reminded them that this *was* supposed to be a difficult time for them.

Or maybe it was because he was also dealing with the bad news that his own father was in the hospital. Yet he was here, picking up his father's work. Mark had unintentionally forced them to have some perspective, and Xiomara wondered when was the last time any of the Abreus had felt such a shift.

Xiomara was the first to find her voice. "Sorry to hear about your father. I hope he recovers well."

Mark gave her a soft smile to mask the crack of worry in his expression. "Me too." He cleared his throat and joined the family in the dining room. Manuel gave the man his own seat, and Mark thanked him.

"Is here fine?" he asked, placing the briefcase flat on the table and undoing the locks. "Now, I don't want to take up too much of your time—not when there's a storm approaching."

As if to underscore the weather comment, thunder roared through the sky, shaking the house. Everyone looked to the windows. Foreboding clouds came with a quick flash of lightning. If rain was getting ready to beat down on the earth, it would no doubt happen in the next fifteen minutes.

Xiomara could see Mark's breath catch in his throat before he let out a "Goodness." Xiomara hoped that she would still be able to order an Uber—one that didn't go too nuts with the surge pricing. Maybe she should have let Papi drive her. Because between asking her relatives for a lift and walking through pouring rain to the nearest bus stop, Xiomara was already trying to remember where the bus stop was. No doubt it was at least three miles out. On a good day, she would have to walk for at least an hour to get to it.

More thunder let her know today was not a good day.

Mark produced a large yellow envelope from the briefcase. "All right, let's see . . ." He opened it.

The family sat up straight, eyes glancing to one another, hands flexing as though they had to quickly snatch what they were due before someone else laid claim to it.

If there was anything Xiomara actually wanted, it was something that would never make it on the will—the books in the library and the old yellow Walkman cassette player she played with when she was a child. She didn't care about playing tapes, she just enjoyed the feel of the large rubber buttons as they clicked down under her tiny fingers. The Walkman was something she alone shared with Papi Ramon.

"Can I have this?" she'd once asked.

"When I'm done with it." Papi Ramon had laughed.

She wished she had never left it behind and wondered if she might still find it somewhere in the house. Maybe it was in the study? Her mind was already trying to track it down when the lawyer broke into her thoughts.

"Huh." Mark stared at the page. He flipped it to the other side and, finding it blank, flipped it again. "Uh . . . okay, this is . . . hm."

It was not that the will itself was empty. Xiomara could see that there was absolutely something written on it. Not a lot, but something.

Manuel and Henry leaned over the man's shoulder.

"Can someone say something?" Marisa snapped from the other side of the table. "What is it? What's going on?"

"What the hell . . . ?" Henry breathed. "Is this a joke?" He looked to his father for answers.

Mark explained. "I am so sorry, it appears there's been an update I was not aware of."

"This is ridiculous!" Manuel yelled as he paced up and down the dining room. Xiomara stepped out of his way, anxiety spiking. Very few things made Manuel move with such fervor. If he was this energized, it was not a good thing.

Aury slammed her hand on the table, stealing everyone's attention. "Hello? Mr. Lawyer, can you just read the damn thing?"

Mark cleared his throat again before reading, "'If you're reading this, one of you is a demon, el bacà, who I made a deal with many years ago when I was young and desperate. I thought I was being careful. I thought I could give you all a better life this way. But demons are crafty. They can even play with your memory if it's long enough ago. You will only have twelve hours after this is read and its presence is exposed to the world. If you do not find and get rid of the demon within twelve hours, you will all be damned. Stab it in its chest, then call it by its name and declare you are ending the bloodline covenant. The name cannot be written—but you will find it in my hiding places. Do not make the same mistake I did. He will not make it easy; he will plant distractions, but do *not* fall for them. He will tempt you as well, but remember that there is *no* satisfaction in dealing with the devil, only damnation. If you need a guide, take the first step. I pray I do not find you where I'm going . . . Hugs and kisses.'"

Silence filled the room. The only sound heard was the placement of the paper on the table, and the screech of a moving chair as Aury jumped up to snatch it. Marisa, Yaritza, and Wanda huddled closely together with her, quickly scanning the page. Clearly, there wasn't much to scan, because soon enough, they looked back to Mark.

"This is a joke, right?" Yaritza asked, echoing Henry from earlier.

Mark scratched the back of his head, removed his glasses, and wiped them again. Anxious energy flowed through the entire room. Wanda went straight to her father and whispered into his ear.

"There has to be another version," Rafael said. "Isn't there? Like a previous version we can refer back to?"

Xiomara almost forgot he was there. She held her breath, trying not to let air escape her lungs. Twelve hours. That only gave them until a little after 3 a.m. *If I'm taking it seriously.*

Would she?

"Under the circumstances, you would be correct." Mark let out a careful breath.

That sounds like there's a but *coming*, Xiomara thought, crossing her arms.

"But I don't have it with me. If one exists, it's probably back at the office." He pinched the bridge of his nose.

"So you have to go get it?" Aury's voice was not only loud but now several octaves higher. Sudden shock had that effect on her.

"What? No." Mark stood up, cell phone already in hand. "I'll just call someone there. Give me ten minutes. I'm sure we can get this figured out quickly."

As Mark maneuvered around Xiomara to get farther down the hall, she came close to the table. Aury threw down the document with a look of disgust.

"I cannot *believe* this. When did he have time to change it?"

"What if he never did change it?" Marisa asked. "The lawyer said 'if one exists'—what if one doesn't exist?"

"One *does* exist." Manuel crossed his arms. "Wanda was with Papi when he first wrote it, and it said nothing like that."

Every pair of eyes darted to Wanda. She shrank back, trying to find solace in her father's shadow.

Yaritza's eyes widened with excitement. "Wait, so do you know what was on the original document, Wanda?" She waved her over. "Come on, tell us! What were each of us getting?"

Aury was quicker, rounding the table and throwing a friendly arm on

Wanda's shoulders. "What are you doing all the way over there? We're your family. Come closer."

Oh, now *we're family?*

Xiomara bit her tongue.

"I . . . don't remember." Wanda squared her shoulders. The movement bucked Aury's arms off. "It was years ago."

"You have to remember *something*." Marisa came to Wanda's other side, cornering her. The young Christian woman sent a pleading glance to her father, who sighed and pulled her away from her overbearing aunts.

"Don't hog her to yourself just because you're her father!"

He put up a defensive hand. "She says she doesn't remember. What do you want her to do?"

"But how can she not remember? It's not like she was five and just sitting on his lap while he wrote it down." Again, everyone looked to Wanda, waiting for confirmation.

"It wasn't *that* long ago!" she shrieked.

"Aha! See?"

"But it was still *years* ago. I think right after . . ." Her voice trailed off and her stare found Xiomara. "After your mom . . ."

Xiomara felt herself go cold. Papi Ramon wrote up a will right after Josefina died? When was that? Xiomara had stayed with Papi Ramon, and she didn't remember Wanda ever making an appearance.

Did he write it after I left? Xiomara felt like she was turning to stone. First Papi Ramon's daughter died, and then his granddaughter refused to help fill an empty house. He was so heartbroken, he thought he would die.

To avoid everyone's stare, Xiomara picked up the will. The A-B Millennium logo sat at the top left corner. A golden medallion with the letters *AB* printed in stylized gothic font. A little gaudy, in Xiomara's opinion, but Papi Ramon thought it made the company look dignified.

Underneath the logo were the same words Mark had read out loud. Xiomara's eyes traced each word and then hung on the last word. It wasn't *going*. The last word was two uppercase letters pressed right against the last period. Anyone else looking at it would misunderstand its meaning.

XO

In English, most people would think it meant hugs and kisses. That's what Mark had read aloud. But to place it at the end of the will was too bizarre, even for Papi Ramon.

No, it wasn't hugs and kisses. It was Xiomara's nickname: Xo. Pronounced like "Zo." Except no one in the family called her Xo—not anyone sitting around the table now. No one but Papi Ramon and her mother would even know about it. When Xiomara was in middle school, she complained that her teachers would always mispronounce her name. Forget the rolling of *R*s; the white teachers wouldn't know how to overcome the hurdle of the Xio part. Their tongues leaned on the *X* hard, pronouncing it like a *Z*. But "Zio" sounded too close to "Zero," and Xiomara didn't want the backhanded nickname to stick. So Josefina had recommended Xo. It was cute, short, and easy enough for a teacher to call on in class without adding a *sorry if I'm butchering your name* disclaimer.

Xo. Xiomara.

This wasn't a will at all. It was a last message, a plea from her grandfather to suss out the demon and remove it from the family—or else they would all be damned.

The only question was this: How was she supposed to find the demon?

No, the question was—what was Papi Ramon thinking?

Xiomara let the paper fall to the table. This was too strange, too ridiculous, too . . . impossible? Did Xiomara even believe in demons anymore? It had been years since she'd gone to a church for anything other than a wake or funeral. Xiomara still had yet to hear her own uncle giving a sermon at his rapidly growing megachurch. And with any luck, she would die before that ever happened.

The family continued to argue, voices rising over one another like crashing waves. Her head felt like it would split the way something pressed on the inside of her temples. The thing about growing up in one religion was that even after you left it, it took a very long time to stop believing in it. They were right when they said faith was like a mustard seed. It only took a tiny amount to keep you in a choke hold of long-held beliefs.

Xiomara felt choked right now, suffocated in the same way she'd felt upstairs not too long ago.

Demons don't exist, she told herself. But her gut believed something different. Because once more she could sense a strange and dangerous presence with its eyes set on her. This time, though, Xiomara couldn't shake the feeling no matter how much she wanted to. She leaned down, holding her head in her hands while an echo of Papi Ramon's voice sounded across her skull.

"Demons are crafty," Papi Ramon had whispered. There had been an edge to it, an impatient tone that was trying to cut through all the red tape and get to the point. It sounded like he couldn't talk fast enough. "I know you think you can fight them, mija, but it takes years and years of—"

A hand fell on her shoulder. Xiomara jumped up, ragged breath caught in her throat.

"Xiomara?"

The family stopped their arguing and looked to her. Naomi retracted her hand.

"Sorry," she breathed. "I just . . ."

Xiomara turned away from the dining room. She suddenly needed some privacy. The chatter of her relatives and the rest of the world fell away. She could barely feel the floor under her feet. She was down the hall in seconds. There was a bathroom right next to the staircase, and she made a beeline for it, hoping that Mark McClaren hadn't taken it for his phone call.

Thankfully, the bathroom was empty. The door clicked shut behind her. Xiomara leaned against the wall, feeling the cool yellow tiles wake her senses. The only sound she heard was the house shaking under howling winds.

One of you is a demon.

The phrasing worried her. If Papi Ramon meant it metaphorically, then she would say most of her relatives were demons. Aury the gossip, Marisa the proud romantic, Manuel the self-righteous snob. Each of her cousins had their own unique flaws that Xiomara could neither forgive nor forget. And Rafael was okay . . . to a point.

Xiomara's stomach clenched, knowing that Papi's message wasn't a metaphor. The brand of Pentecostalism he'd grown up in held a very deep belief in the literal message of the Bible. Nothing could not be evaluated in its historical and socioeconomic context, because "Jesus Christ is the same yesterday, today, and forever" (Hebrews 13:8). The strict adherence to the letter of the law and not the spirit of the word meant they also believed in the existence of demons—and that many were still possessing people to this day. Most other denominations moved on to believe demons were simply an analogy for troubling mental health—or at least that they were less active now than before. Not Pentecostals.

And not Papi Ramon. No, he meant *exactly* what he said. Someone in the family was an actual demon. But she had known them all her life—how was she expected to figure out who the demon was?

How was anyone *supposed to find out who was a demon in hiding?*

She approached the mirror and stared at her reflection. It was a lot more solid than the reflection in the windows upstairs, and her lips parted as she panted, attempting to regulate her breathing. She focused on the dark of her eyes. Large, black eyes that sucked in all light and gave nothing in return. She'd heard once that her stare made people uncomfortable, that she had a cold calculation about her that scared them. Was that why Papi Ramon thought he could trust her to do this? Did he think she was holding back some special talent that could help? Use her observational skills to drag the demonic presence from the family?

Xiomara couldn't. She *literally* couldn't. The smallest part of her might still have been holding on to old beliefs, but that didn't mean there was some great task ahead of her. What did he expect her to really *do*? It was stupid, what he was asking of her—she'd never say it to his face, but Xiomara felt the stupidity like a coat. Like something she *chose*. And if she chose to believe Papi Ramon, then she was choosing to feel stupid if it didn't go like she thought it would.

Going upstairs probably just spooked me. Xiomara decided not to consider it. It was easier to believe Papi Ramon entered a senile age before she knew it than to reckon with the idea of her hero of a grandfather making a deal with a demon.

After splashing her face with water a few times, Xiomara turned and opened the door.

Yaritza stood right there, a fist half raised as if to knock. She blinked. "Oh, sorry. You're done, right?"

"Yeah." Xiomara gave up the bathroom.

"Wait, don't go nowhere, I want to talk to you!" Yaritza waved at her to stay close even as she was shutting the door in her face.

About what? Xiomara wanted to ask, but the door was already closed. She heard the slight smack of the toilet cover hitting the tank and decided to stay put out of mild curiosity. Maybe Yaritza already knew who the demon was. Xiomara would laugh if that was the case.

Minutes later, after a suspiciously short rinse at the sink, Yaritza was back at the door, her phone in her hand.

"Okay, so I was thinking about the demon—"

Xiomara raised an eyebrow. *Does she really think there's a demon?* Color her surprised.

"I don't know about you, but I don't think a demon can, like, procreate with humans, right? I mean, there's a whole story in the Bible where angels couldn't and if angels can't then why would demons be any different?" She spoke as fast as her fingers moved across the screen. "Demons are supposed to be fallen angels, so *technically* it makes sense and—"

"What are you talking about?" Xiomara cut her off.

Yaritza looked up from her phone, a wry smile on her lips and a furrowed brow like she was pleasantly surprised her cousin couldn't keep up. "I'm trying to narrow down who the demon is. Think about it—who in the family don't have children?"

That was an easy one. The entire last generation—Henry, Wanda, Xiomara, and Yaritza, along with their aunts, Marisa and Aury. That didn't exactly narrow the list down by much.

"Let's just hold on for a second . . ." Xiomara pinched the bridge of her nose. It was a little startling how eager her cousin was to join in the whole demon hunt. Xiomara might have even considered that Yaritza *was* the demon and just trying to get suspicion off herself. But that would've been too easy, and demons were supposed to be craftier than that. "Can we start with something a little simpler?"

"Like what?"

"That Papi Ramon might have been a little . . . *unwell* when he wrote that will."

"What?" Yaritza's smile fell into a flat line.

"Just think about it. We're standing here talking about *demons*."

"Yes . . ."

"Well, Naomi just told me about how paranoid he got in the last couple of years. Wouldn't let her in the house unless she proved who she was." Xiomara's throat constricted. She couldn't tell if she was telling a lie or the truth about Papi Ramon's mental capabilities. Sure, he might have been a little out of his mind, but was it so bad he manufactured the threat of a demon in his family?

"But . . . wouldn't we have known?" Concern colored Yaritza's face, and she lowered her phone as she held Xiomara's stare.

Guilt growing, Xiomara turned away from her as she dealt the final blow. "I don't think we would have. I mean, when was the last time any of us visited him?"

When was the last time I *visited?*

Her cousin was stunned. Xiomara could practically hear her face twist in hurt as she considered the implication. Were they awful grandchildren? Would any of this have happened if they'd paid more attention to Papi Ramon? Spent more time with him? Would they be arguing about a past will written years ago if they had just taken a few hours out of their day to see how he was doing?

Yaritza's heels scuffed the floor as she went back to rejoin the family.

Minutes later, Naomi's head poked out of the library and she locked eyes with Xiomara.

"Did Mark say anything yet?" Xiomara asked. The two lingered by the doorway, facing the dining room. Manuel was still pacing, and Aury was talking Rafael's ear off. Marisa stood off in the corner, her cell phone pressed against her ear. She laughed loudly, as if trying to get everyone's attention while they all did their best to ignore her.

"He's still in the other bathroom," Naomi responded. "I'm pretty sure he's stalling. How long does it take to confirm that there's another version of the will and have someone just read it out?"

Xiomara had to agree. If he was stalling, she could only imagine the reason was not good.

If we don't do the will reading today, do I have to come back here again? God, she really didn't want to. Next time, Papi might really decide to accompany her, and she didn't have the energy to play chaperone for every conversation he'd have with this side of the family. She already knew someone would say something slick about her mother, and Xiomara would immediately crack a wine bottle over their head.

And then I'll go to jail for manslaughter, and then Papi will have to visit me and bring me good hair conditioner and—

Xiomara shook her head. Imagining pointless hypotheticals was not a good use of her energy or time. She considered how much of her thoughts she'd already put toward the preposterous idea of there really being a demon and shook her head in disgust. Instead, she pulled out her cell phone and considered getting a rideshare driver well in advance. Was twenty minutes enough time for Mark to finally tell the family the bad news?

"Oh, there he is." Naomi nudged Xiomara. "Come on, let's go."

"So?" Aury's hopeful eyes were pinned to him. Marisa's phone disappeared into her pocket.

Mark took a deep breath.

Uh-oh.

"Unfortunately, everyone has already left the office for the day."

The tension in the room became desperate.

"Someone can't go back?" Marisa asked. "How far is the office?"

Mark raised a hand. "The office is only thirty minutes away—forty-five if there's traffic. I can go and come back quickly. Unless you'd rather we reschedule—"

"No!" Aury jumped to her feet. The rest of the room looked at her in mild shock, as if to say, *damn, you really want to know what you got that bad?* She ignored their judgmental looks. "I'm just saying there's no reason to reschedule if we can just do this today."

As if in response, the house creaked under the pressure of billowing winds. It came with the sound of static, and when Xiomara looked to the nearest window, she could see why—the earlier drizzle had turned into definitive rain.

Or a torrential downpour. Xiomara's mouth fell. It was hard enough seeing the street from the house. Were they really going to force this man to drive through all of that?

"Just drive slow and keep your headlights on," Aury said as if voicing everyone else's thoughts. "This isn't as bad as the rain in DR. We've driven through worse. You'll be fine."

Xiomara's stomach coiled tight. She really didn't think it was a good idea to drive in such violent weather. But the idea of having to meet her family once more gave her pause. This was supposed to be the last time she'd ever be with them. After all, unlike so many of them, she didn't work at A-B Millennium, nor were her funds tied up in the company. She didn't hold any official position that would force her to remain in close proximity with them. Xiomara had just graduated from college with a degree in computer science. She would rather do lowly IT support than work with anyone in her family.

Still . . . to drive in this rain? Even if everybody else in the area stayed off the road, it would only take one bad break to hydroplane into a tree. Or worse.

Xiomara sighed, common sense winning out against selfishness. "I don't think this is a good—"

"Is it okay if I call you from the office?" Mark interrupted, the question surprising everyone.

The room erupted in affirmative sighs and murmurs.

"Naomi, go find an umbrella for him and walk him to his car," Marisa said.

It was subtle, but Naomi's jaw clenched for a moment. She turned to Mark and said, "Just one moment, please."

While they went, Xiomara watched Wanda quietly head to the kitchen. She didn't seem to be the only one who noticed, however, as Manuel also followed her with his eyes.

"Are you hungry, mija?" he called out.

"Oh, you know what would be good?" Marisa's face relaxed into a pleasant smile. "Sancocho. Remember how Mami used to make it when it rained like this?"

The older generation made noises of affirmation. Henry nodded to himself and patted his stomach.

"Not gonna lie," he said, "I could go for some sancocho right about now. Do we have any of the ingredients?"

"Why? Do you know how to make it?" Aury teased.

"Nah, but my sister does!" Henry pointed a thumb toward the kitchen. "Yo, Wanda! Can you make us sancocho?"

Marisa tsked audibly, fingers already dialing a number on her phone. "This is why we call you Chico."

"Yeah, okay, just go call your boyfriend." Henry waved her off.

"Ah!" Her face flashed with shock. "Manito, did you hear what your son said to me? You better say something to him before I do!" And then she pushed her seat back and jogged to the corner of the room, phone pressed to her ear again. Manuel, Rafael, and Aury shared a look before snickering to themselves.

The scene was playing out exactly how Xiomara had expected it to go. Henry being immature and spoiled, Marisa and Aury demanding respect at all costs, Wanda quietly keeping to herself, and Rafael just enjoying the chaotic family dynamic. Yaritza was scrolling on her phone, and Xiomara wondered if she was still thinking about what she had said by the bathroom.

"We got mail." Naomi returned, waving an envelope.

"Ay, if it's not the will, then we don't care." Aury scoffed. Naomi looked to everyone else in the room and was met with total indifference. No, not indifference. It was like she wasn't there. Rafael and Manuel didn't so much as spare her a passing glance. Wanda did not return from the kitchen. If Marisa didn't need something done, then she wouldn't even remember Naomi existed. Everyone found one reason or another to completely disregard her entire existence.

Naomi's hand fell to her side. Guilt bloomed in Xiomara's chest.

Once again she thought, *I should have visited more often*. It was easy for her to avoid the family. Naomi didn't get that same choice. She never knew her father, and Julia died when she was eighteen. The only option she had was taking up the same job as her mother and working for Papi Ramon. Even so, the family wouldn't acknowledge her.

Naomi pursed her lips tight and looked down at the envelope.

Xiomara held out her hand. "Who's it from?" She flipped the envelope over twice. It was thin, with seemingly just a single page in it. And no return address.

"Huh. It just says, 'To the Abreus.'" Xiomara's palms grew sweaty. There was that feeling again, the need to freeze because something was watching her. Or was she already on edge because of the failed will reading?

She focused on the letter and opened it. Unfolding the page, Xiomara gasped audibly.

Sensing drama, Yaritza looked up from her phone. "What is it? What does it say?"

Xiomara twisted it around to her family. The chatter slowly stopped. Wanda returned from the kitchen and even Marisa lowered her phone.

In thick black Sharpie marker were the words:

Confess your sins, or I will confess for you.

3:37 P.M.

Lightning crackled. The room stilled. Xiomara's eyes swept the room. What were those looks on her family's faces? At first glance, they seemed blank. Neutral. But Xiomara knew them better than that. No sudden reaction meant they were still processing. They were thinking.

What was there to think about if they were innocent?

Was *I* innocent?

Xiomara thought through every mistake she'd made, every curse she'd spoken, and every lie she'd ever told. None seemed so grievous that someone would venture out to Papi Ramon's house to leave a vaguely threatening letter.

Yet it said "To the Abreus." Maybe this was meant for the family as a whole. Maybe it was about a bad decision the company made that impacted someone else's life. Xiomara wasn't sure, and it was the uncertainty that made *her* freeze. She didn't know if the same could be said about the family.

Yaritza was the first to break. She let out a sputtering kind of laugh, one that sounded like she was between a snort and chuckle.

"Who wrote *that*?" she asked. Her amusement quickly changed the tone of the room. Henry's eyes glazed over, and Marisa went back to her phone. Aury sneered and marched to the window, as if hoping to catch the culprit in time. Manuel went to the front door.

"Someone's probably just trying to cause trouble." Aury drew the curtains and caught Xiomara's stare. "What?"

She shook her head and looked back at the envelope. "There's no return address." And the envelope was completely dry. How was someone able to put it in their mailbox during a downpour without it getting wet?

As if answering her question, Naomi said, "The mailman comes every day around one p.m." Meaning it had to have been sitting there since before any of them arrived. Did someone know they would all be here for the reading of the will?

Or is this from Papi Ramon? It seemed to be related to the message in the will. Demons and sins—it didn't take much to see the connection. But what did it mean? Did they have to confess their sins to find the demon? Xiomara chewed her bottom lip as she thought. This was all such bullshit . . . and yet it was bullshit that they'd held in their hands, twice. *Something* was happening, and demon or no, it was unsettling.

As was the command itself. Because if she had to get her family to confess to any number of their shortcomings or risk a ticket to hell, she might as well have begun packing the extra sunscreen.

The front door shut with a loud thud, and Manuel returned with a grumble. "We should sell this house as soon as we can."

"We don't even know who's getting the house!" Aury argued.

"He's probably leaving it for all of us," Manuel said. "Which is why we have to sell it. It's a bad idea for people to know where we are."

"Ay, look at the preacher not wanting people to find him." Aury wrinkled her nose in disgust. "That's not very Christian of you."

"My flock can find me whenever they need—"

"Your *flock*?" Aury laughed. "Look who's all high and mighty—"

Tuning out the rest of their argument, Xiomara looked over the rest of her family. Yaritza had taken to the lamp in the corner to take pictures of the letter in better lighting. Marisa was cooing Spanish terms of endearment into her cell phone. Rafael and Henry were now talking about women.

"Settling down yet, Chico?" Rafael asked with a playful bop on the shoulder.

Henry was bashful. He rubbed the back of his neck. "I don't know about *settling down* . . ."

She looked at it all in disbelief. One strange incident—the will—was something you might dismiss. This lot clearly had. But two . . .

How are you not taking this the least bit seriously?! she wanted to shout.

And what she really wanted to say aloud was, *What if it's the demon?*

Because even as she had dismissed the will as Papi Ramon's senility, she couldn't dismiss this letter saying what it said and appearing as it did.

Or I will.

Who—or what—could do such a thing? Blackmail wasn't out of the realm of possibility, but how would a blackmailer have slipped that new will into the lawyer's files? Maybe it was the lawyer, but Xiomara couldn't figure how he'd get away with it. What—put a fake will, and then he'd somehow inherit everything, as if no one would notice? And sure, hackers could get access to all sorts of information, but that alone should be enough to get these people to shut up and focus. Because whether it was a metaphor or literal, there definitely seemed to be *something* coming after them. It had basically knocked down the front door with this letter . . .

A flash of realization hit her. The front door. That was it.

"Naomi, do you know how I can get the security camera footage?"

It didn't take long to get access. The security camera was apparently linked to an app called SureSecure that Xiomara had to download to log into the account. According to Naomi, Papi Ramon had apparently never changed the default password from 12345 (the computer science major in Xiomara winced at that lack of password security, but she put that aside for the moment), so once she was able to log in, it was just a matter of finding the latest footage from that day and rewinding.

She rewound far back, until the sun began to rise. The security camera was switched to night vision mode, casting Xiomara's entire screen in dark green and black pixels. She could somewhat see the road, though the large trees practically melted into the night. She fast-forwarded. Hours later, the person who came first was Rafael. Naomi had mentioned that once before. Xiomara paused the video just as Rafael came to the door. She zoomed in on his hands and felt a pang of disappointment when she realized he wasn't holding anything. When she tried to parse that particular feeling, it struck her that it would have meant they had found their culprit, that they could put all this nonsense to bed and get to the task of figuring out what the hell Rafael was up to.

What has he been looking for? she wondered.

Xiomara fast-forwarded the video again. There was Naomi, coming by Uber. The drizzling had started by then, and Xiomara watched the young woman pull her North Face rain jacket tighter around her body and prop up her hood. Then she lingered by the doorway, hands disappearing into pockets. Xiomara's breath caught in her throat.

Was it her . . . ? No, it couldn't be. Granted, Naomi had reason to greatly dislike the family, but Xiomara didn't want to imagine she was capable of such cruel manipulation during a mourning period.

As if to prove that, Naomi pulled out the house keys. Xiomara sighed in relief as her ears burned with shame. This was why she wanted this over. It was embarrassing to start pointing fingers without any kind of proof. More than that, the disappointment was crushing. If there wasn't a rational explanation for this, she could only consider the impossible.

That among the family was a lurking devil.

Or maybe it's a hacker, she thought. One with really good AI software.

With AI-generated images, there were always telltale signs that it was simply a bastardized creation, a collection of pixels slotted together like puzzle pieces to create a facsimile of whatever the prompt was. Extra fingers on hands, objects suddenly blurring into other items, the list went on. Having taken a course on AI generations and the pitfalls of such technology, Xiomara knew this. Something so obvious wouldn't have escaped her notice. She held on to the possibility of tampered footage. Sure, it was *incredibly* improbable, but if she was going to go out on a limb and say that *demons* were involved, then a dedicated hacker could *not* have been her line in the sand.

Xiomara pressed play, watching Naomi disappear into the front door. She sped the video up again. On the street, several cars whizzed by, and the trees waved and bristled in the wind. The clouds above were brewing something fierce, and Xiomara stopped the video an hour later. There were Marisa and Aury arriving together. The two seemed to be laughing loudly about something while Aury reached into her purse. The peach Michael Kors handbag looked overloaded and stuffed to the brim. Aury dug so much into it, Xiomara could see the edge of a piece of paper sticking out.

Well, that's interesting. And out of all of them, it wouldn't be at all surprising for Aury to start unnecessary drama. After all, she *was* the one who started the rumor that Josefina had been having an affair and was sick with a stubborn STD, while in fact she had been getting seen for the hernia developing in her lower back. When the truth came to light, Aury feigned innocence and claimed she was just worried since Josefina never mentioned having back pain.

Xiomara gripped her cell phone tight. If there was anyone who deserved to be damned to hell, it would be Aury. Papi Ramon should just let the demon take her.

But no, it wasn't Aury who left the letter. In the video, she only pulled out a ring of heavy keys and unlocked the door. Marisa followed her inside. Xiomara fast-forwarded again until she saw herself, making a straight line for the door.

Xiomara put down her phone with a sigh. It didn't look like the post office had anything to deliver that day.

Could the mystery writer have come another day? And if so, how long had the letter been sitting there? Xiomara continued watching the footage. Eventually, Manuel and his kids appeared, hardly waiting long before being let in. Fast-forwarding once more and there was Yaritza in her fur and sunglasses.

A knock at the door pulled Xiomara from her thoughts. Naomi entered the library just as Xiomara stepped away from the wall, shoving her cell phone into her cardigan pocket.

"Nothing still?" Naomi asked, closing the door behind her. Exasperated did not even begin to describe the look on her face. Xiomara imagined that Marisa was still bossing her around while the others ignored her.

"I only got through one day." This was going to be difficult. *They have to be caught on camera somewhere,* she told herself. Xiomara cursed under her breath.

"Has the rain let up at all?" she asked. Xiomara was beginning to feel claustrophobic with her family in the house. Naomi shook her head.

"It's still going strong. Marisa's worried it's going to take down the telephone poles."

"She'll be fine as long as the cell tower stays up." Xiomara couldn't imagine Marisa wanting to go too long without talking to her boyfriend. She hoped Mark would call soon. Maybe she wouldn't be able to get back home tonight, but knowing the rest of them, they would rather risk death than stay a night. If she got lucky, she may be able to at least be alone.

Before Xiomara knew it, her hand was already wrapped around the doorknob.

"What are you going to do now?" Naomi asked, watching her stand at the door with such a nervous energy, Xiomara was sure she could brush shoulders with her and feel the sting of static shock.

She sent back a look of calm calculation.

"I'm going to talk to Wanda."

The sound of clanging metal echoed down the hallway. Water ran from the sink in short bursts, and Xiomara swore she could hear the stove clicking on. Inside the kitchen, Wanda all but sprinted from one side of the counter to the other. A bowl held to her hip and a knife pointed outward, the woman seemed to be moving on autopilot. Wanda didn't notice when Xiomara popped her head into the door, and she didn't stop her circuit from a cutting board to a pot boiling on the stove when Xiomara cut across her path. Wanda simply rerouted, treating Xiomara as an inanimate barrier and not a person moving with intention.

"Wanda? Wanda!" Xiomara waved her hand in her cousin's face until she was swatted away.

"*What?*" Wanda snapped. "I'm trying to cook." She made a subtle frown and chopped plantains into halves.

"Do you know about the letter in the mailbox?" Xiomara asked. Wanda raised an eyebrow and clicked her tongue.

"Ah, I think Yaritza mentioned something like that. Someone wants us to confess?"

Xiomara nodded. That was the gist of it. But what she really wanted to know was if Wanda could sense the connection between that and the odd will. If anyone was capable of appreciating the obvious biblical language link, it was the literal choir kid.

"Sure, why not." She shrugged apathetically. "You should all repent more. Maybe then your lives wouldn't be such a mess."

The insult hit Xiomara cold and hard. She forgot that Wanda had a poison tongue. This was why she disliked the girl. She took after her father in more ways than one.

"So *you* don't have anything to repent for?" Xiomara asked, turning just as Wanda lowered the flame on the stove. Dipping a wooden spoon into the pot, Wanda slowly stirred.

"Of course not. When have I ever disobeyed the Lord?"

Xiomara wasn't sure why she'd asked. Instead, she changed the topic.

"What do you think of Papi Ramon's message?"

"Message?" Wanda's stirring paused.

"His will," Xiomara self-corrected. "Why would he say one of us is secretly a demon?"

On some level, she felt like she was grasping at straws. Maybe it was her own misconception about demons or something, but she genuinely couldn't imagine it taking the form of a pastor or a vigilant church member. Even if Wanda acted like she was sent from hell purely to annoy the family.

For a long while, Xiomara's cousin was silent. A sudden bout of the cold shoulder was a bit passive-aggressive, in Xiomara's opinion, but it wasn't like the two were ever friends. The thick wall between them remained as permanent as it was imaginary.

". . . don't know."

Xiomara thought she saw Wanda's lips move. "Did you say—"

"I know one thing, though." Wanda tossed a look over her shoulder. "If anyone's the demon, it's not me or Papi." Her eyes blinked up and down Xiomara's entire being, lips curling downward.

Xiomara could sense the hostility hardening with every second. She took a step back, getting as far out of range as possible, because she knew this feeling—it wasn't the first time. No, Xiomara remembered the day she came to understand that Wanda didn't like her. And it would not matter what Xiomara did, her cousin would still not like her. It hurt, that moment of understanding. She was young, too young to process the sting of unconditional rejection, so she carried it as a scar.

It was when Wanda finally looked away from Xiomara that she realized Wanda had never mentioned Henry. She kept the thought to herself. It was obvious Wanda had inherited her father's air of superiority. There was no grace or mercy extended to others unless they were ready to kneel to God—in that way, the concept of unconditional love was very much conditional.

Why did I even come here in the first place? Let alone stay. Even if Mark managed to get the previous will and returned safely, she was feeling less and less interested in whatever Papi Ramon left for her. She would much rather protect her peace of mind than protect her inheritance.

Back in the dining room, Aury shook Rafael's arm with a laugh.

". . . and she wanted me to eat the whole pot of rice!"

Rafael couldn't help but crack a smile. "I still don't know how you did that."

"I was hungry!"

Xiomara looked away from them. Henry and Yaritza were both scrolling on their phones. Manuel was at the wall-mounted TV, pressing the on button. The screen blinked to life, filling the room with background noise as it settled on a news channel. Xiomara recognized it easily: the exact same brand as the last TV from before the break-in.

Wait . . . Xiomara squinted, seeing a familiar chip on the bottom right. Once, when she was small, she tripped in the living room and fiercely launched the remote overhead. The resulting crack earned her more than a smack from Mami when she got home, yet Papi Ramon never replaced it, even though he could. This was that exact TV.

"Does anyone know where the remote control is?" Manuel scratched his head. He went on a search, looking between couch cushions and telling his son to help him look.

Marisa slipped past Xiomara, pressing a hand against her other ear as she went.

"Soy yo . . ." was all Xiomara caught before she was out of range. With the way her aunt's voice softened, Xiomara assumed she spoke to the aforementioned boyfriend. She looked to Aury, who wore displeasure like a shawl.

"I thought this TV was stolen during the break-in." Xiomara gestured to it.

"I don't know, maybe it was the one upstairs." Aury shrugged. Then she roped Yaritza into a conversation with her father. Neither of the two looked ready to acknowledge the other, so while Yaritza kept her eyes glued to Aury, Rafael's head was turned the other way.

What happened there? She recalled they'd stood on opposite ends of the casket when Papi Ramon was being lowered into the grave. She didn't think anything of it at the time—but now she was wondering if they'd had a recent argument and were still cooling off. Growing up, Xiomara always thought that Rafael was such a reasonable dad. Not overly protective or completely out of touch. He could read the room and know when he wasn't needed, then make himself scarce. Yaritza was a little bit of a party girl. Her Instagram stories alone showed her bouncing from club to club, and now that she was legally old enough to drink, the habit had worsened.

Maybe he confronted her? Whatever it was that soured their relationship, it was clearly lingering in both their minds.

Confess your sins . . . Was that message specifically about them?

What even were they supposed to be confessing? That they'd gotten bags from the grocery store without paying the ten cents? Or was someone hiding a seriously heinous secret? Xiomara wasn't sure she even wanted to know. But with those phantom eyes seeming to glare at her, she also knew she couldn't just sit there like nothing had changed in the last hour. She didn't have long until Mark returned, so if she was going to do something, she would have to get moving. And once she came to that conclusion, it felt like a bit of the weight of those eyes lifted, just a little.

Like they approved . . .

I'm going to go crazy if I stay here too long, she thought.

Xiomara joined Manuel in looking for the remote. At least this was an activity, something with a purpose. Besides, she needed to ask him what he thought about the letter and will. Her hands collected sweat, and she wiped them on her jeans. She wasn't a secret agent. What the hell did she know about pumping a suspect? More, was Manuel even considered a suspect?

To calm her racing thoughts, she focused on looking for the remote. If memory served her correctly, she would find it inside the ottoman that was right under the mounted television. Papi Ramon thought it only made sense to leave it close to the television without mounting an extra shelf himself.

Xiomara opened it. The ottoman was half-filled with unsealed envelopes, old DVD cases, rogue pens, rewards cards, a little pig figurine that had probably come with a set, three long HDMI cords, an old laptop that was missing its battery, a gold bangle bracelet—and there was the remote. Tucked into the far corner, peeking out from under a stack of bills.

"I found the remote," Xiomara announced. She passed it to Manuel, who tested it out.

"Hm. Thank you," he said, satisfied. Xiomara braced herself. "Tío, do you know what Papi Ramon was talking about?"

The man's face flickered between annoyance and confusion. "What? About what?"

She looked back at him in bewilderment. *What the hell do you think I'm talking about?* "El bacà. He said it was a demon. Do you know anything about that?"

Xiomara could feel other eyes on her. She imagined it was Aury, already bored of the tension between Rafael and Yaritza.

"Why would I know anything about demons? I'm a man of God."

Manuel settled into his seat again, attention set squarely on the television. Xiomara studied his expression. He didn't appear to be lying. Maybe she'd overestimated his knowledge on the supernatural.

"Then why did Papi Ramon write that?" she asked. It was as good a question as any. Manuel's expression deepened for a moment, a V forming on his forehead as he knit his brows together.

"He was . . . old," he offered, in a voice so gruff it sounded forced. Like he was trying to bolster a confidence that just wasn't there. "Sometimes you get old and you just start saying stuff."

Sometimes you just start saying stuff? What a way with words this megachurch pastor had. Xiomara tried again from another angle. "It reminded me of when he was an exorcist and—"

"What?" Manuel put the remote down, shifting his attention in the flash of a blink. "What are you talking about, exorcist?"

Xiomara's mouth fell open, stuttering through the start of a sentence three different times. Abashment found her quick. "Exorcists, you know, uh, deal with demons, and Papi Ramon was an exorcist, so I thought—"

"Papi was never an exorcist."

It wasn't how fast Manuel said those words that shocked her—like a reflex, an answer that didn't need to be prepared—but rather the certainty in delivering it. It passed under her radar and she nodded like, *of course, you're right, he was never a—* Wait.

"Yes, he was." She passed a look among each of her relatives, searching for just one person to confirm. "He told a lot of stories—remember?"

"Papi and his stories!" Aury let out the kind of laugh that made her shift in her seat. "He was always exaggerating those, trying to get us to behave."

"No, no, he said he was a full-time exorcist." Xiomara insisted on what she *knew*, and what she knew was that when Papi Ramon *said* he was an exorcist, he fully meant it. Doubt trickled in, eroding certainty until its sharp edges were all smoothed down.

Oh my God, was he exaggerating the whole time?

Manuel had already turned from Xiomara, plugging away at the TV.

She followed his line of sight, settling on the news cycle. The report lingered on the topic of the storm outside, urging everyone to stay in their homes. Certain areas closest to the Bronx River were in danger of flooding. It was estimated that the weather wouldn't subside until morning, and Xiomara once more cringed at the thought of spending the night with her family.

If it came to that, she would likely stay in the library rather than her mother's old room. Nobody would want to stay in the library, guaranteeing her privacy. And there were other benefits to staying on the first floor . . . namely that the floorboards didn't creak as much, so Xiomara would be able to sneak around, gathering information and clues without anyone getting in her way.

What she would gather, she didn't know. If nothing else, maybe she could figure out if her grandfather was crazy or if they were in actual danger—and if that danger was a greedy human or a hungry demon.

She almost laughed at that last thought, but something held it in. Belief in it or not, she decided she was done tempting any kind of fate until this all got sorted out.

She checked the time—it was about 3:30 p.m. Wanda would be busy cooking for at least another two hours, and if everyone had their fill and Mark still wasn't back, they would likely retire upstairs, the older generation reclaiming their old rooms while everyone else considered who they would rather double up with. The process would be quick, with the heaviness of the stew lulling them to sleep. Maybe she'd have time to sneak around at 7 or 8 p.m.?

Manuel flipped to a sports channel, the roar of a crowd catching Rafael's attention.

"Wait, turn that up!" he said. Rafael twisted his seat around to face the TV, already enthralled by the soccer players.

Well, at least it'll be easy keeping these two busy. Xiomara sat down next to Yaritza. The young woman was absentmindedly scrolling on her phone, hardly passing a glance to her cousin.

"What's up, cuz?" Yaritza murmured. Ninety percent of her attention was definitely on her phone.

"Nothing," Xiomara answered quietly. She waited until the sports announcers were sufficiently loud enough to distract her uncle. "What's up with you and Tío Rafael?"

Yaritza's thumb paused mid-scroll. Her mouth twitched, and she pressed her tongue against the inside of her cheek.

"Nothing," she answered, smacking her lips. "What's up with you and Naomi?"

Xiomara's heart jumped.

"What do you mean?"

"I mean, why is she *here*? Why did you bring her?"

Xiomara blinked. "I didn't. She was already here when I got here."

Yaritza's eyes finally met hers. She narrowed her eyes, searching Xiomara's face for a long time.

Does she not believe me? It wasn't like Xiomara didn't have the video evidence to prove it. Suddenly, Yaritza's face relaxed and she smiled. That was when a realization struck Xiomara.

"You knew she was here already," she remembered. "It was the first thing you asked me when you got here."

"Of course I did. Marisa sent a picture to the family group chat," Yaritza said.

There's a family group chat? Xiomara thought, surprised.

As if in response, Yaritza showed her the photo. Marisa and Aury sat with an arm around each other, smiling at the camera. Rafael leaned into the camera frame with a half smirk. Yaritza zoomed into the back corner—there, she saw Naomi, completely oblivious to the camera and carrying a box out of frame. "Still, I assumed you'd brought her. Why else would she be here?"

"To . . . help clean things up?" Xiomara lied. For as long as she'd known, her cousin held a strange animosity toward Naomi—it wouldn't be beneath Yaritza to try blocking her from receiving anything from the will. Or worse—force her to leave. And if Xiomara was going to have to share the house with a family like this, she would prefer to keep Naomi around. *Just because they look down on her, doesn't mean that Papi Ramon did.* For all she knew, the two had probably had a close friendship like he'd had with Julia.

Xiomara frowned. That made it seem like Papi Ramon had a habit of treating children like the stand-ins of their mothers. *Or replacing them . . .*

She pushed the thought from her head.

"Ha! Since when has she ever helped lift a finger?" Yaritza snickered.

In that picture, you can clearly see her cleaning up. However, Xiomara kept the thought to herself. Nothing she said was going to improve Yaritza's image of Naomi. It was better to move on.

"Hey, so . . ." Xiomara leaned closer to Yaritza and dropped her voice to a whisper. "I've been thinking about the demon. Why do you think it's Marisa or Aury? Why not Wanda or Henry? They don't have kids either." *And neither do we.*

Yaritza lowered her phone. "Hm. Good point. Hey, Henry!"

Their cousin perked up at his name.

"Got anything to confess?"

Henry's face scrunched at the question. "Why you asking?"

"It's a yes-or-no question." Yaritza pressed with a smile. Not wanting to be caught between them, Xiomara turned away from them just as Manuel began flipping channels.

"What are you doing? Leave it on," Rafael complained.

"It's just a commercial. I'll change it back in a few minutes." Manuel continued surfing, while Henry got up and left the room. The screen quickly went from Home Shopping Network to a Lifetime movie to a news channel returning from another commercial. Manuel clicked again, just as a familiar image came on-screen. Xiomara jumped to her feet.

"Wait, what was that?" she asked. Her chest felt weirdly tight, like a premonition taking hold. "Go back."

Manuel scowled but obeyed. The female newscaster wore a bright yellow suit while standing next to a candid photo of Xiomara's cousin Henry exiting a Tesla.

". . . Several women have come forward with accusations against the influencer, ranging from sexual assault to overt sexual trafficking. The story began originally circulating online, in part due to his father's role in covering up the alleged crimes."

The room fell silent as Manuel's headshot appeared next to Henry's. The man of God held a gentle smile on-screen.

"Manuel Abreu," the newscaster began, *"appears to have been embezzling money from his church in order to pay off the women his son allegedly targeted."*

Footsteps breached the dining room entrance.

"Oh, is the game on . . ." Henry sauntered in with a glass of water in his hand, casually grinning until he looked to the TV. His jaw immediately dropped. The family slowly turned to him—and Manuel—with questions spinning in their heads.

"Is this true?" Aury's face hardened. Henry's eyes flicked to her, to his father, to everyone currently in the room. Yaritza averted her stare as her thumbs moved quickly across her phone.

"Hey, what are you texting?" Henry snapped, coming toward her. Aury cut in front of him.

"Answer the question!" she demanded. "Is what they're saying true?"

Henry scoffed. Refusing to answer, he stomped away, but Manuel held Aury's stare all the same.

"Manuel?" she demanded.

Confess your sins, was all Xiomara could think. *Or I will confess for you.*

3:58 P.M.

When Xiomara had been much younger, too young to understand the animosity between the older generation, Josefina had tried her best not to isolate her from her cousins. It had been important to her that Xiomara had a healthy relationship with some of her relatives, of course, and she'd felt it necessary for the children to socialize with one another whenever possible. That meant near-weekly visits to the park with Yaritza, semiregular get-togethers during holidays or even just being sent to stay with Manuel while her parents ran errands. Wanda was closer in age to her, practically a peer—but Henry had always been an enigma. When Xiomara was nine, Henry was already eighteen. He had graduated high school and was looking forward to college. (At least, that's what Xiomara had assumed he was doing.)

"How am I supposed to go without a car?" he had argued on one particular Friday afternoon. Xiomara's mother had a doctor's appointment that started right before school let out, and Papi worked a late shift, so she begged Manuel to pick up her daughter and watch her until she was done.

"You're too young." Manuel shook his head. "You'll get into a car accident and then your insurance will get too high for you to pay off."

"I have to *pay* for my own insurance?" Henry balked.

Xiomara was sitting in Wanda's room, pretending to play with dolls while their voices carried through the house. Wanda, at age fourteen, busied herself with the television, flipping through the reality TV channels to get to a Disney movie about teenhood and responsibilities.

"Why are they arguing?" Xiomara whispered, as if her curiosity would shatter the walls.

Wanda shrugged. "Henry wants a car so he can drive around the university."

Xiomara's eyes widened. "I didn't know Henry knew how to drive."

"He doesn't."

The argument went on and on outside of Wanda's room. Xiomara didn't remember how it had ended. She assumed he'd gotten his car because he always got what he wanted—from the expensive Burberry coat to the unique pair of Yeezys. At first, Xiomara thought Henry was the odd one out in his family. After all, Wanda seemed content with plain clothes, whether they were from Walmart or Target. And Manuel was a pastor who seemed to dress modestly. But one time, while Wanda was ironing Manuel's button-up shirt before a sermon, Xiomara snuck a look at the tag and looked up the strange Italian words. The price made her hair stand on end. It was the first time she'd learned that even the most unassuming clothes could still cost so much.

After Mami had picked up Xiomara and made her way down the street, Xiomara told her about her findings.

"Well." Mami clicked her teeth, a mysterious look in her eyes as she stared straight ahead. "The apple doesn't fall too far from the tree."

Now, there they were, in Papi Ramon's house, as silent as the aftershock of a nuclear bomb. Aury's fury showed itself in her eyes. They were twisted with venom while Manuel remained as stone-faced as ever.

"Manuel!" Aury shouted. "Answer me!"

"I don't answer to you!" he shouted back. The boom of his voice reverberated around the room.

"Papi . . . ?" Wanda's voice was small. He turned and she flinched, clearly choosing to interject at the wrong time.

"Go back to the kitchen," he said sternly. She obeyed and disappeared.

Aury laughed scornfully. "*Now* I see where he gets it from." She gestured between Manuel and his son, earning a sneer from Henry. "Oh, did you see that? Did you see that look he gave me? It's true, isn't it?" Aury nudged Yaritza and waved at Marisa to join in. From the looks on their faces, neither wanted to. So she turned to the only other woman in the room.

"Xiomara, you saw that, right? No wonder he thinks he can do whatever he wants. He doesn't respect the women in his own family!" Again, Aury laughed, indignant. "I cannot *believe* you would do something so despicable. Ha! It's a good thing Papi Ramon isn't here to see it. You would've killed him with a heart attack!"

"Okay, calm down . . ." Rafael stood up.

"Don't tell me to calm down!" Aury smacked his arm. "Your nephew was just caught molesting women and our so-called godly older brother was paying for them to be quiet!"

". . . and he took it from the church," Yaritza mumbled, adding fuel to the fire.

"*And* he took the money from the church!" Aury screeched. "How long has this been going on, huh? Since last year? The year before? Give me back my ofrenda!"

"What, your little twenty dollars?" Manuel mocked.

"Everyone stop!" Rafael tried again. "We still don't know if it's true . . . or that it's as bad as what they say." Whoever's side he was supposed to be on didn't appreciate the fence-sitting. Aury's face fell, and Henry pushed past Xiomara on his way out.

She hit the wall with a thunk.

"You don't know if it's true?" Aury pointed to Xiomara. "Look how he treated Xiomara just then! Xiomara, come over here. Don't stand so close to those men."

With her name being called, Xiomara felt a great spotlight on her. She began to sweat, already feeling Manuel glowering at her when she took a half step toward Aury. What else was she going to do? Either Manuel was going to be upset with her or Aury was going to yell about how the men were intimidating her.

Before she could take another step, Xiomara felt a tug on her cardigan sleeve.

"Hey, Xiomara, I need some help in the library."

Thanking God, she followed Naomi away, eager to escape the imminent explosive argument that she could feel was underway. Xiomara wouldn't be surprised if it ended in an actual fight, with Aury descending on Manuel like a crazed banshee while Rafael tried to keep the two away from each other. Manuel was short and much older, but that didn't mean he didn't have the strength to knock her down if he really wanted to. She wiped her sweaty palms against her jeans.

Once Naomi closed the door behind them, Xiomara looked around the room in confusion.

"What did you need help with?"

"Nothing," Naomi admitted. "I just thought you needed to get out of there."

There weren't enough words in the English language to describe the weight of the relief Xiomara felt.

"You heard all of that?"

Naomi gave her a look that said, *how could I not?* "Your aunt's voice travels."

That was an understatement. Even now, Aury's voice shot through the wall, each syllable like a bullet.

"Do *not* defend them!"

Xiomara winced. Naomi rolled her eyes as she went back to her reading nook. An unfamiliar book sat half-open on the floor, and when Naomi picked it up, Xiomara saw that it was Elizabeth Acevedo's *Clap When You Land*.

"How can you be reading when they're about to tear one another apart?"

"They aren't going to tear each other apart." Naomi flipped a page. "And even if they were, what am I supposed to do about it?"

Xiomara opened her mouth and shut it. Naomi wasn't wrong. There wasn't a damn thing anyone could do to stop them from getting at one another's throats. Rafael and Marisa would probably try anyway, but Aury was definitely a fighter, and Manuel liked to swing his weight around to establish dominance. It wasn't the first time Xiomara had seen a fight brew between her aunts and uncles. It was just the first time the fight wasn't directed toward her mother.

Was it always so easy for siblings to duke it out?

"You should lock the door behind you," Naomi said. "Make sure Henry can't come in."

And then there was that. Xiomara's shoulders dropped.

"You think he really did all that?"

Naomi countered with a question. "You think he didn't?"

Xiomara pursed her lips. It was hard to say yes. Damning, even, to look at someone and go, *yes, you look like you would actually be a shithead*. And worse to say that about a close relative. Henry was her *cousin*, after all. She'd stayed in his house several times. A few of those times, he'd even been in charge of her and his sister. He'd babysat her when needed, and made sure she was fed and not in any immediate danger.

Granted, *he* hadn't fed her so much as he'd told Wanda to fry a couple of eggs with plátanos. Which she had, so Xiomara had definitely been fed. He'd been otherwise indifferent about her, now that she thought about it. As a kid, he'd just seemed nonchalant, cool even. Taking nothing and no one seriously.

But he'd never really talked to Xiomara. Never asked how her day was, or what she was learning in school. None of the usual questions that adults normally asked her, if only to feign interest.

In hindsight, Henry might have just been regarding her the same way as someone regarded a potted plant: It was there, and as long as it didn't get in his way, that was fine. All he was required to do was pour water in the pot every so often and leave the plant out in the sun.

Still, to think he was capable of such cruelty! Sexual assault? *Sex trafficking?*

They said the stories originally circulated online. Xiomara quickly fished her phone out of her pocket. The first page of Google came with similarly written articles about Henry. He had no fewer than six victims, each one with a very similar story about how he'd originally flirted with them on Instagram, eventually propositioning them and getting them to start an OnlyFans.

The loverboy method, it read. When one of the women seemed unsure about doing any of this, that's when the sexual assault occurred. Xiomara put away her phone. She didn't want to know so much about Henry. She hadn't known much about him before, only what she could see on the surface, and that had suited her just fine.

Now, everything was exposed, and it somehow made *her* feel exposed.

Maybe Henry is *the demon.* Yet as simple as that would make things, Xiomara struck that thought down. It was tempting to think so, to think that the worst person she knew was a descendant of hell, but she was still on the fence about the existence of demons.

It's just a coincidence. Just a coincidence the story broke when it did . . .

"Honestly, I'm surprised we didn't find out sooner," Naomi mumbled. Xiomara had to agree. For this to hit the news on a Friday afternoon could not have been a coincidence. To go from a will reading to a thinly veiled threat and then a scandal all within an hour? A normal person could not have orchestrated all that.

Unless it wasn't a person . . . Xiomara felt a chill run down her back.

There was a crash coming from the dining room. Xiomara flew out into the hallway just as Manuel stomped down toward her. Not wanting to be shoved again, Xiomara pressed herself against the wall to give him space. He didn't so much as look at her and only went up the stairs to the second floor. Not a moment later, a door was slammed.

Xiomara treaded carefully to the dining room. A chair was flipped over, and the table had been shoved aside. Rafael stood with hands on his hips, shaking his head at the floor. Marisa was by Aury's side, cooing as the woman sniffled. Aury's hair was a mess.

And Yaritza was tense. She pressed her phone to her chest and locked eyes with Xiomara.

Don't say anything, she mouthed. Xiomara nodded and backed away into the kitchen.

A subtle heat ballooned from the kitchen. Inside, Wanda looked to be twice as focused on making the sancocho, an array of ingredients out on the counter while a pot sat on a lit stove.

Xiomara approached the counter. She recognized the oxtails in an open Tupperware container, and the open jar of sofrito next to it with a dark green glob running down its side. But the rest of the counter was a mess of peels and spills that told Xiomara the woman was struggling to keep it all in order.

It looks like she has all of the ingredients, though. There were the yautia malanga, yucas, and half a calabaza waiting to be boiled. Three peeled plátanos, each cut in quarters while the discarded skin partially obscured the Doña Gallina cubes. She did wonder why there was a blob of dough sitting on the cutting board, though.

"You need some help, Wanda?"

The frenzied look in Wanda's eyes could have been its own answer. She looked at Xiomara up and down before frowning and shaking her head.

"I'm fine," she said. A bead of sweat rolled down her forehead.

"Are you sure? This just seems like a lot—"

"Oh, *this* seems like a lot?" Wanda spat. "Is that what you came to talk about?"

Xiomara put her hands up defensively. "I was just asking—"

Wanda interrupted. "I *know* what you were just asking. I'm *fine.* Go gossip with Yaritza like you always do."

Like I always do?

Stunned, Xiomara didn't move. She watched Wanda dump the oxtails into the pot and jerk back as a sizzling roar released a large cloud of steam.

Wanda grabbed the nearest yuca and a knife. Right as she positioned the knife over the root vegetable, she sent another vicious look to Xiomara.

"Can I help you?" Wanda scowled.

Xiomara backed away, and the knife came down. Xiomara lightly touched her neck, imagining it to be on the cutting board, and Wanda going, *off with her head!*

She tried not to take it personally. Wanda was clearly reeling from the news about her family. Henry was one thing—she had implied as much earlier. But Manuel was supposed to be above such things. What would the congregation think? What would they *do*? Xiomara couldn't imagine he'd have much of a flock anymore. Unless they were incredibly forgiving . . . but if they had been taking cues from him on how to behave as people of God—a lot more Old Testament than New—then the last thing they would be was forgiving.

Xiomara's pocket vibrated. She waited until she was farther down the hall to pick up her phone.

"Papi?" she whispered.

"Xiomara! Are you okay?" Papi's voice sounded like heaven. Well, he sounded concerned—but it was heaven nonetheless. The house was filled with either tension or aggression, and this was a needed break from it. Xiomara rubbed her face in a soothing motion.

"I'm fine, Papi. The weather is bad, but I'll be fine as long as I stay inside."

He was quiet on the line. Then, "Have you seen the news?"

Xiomara closed her eyes and held her breath. She'd been hoping he didn't know.

"Yes," she answered on a sigh. "The whole family has."

"Do you want me to come get you?"

"No!" Xiomara said. Thunder crackled outside. Or was that a tree being hit by lightning? Xiomara looked out of the front door's peephole. The weather continued to rage like God Himself had forgotten His rainbow promise. "You can't go out in this!"

"Mija—"

"Don't worry," she said, trying to inject as much calm into her voice as possible. "I'll be heading home as soon as the rain lets up, but *do not come here*. Especially now—it's still really bad."

"It is really bad—"

"I meant the weather."

"I don't like you being there," Papi said. *Me either.* But as Xiomara leaned her forehead against the door, she realized he wasn't talking about the normal family dynamic, but the specific threat they were suddenly aware of.

You believe it, too, huh? Not that she could blame him. He didn't know Henry as well as Xiomara did—and it turned out that Xiomara didn't know him at all. Anyone in Papi's position would be nervous about being under the same roof as someone with those kinds of allegations hanging over them.

For some reason, though, those worries seemed small compared to the bigger issues exposed in this house. "I'll be fine, Papi," she reassured him.

"It's been almost two hours. You should already be back by now." He switched subjects. "What happened with the will?"

Ah, right. Papi didn't know the situation. How was she going to fill him in?

So, actually, Papi Ramon left me a really cryptic message about a demon infiltrating the family, and he wants me to figure it out, so the lawyer left to find another version of the will that doesn't mention demons . . .

Mm-hm. *That* will convince him that she was perfectly safe.

Or insane.

"The lawyer got stuck in traffic when the storm began," she blurted. "We're not sure if he'll be able to make it at all. We might have to reschedule."

Technically, it wasn't a lie. Mark really *did* have to get the will. And the storm really *had* started when he drove out. Xiomara's anxiety prickled at the thought of him driving around in that vicious weather—but fear made her selfish and hopeful that he would be back very soon. At the very least, with the lawyer present, the family would be back on their "best" behavior, and Xiomara wouldn't have to worry about another fight breaking out. The longer she sat with the news of Henry in her head, the more her fear skyrocketed. If he was capable of sexually assaulting multiple women, what else could he be capable of?

"Oh, mija . . ." Papi sighed, bringing Xiomara back to the present. "I'm sorry. I know you wanted to get this over with. Just . . . promise me you'll stay away from him, okay? Stay with your aunts. They'll keep you safe."

Xiomara swallowed. There was a lump in her throat that she swore wasn't there before. "Okay, I will. I'll call you once I'm on my way back, okay?"

She hung up. First she'd promised a text. Now she was promising a call. Xiomara hoped her urgency had slipped underneath Papi's radar, otherwise she couldn't be surprised if he showed up in the torrential rain to rescue her.

Truth was, part of her *did* want to be rescued.

I'm sorry, Papi Ramon. With their secrets being revealed, Xiomara wasn't sure if she wanted to crawl around in the dark looking for clues anymore. At least now the letter made a little sense. *Confess your sins.* She'd thought it was about Yaritza and Rafael, but now it was clear it was meant for Manuel and Henry. The two's sins may have been tied up in each other, but that still made them two separate sins.

Unless there's still more. Xiomara's spine stiffened. More sins to uncover? More secrets? Xiomara didn't want them to be revealed. It would be hard enough dealing with her uncle and cousin for the rest of the night. If more of the family were in the same foul moods, Xiomara would rather take her chances in the storm.

"Let go of me!" Naomi shrieked.

Xiomara sprinted to the library. The door was thankfully ajar, and when she pushed it open, she saw Henry gripping Naomi's shoulder.

Xiomara's nose flared. "Hey! What are you doing?"

Henry amazingly let go of Naomi, yet didn't move away from her. Naomi backed into the wall.

"I'm asking *this one* who gave her the letter."

"No one gave me the letter!" Naomi gritted her teeth. "It was in the mailbox with all the other junk mail!"

"*Bullshit.* Someone had to have given it to you, so who was it?" He now had her cornered. "Was it Clarissa? Was it Eden?"

Xiomara forced herself between them. Henry barely registered her. He only glared at Naomi, jaw flexing.

"The letter was in the mailbox, Henry." Xiomara invaded his line of sight. "I checked the security camera. It must have been sitting there for days."

For a second, it was like Henry was looking through Xiomara. His anger wasn't directed toward her; she wasn't even there, not to him. Once more she was a plant, at most.

Until she wasn't.

He blinked and turned his attention to Xiomara. The whites of his eyes had grown red and veiny, little roots crawling inward to the pupil. His shoulders came up and down with each quiet breath, and in his eyes, Xiomara could see how quickly she'd transformed from a plant to a roach.

He'll kill me. An alarm rang in her head, as she took inventory of every possible weapon she could use if push came to shove. Hammer or drill in the toolbox, a knife or fork from the kitchen—how much force would she need to use to turn the blunt end of a glass bottle into jagged teeth?

"Henry. Leave the girls alone," Rafael said. Xiomara hadn't known that he'd come to the library, but there he was, at the door. He crossed his arms, keeping a stern eye on Henry. *"Now."*

Without turning his back, Henry smirked and stepped away.

Rafael looked between the girls and held up a hand, a gesture that was supposed to mean, *just stay away from him.*

Xiomara shot him a look in response. *Why don't you keep* him *away from* us? They weren't doing anything. Henry was the one who was on a rampage, turning every woman in his family into his enemy. As soon as Rafael closed the door behind him, Xiomara leaped to lock it. There was a brief moment of shame, where she recognized the action as painting Henry as dangerous. But she shot the feeling down, the idea that familial solidarity held sway anymore. Henry *was* dangerous. He had clearly long been a danger to other women, and now Xiomara was getting the chance to view that side of him. It surprised her that she'd missed it so long, the selfish anger that poured out of him like sweat. As much as she hated that he wasn't the one being restricted, she knew she would have to steer clear of him from now on.

Xiomara turned to Naomi. "Are you okay?"

Naomi rolled her shoulders in relief. "I'll be better once I'm far away from this house."

That was fair. Xiomara wanted the same thing. The storm outside wailed, though, reminding her just how treacherous the roads must be.

Like mother, like daughter, she thought morbidly. To keep her mind off Mami's car accident, she went across to Naomi's reading nook.

"Can I ask you something . . . weird?" Xiomara asked. "Have you ever felt something was off about this house?"

"Like something was always watching?"

Xiomara tried to contain her heart. "*Yes.* But also . . . gaps in your memory? Or just things that don't feel quite right?" It was hard to put the feeling into words. "You try to think about something, but the more you look at it, you feel like you shouldn't—or you feel your attention being directed elsewhere . . ."

Naomi frowned. Though she sat down next to Xiomara, the look on her face told her she wasn't looking forward to whatever conversation Xiomara wanted to have.

"Are you sure it's not just your grandfather's exorcism stories getting in your head?"

"You remember that?" Vindication shot through Xiomara and settled in her bones, strengthening her resolve. "That Papi Ramon was an exorcist?" She couldn't believe how easy it was for her family to gaslight her, make her think that Papi Ramon had either lied or exaggerated his time spent in religious fervor. Xiomara thought that she'd been able to spot when her family was lying to her, but clearly that skill had eroded over time.

"Why wouldn't I remember?" Naomi scoffed. "It's the one thing he bragged about constantly."

"And you remember all the stories he told?" Xiomara hoped that Naomi's memory was better than hers.

"You mean the stories he only told *you*?" Naomi pointed out. "I was never part of those conversations."

"What? But . . ." She thought back, all those years ago: Every Sunday she had sat on her grandfather's lap. She remembered the smell of his cologne, the bony feel of his knee as he bounced her up and down, the way sunlight trailed in through the windows . . . but no Naomi.

"I thought you were there." Xiomara chased the memory like she was trying to keep sand from slipping through her fingers. Only grains were left behind, lodged underneath her nails. She tried to pick at it, feeling something was not quite right, but all that came was the dull beat of a headache circling her skull.

The home aide shook her head slowly. "Why would I be there? He was *your* grandfather. He always shut the door when you were in his study. Ma told me not to go in. The only reason I know anything about that is because . . ." Naomi stopped short.

"Because what?" Xiomara pressed.

"In the last few years . . . he would get confused." She looked away from Xiomara. "He'd look at me and think I was someone else, and for a while I thought he thought I was my mom, because, well . . ." Naomi gestured to her face. "But then I realized, when he was laughing hard about the way I used to pronounce certain words, he didn't think he was talking to my mom. Because I know he used to talk to her, and it wasn't like that. The only time he laughed like that was when he was with you."

If guilt was an ocean, Xiomara resided at the very bottom. It was one thing to remember Papi Ramon's voice and the feel of his hugs—it was another to be told that his laugh was exclusive, and that she was one of the very few privileged enough to hear it.

As if to steer grief away from herself, Xiomara mustered up all the moisture in her mouth to ask, "How did Papi Ramon talk to Julia?"

"Quiet." Naomi shrugged. "And in private." To mark the end of the conversation, Naomi went scrolling on her phone.

Xiomara leaned her head back until she was staring at the ceiling. Though Manuel was somewhere up on the second floor, it felt strange for there to be no noise coming from above. She'd thought she was remembering it wrong before, but now she was certain. Even when no one was on the second floor, there was a consistent pattern of thuds followed by light scratches.

It wasn't rats. Xiomara felt her stomach tighten as the memory sharpened. It wasn't rats, and she knew it for sure, because one day, she traveled all the way up to the second floor—to the source of the sound. It was right above the library, which meant it had to be coming from her mother's childhood bedroom. The thudding stopped just as her right foot settled on the first step. She held her breath. There were the eyes; she felt them then—and she was feeling them now.

Xiomara glanced to Naomi. The home aide was not even looking up. Still, her own pores opened up, and the deer alarm rang in her head as she tried to remember what happened next.

I walked inside. Xiomara swallowed. She leaned against the wall, her legs shaking as she traveled down memory lane.

Xiomara, at barely eight years old, went into her mother's old room. The room at the time wasn't just stale—it was a vacuum. Not even a fan could stir up dust; that's how strange the room felt.

I must be remembering it wrong. But intuition refused to acquiesce. Xiomara had felt the wrongness of the room to her core, and it was still fresh to this day. Once again, a thought scratched away:

How could I have forgotten about it? But she was remembering now, or at least she was remembering something.

So what then?

She was kneeling in front of her mother's bed. Despite the utter stillness of the room, the end of the sheet hanging over the bed was billowing, a warmth flowing out toward her.

It was probably an air vent, Xiomara thought, attempting to tamp down the prickly sense of unease that was rolling over her skin. At eight years old, Xiomara peered under her mother's bed.

And something said, "Hello, Xiomara."

A knock at the door made Xiomara jump. Naomi glanced at her with a raised eyebrow before Xiomara answered, "Who is it?"

"We've got a situation," Yaritza replied from behind the door. *That's an understatement.* Xiomara went to open it.

"So, that lawyer?" Yaritza pressed her hip into the doorway, typing away on her phone with indifference. "Yeah, he's not coming back tonight. Lot of blocked roads because of trees and car accidents."

"Can't he just call?" That seemed like such an easy solution to at least one of their problems. "He can read off the will over the phone."

"He was going to, but then his phone cut off." Yaritza shrugged. "Aury's trying to call him back, but it keeps going to voicemail."

Xiomara pressed her head into her hands, and felt the full weight of dread falling over her. She could read between Yaritza's lines. It was obvious, after all.

No matter what, Xiomara was going to have to spend the night with eight people who were either upset with her or just didn't like her.

And one of them was almost certainly a predator . . . and maybe worse.

"Hey." Yaritza lingered. "You mind if I sleep in your mom's room?"

5:36 P.M.

The arrangements were made. Yaritza and Xiomara would both be sharing her mother's old room. Marisa and Aury would take their old room, sharing with Wanda. Rafael would take his old room. Manuel and Henry would take Papi Ramon's bedroom. There was a brief argument about why those two wanted Papi Ramon's room, but it was quickly buried when no one else offered to swap instead. Naomi was happy to stay in the library, not that anyone asked her.

Standing in front of her mother's door with a fresh bundle of blankets and an extra pillow under her arm, Xiomara's chest tightened.

She thought a little more deeply about her last visit, the entire week she'd spent helping Papi Ramon through his grief and burying her own, walking through the house like a ghost, like *she* was the one who'd died, and she remembered one thing—how utterly afraid she was of Mami's room. It came to her in flashes, the feeling of being watched all over again. Despite being alone in the room, she could never keep her back to the walls. She always imagined there were a pair of hands reaching out to snatch her and that even the floorboards were conspiring against her.

Yet here she was. She told herself it was to keep an eye on Yaritza, to make sure she didn't go through her mother's belongings. But the truth was, it was that voice—the voice that had spoken to her from underneath her bed. She didn't remember anything after that moment, didn't like that it had taken her *years* to recall it at all, and most of all—she didn't like the sound of it.

All Xiomara knew was that she shouldn't leave her cousin alone in that room.

Yaritza tapped her on the shoulder. "Are you gonna go in or . . . ?"

Xiomara stepped aside, letting Yaritza be the one to open the door.

Josefina's room was a 13 x 13 square space with a sizable closet and a full-sized bed made flush against the wall. It was obvious the room hadn't been occupied in some time, with a coat of dust over the nightstand and dresser. Even the floor felt sandy underneath Xiomara's feet. She thought about grabbing a broom, then decided against bothering Naomi for its location—she'd already upset the home aide earlier; the least she could do was give her space. Instead, she took in her mother's room again, comparing how it had looked the last time she stayed to now.

Time had rendered it muted in all aspects of appearance. The bright yellow stripes of the bedsheets were dull, almost piss-colored. The patchwork quilt folded at one end of the bed was now only loosely connected by threads, stretched nearly to its breaking point. On the other end of the bed, two pillows lay side by side, flattened. Under the bed were a few rows of Josefina's old shoes and sandals. If Xiomara bothered to look in the dresser or closet, she was sure she would be face-to-face with more of Josefina's clothing from another era.

She stayed away from those, especially. Xiomara knew herself too well. She knew that if she so much as saw another one of Mami's dresses or blouses, she'd want to touch it, smell it, feel any lingering essence of her deceased mother. The action never brought closure, just hurt.

Xiomara plopped the extra sheets and pillows on the bed, biting her tongue when Yaritza quickly sat down. Her legs dangled over the side of the bed, brushing carelessly against the bedsheet. Xiomara felt panic rising like a tsunami, a deep knowledge that there was something *dangerous* in the room, something that knew her name and could speak it.

There couldn't have been a voice. It was ridiculous just to imagine it. She was clearly misremembering the moment, which was probably just a scene from a horror movie or a story she'd read.

But just in case . . . Just in case, she was there, with Yaritza, in the same room that used to terrify her. She looked out the window, watching the trees bend under the force of an angry sky, like they were bowing to a tyrant. The winds continued to howl, and the house was mercilessly pelted with rain. Between the room and the weather outside, Xiomara knew where she was safest.

Yaritza sighed. "That was crazy, wasn't it?"

Xiomara pursed her lips together.

Go gossip with Yaritza like you always do. She hadn't understood why Wanda accused her of gossip, but maybe this was what she meant.

This is hardly gossip, though.

She answered Yaritza with a question. "What even happened? I was in the library, and when I came back, a chair was flipped over and Aury was a mess."

"Oh my God, you missed it," Yaritza said, eyes as wide as dinner plates. "Aury got in Manuel's face and said it was no wonder Claudia left him."

Xiomara let out a deeply disappointed sigh. *Of course she did.*

It was an unspoken family agreement not to bring up Manuel's ex-wife in front of him. The divorce was *not* amicable. It was so bad that even Henry and Wanda didn't talk about their mother. And to throw it in Manuel's face? Xiomara expected nothing less from Aury's razor sharp tongue.

"So he threw a chair at her?" Xiomara asked.

"What? No. He just pushed her so hard, she tripped over it."

While that wasn't what she'd expected, Xiomara could see that happening—as well as Aury bringing on crocodile tears.

Bet she regrets saying that now. Aury and Manuel would be stuck under the same roof for an entire night. Seeing each other would be unavoidable, especially for dinner. Wanda was still in the kitchen, working on the sancocho. The house was pleasantly filled with the smell of a savory stew that made Xiomara's stomach rumble. The meat alone made her mouth water.

But imagine eating right between Manuel and Aury. Her stomach would curdle from the tension.

Xiomara's cell phone buzzed again. She took one look at the caller ID and frowned.

She decided to pick up and cut him off. "Marcus? Is something wrong?"

"Did you see the news?"

Xiomara clenched her teeth. All at once, she realized what it was about Marcus that *really* irritated her. She'd experienced bits and pieces of the issue during their relationship—Marcus's propensity for being *helpful*. To the point of overstepping. Marcus was a self-proclaimed "problem solver," and no matter what the issue, whether it was Xiomara's fraught relationship with her family or her struggling grades, he was determined to help her fix it.

Or pretend it was also *his* problem.

It was patronizing, was what it was. One could only be sympathetic to a point. After that, it felt like he was hijacking her situation.

Worse was when he made assumptions about what she knew or felt. If Marcus ever wanted to ask a question, he would spend at least ten minutes giving context instead of getting straight to the point. He couldn't just start a conversation; he had to make sure she was sufficiently knowledgeable about the topic first. It wasn't so much mansplaining as it was showing off just how kind and supportive he could be.

Like he was doing now. Calling to make sure *she* knew that *he* knew about her family and that he was available as a shoulder to cry on. He expected Xiomara to be deeply affected and entirely emotional. He wanted to *help* Xiomara, because if she was sad, then he would be sad on her behalf.

Marcus could be very annoying.

Annoying, Xiomara thought. *Not malicious.* She tried to forgive him and uncurled her fingers. Thank goodness he couldn't see her. He'd find a way to turn her obvious anger into evidence for sorrow.

"Yes. I saw the news," she said. "What about it?"

Marcus went quiet, unsure how to follow up with that. Deciding that she must not *really* know, he broached the subject again. "So you know about your cousin . . . ?"

"And my uncle, yes." Xiomara pinched the bridge of her nose. "Did you want to talk about it or something?" She flipped it on him. It would take someone truly dense to mistake proximity to a situation for ownership. Whatever was going on with Xiomara's family was *Xiomara's* business. Well, technically, anyone with internet access would know what Henry and Manuel had done, but that did not give everyone the right to pry even further.

She hoped that Marcus would understand that.

Seconds passed. Xiomara wondered what was going through his head. Perhaps it had dawned on him that she was not as distraught as he'd expected her to be. Maybe if it was the only thing going on today, she would be. But considering Papi Ramon's message-slash-will, she had to compartmentalize if she was going to make it through the night.

"I thought *you* might want to," Marcus said quietly.

"I don't," Xiomara admitted. What was there to even say? Her cousin was a criminal, her uncle was a hypocrite *and* a thief, and she regretted having shown up at all. Why couldn't they have done the reading of the will over Zoom? She still would have had to deal with Papi Ramon's message, but at least she would have been at home.

"Are you okay?" he asked.

What kind of question was that? Xiomara stopped herself from asking that out loud. *Annoying, not malicious*, she repeated, like a mantra to keep calm. She closed her eyes and pretended to go into a half-meditative state.

"I'm fine," she answered. Would that be all? Was he going to finally leave her alone—

"Are you safe?" Xiomara's eyes snapped open. She resisted the urge to ask him what he was going to do if she wasn't. Doubtless, he would make an unnecessary promise to rescue her from her family. While she would welcome that from her father, an ex-boyfriend was not someone she wanted to hear that from.

"Perfectly safe," she confirmed. The line went quiet again. Yaritza stared at her from the bed, eyebrows raised in interest. Great, now her cousin was going to start prying too—except it would be about her relationship, not the family. She would have to end the call sooner rather than later.

"Marcus, I have to go, so if there's anything *important* you want to say," she said, emphatically, "you can just text me. Okay?"

"Okay, I just—"

Xiomara hung up. Not a minute later did her phone buzz with a new text.

Let me know if anything changes

He was persistent, Xiomara could give him that. She answered with a thumbs-up emoji. Less of a promise and more of an acknowledgment of the text.

"So . . . who was that?" Yaritza casually fell on her side. Her elbow dug into the pillow, and Xiomara did her best not to wince. At least the girl had the decency to kick off her shoes before putting her feet on the bed.

"Just an old friend." Xiomara put her phone away. If she acted with extreme nonchalance, Yaritza might just lose interest.

"Uh-huh. An old friend named Marcus?"

Xiomara mentally kicked herself. She shouldn't have said his name at all.

"Yup." She nodded, stepping to the window. Outside, the weather was raging, and the backyard looked more like a swamp than it did part of a suburban landscape. "Has anyone gotten in touch with the lawyer?"

Yaritza snorted. "Are you kidding me? If anyone had, we'd all be out of here. Hell, I'd be walking out, storm or no storm. I don't want to be stuck inside with *Henry*."

Neither did Xiomara.

"Wish the storm would let up . . ." she mumbled, still staring out of the window. She met her reflection with a sour expression, massaging the back of her neck with both hands. As temporary as it was, it soothed her, and she rubbed in small circles up into her roots—

Xiomara's eyes snapped open. *What is this . . . ?* Her fingers went over it again: a hairless dent that curved through her skin. She turned into the window, pulled at her skin until she could confirm with her eyes what her hands felt. "Is this a fucking scar?"

"Huh?"

In three wide steps, Xiomara was crouching in front of her cousin. "This." She pointed. "I can't see it, but I can feel it. There's a wide split here, right? Is it a scar?"

"Oh, shit," Yaritza said, pressing a finger into Xiomara's skin. She ran the length of it, ending at the nape of her neck. "Yeah, no, that's a scar for sure. How'd you get that?"

"*I don't know!*" Xiomara cried, alarmed by its sudden appearance. It was a suspicious place for a scar to be—a *vulnerable* place. She would not forget an injury so severe that it killed the roots of her hair. When would it have happened?

Was I really young? That was the only explanation. Pulling out her phone, Xiomara started dialing. Papi would know—he was her father; of course he would have an answer. The call immediately went to voicemail, but Xiomara didn't leave it there. She sent a quick text, a question about the origins of the scar.

"Jesus, calm down." Yaritza snorted.

How could she? This wasn't even the first of the long line of memories obscured, omitted, or altered. First, Xiomara thought—no, she *knew*—that Papi was an exorcist. Maybe he exaggerated the details, but she knew that it was a large part of his life. Then she *knew* that the window at the end of the hall used to be open. It was glued shut now, and the story of why was escaping her. (Was there even a story?) And now this scar had appeared on her body, seemingly out of nowhere.

The demon can even mess with your memories if it's from long ago enough. That was what the will had said, right? Was this what it felt like?

No, Papi Ramon was just sick. Old. There was no way he'd made a deal with a demon. He was an *exorcist*—okay, even if he *wasn't*, his loyalties were to God first, and everything else second.

Xiomara glanced at her cell phone. Still no response from her father.

Great. Now she was going to be anxiously awaiting an answer all night. Xiomara pulled away from the bed and sat on the floor with her back against the wall. She had a perfect view of the underside of the bed from there, and while it was empty of all but dust bunnies, her core was still tight with questions.

She thought about Papi Ramon and the time she'd spent with him. Sitting on his lap, listening intently as he described the way a demon hissed and spoke in a garbled language that set his teeth on end. The way they contorted the human body, pressing bones against the skin until the protrusion risked puncturing. She had nothing to compare that pain to, so she often didn't linger too much on the description—only how Papi Ramon had fought valiantly against the creature and eventually expelled it from the victim it possessed.

And yet . . . the *how* was still missing from her memories. The more Xiomara thought about it, the fuzzier the memories became. How *had* Papi Ramon exorcised demons? Was it with a rosary? Had he just yelled Bible verses? Had he used holy water? Had he even told her?

Xiomara frowned. Something about that didn't feel right. It was like a good-natured adult was playing *got your nose!* Except Xiomara wasn't a child and the nose was that memory. She still had it, could recall every other part of the moment and almost feel the slope of her grandfather's legs against her bottom. But that bit of information? It snuck away from her.

I just need to jog my memory. Yes, she could do that. Find something that put her thoughts and feelings into context. If she was going to be stuck in this house all night, the least she could do was not feel like she was fighting it.

Xiomara glanced between Yaritza and the door. Her cousin had a hand pressed to her mouth as she let out a long yawn.

"God, I wish Wanda would hurry up with that sancocho," she whined. "I want to eat before I sleep."

"I'll check in on her," Xiomara announced as she crossed the room. Unease grew at the thought of leaving Yaritza alone—but what was the girl in danger of? Nothing. The room was empty of everything except mothballs and dust. Xiomara stomped down on the childish fear as she left—all while ignoring the prickling feeling of being watched.

Once outside the door, she took a moment to listen carefully. Across the hall, she could hear footsteps behind the door of Papi Ramon's old room, Henry or Manuel—or both—pacing back and forth, as well as a set of hushed voices conversing secretly. It was too difficult to make out what they were saying. Xiomara took a half step toward the door when the floor creaked loudly, giving away her position. The talking hushed, and Xiomara quickly darted down the hall.

The next room over was Marisa and Aury's room. Xiomara could hear the older aunt much more clearly. A flurry of Spanish spilled into the hallway, as well as high-pitched laughter that felt like nails on a chalkboard.

"You're being too loud!" Aury complained, like the pot to the kettle. At least Xiomara knew where most of her family was. As she descended the stairs, movement in the kitchen confirmed that Wanda was still working on the stew. And Naomi was likely in the library. That left the storage room, the dining room, and Papi Ramon's study completely free.

Assuming Rafael wasn't still searching for whatever he was looking for. Xiomara hoped she wouldn't come across him now.

Her hand landed on the knob to Papi Ramon's study. *Breathe in, breathe out.* There was no reason to be nervous. This was her grandfather's study, and it wouldn't be the first time she was inside. No one would fault her for it, or interrogate her. Xiomara wasn't there to steal company secrets.

Yet her joints locked in place, becoming as rigid as iron. Like the library, Xiomara feared a permanent change behind the door, a difference in appearance so big there was a gaping chasm between *before* and *after.* At least if she never went in, she could pretend that everything was in its place—and by extension, Papi Ramon was in his place. And his place was not in a casket, six feet underground. Xiomara squeezed her eyes shut, willing away tears.

The doorknob clicked and released the bolt, allowing the door to swing open. Xiomara stood in the doorway with her breath caught in her throat.

There was something to be said about how certain senses awakened the *feelings* of memories rather than *actual* memories. For example, sight. Looking into the study, she remembered the exact placement of every bit of furniture in the room. The large bookcase that stretched to the ceiling, looming over her like a tower. The wide mahogany desk that took up the length of the room in front of a leather chair that squeaked with every movement. The double windows, and long curtains flowing down like a waterfall. The plaques and framed awards on the wall to the right, mimicking eyes in the way they watched her.

Xiomara remembered the *feeling* the furniture gave her. It was the same as the rest of the house—it made her feel small. A creature the size of a bug exploring a large cavern. There was always more to see, secrets to unearth, the need to map out every square inch of the room even if it was, well, just a room. It was the feeling of endless discovery, for a child like Xiomara.

Then there was *smell*. That Polo EDT—tobacco and pine and leather—unlocked further memories of Xiomara hanging around his neck as he spun her around, the feel of being carried to the car in a sleepy daze, the sound of the glass bottle being spritzed on her wrist when she decided she wanted to try it on for once. The scent was too mature for her but dazzling nonetheless. It was like Papi Ramon had never left.

Xiomara felt loved. Until she realized the person who'd made her feel that way was no longer around.

She stepped inside and closed the door. She almost reached a hand out to the light switch but thought better of it. The whole point of this excursion was to be discreet. She whipped out her cell phone and turned on the flashlight app. A circle of light appeared in front of her feet, and she used it to search the room more carefully.

To her left was the same looming bookcase—though it no longer felt like a tower. Her own head was halfway to the ceiling.

Xiomara searched the rows of the bookshelf—they were entirely empty. Her hands came away with dust. The pit in her stomach hardened. For the bookcase to have collected dust so quickly, it had to have been empty for a while.

Okay, there's nothing here. That's fine, she told herself. It *had* to be fine, because she was okay with her library turning into a mountain of boxes and her memories of this home turning sinister—why couldn't she be okay with this too? Her shoulders ticked up, lungs swelling with air. Things changed, people died, it was all fine! Well, maybe not fine, but it was *natural.* A normal thing to expect. Xiomara just had to suck it up and brave it.

She went to the other wall. Despite the surprising desperation moving about in her body, she carefully removed and flipped over each plaque. She undid the frames, sliding the award out from between the wood or golden edges and held each one up in the dim sunlight, hoping to find something written along the backs.

There was nothing. Each time, each plaque, each frame—there was nothing written on the backs or etched in the wood, nothing sticking out from the corners or beckoning her attention. What was she even looking for? More hidden messages from Papi Ramon? Her body seemed to move on its own, less muscle memory and more like she was simply imitating something she had seen once, from someone she greatly admired. She imagined him bringing his finger up to his lips, tightly drawn together, like he was holding back a secret.

Remember my hiding places.

Xiomara's skin rippled, a deep displeasure taking root beneath her newly discovered scar. *Wrong.* She gritted her teeth, jolt of nerves taking her by surprise. Something was *wrong*, truly wrong, and she might not have known what it was, but that did not mean it couldn't set her off, wave after wave of profound terror, she would be fine if she could just *get her skin off*—

Xiomara's hands shook as she held a frame high, eager to launch it clear across the room.

She stopped herself in time. A subtle rotten smell wafted through the room, melting her silent breakdown. She regained control of her lungs, a sensation she hadn't realized she'd lost in the first place, and focused on the scent.

Eggs? No, it was much more pungent. Was it sulfur? Xiomara put down the frame and tried to follow the smell with her nose. With every breath, it became less faint, nearly out of grasp, and she wondered if there was a strange gas leak or she was having a stroke. The smell brought her back to the empty bookcase. It was strongest toward the bottom, and she knelt down far enough for her temple to kiss the floor.

There. Underneath the bookcase, something remained. A strip of white that illuminated with her handheld light. Xiomara reached out to grab it, surprised to feel leathery skin enclosing something with definite weight.

A book. Gold cursive was etched into the cover. Xiomara shined her light on it.

The Holy Bible.

It was hard to tell how she was feeling. Relief? Exasperation? Definitely confusion somewhere in that mix. What was the Bible doing underneath the bookcase?

". . . I'm telling you, there's nothing to worry about," a voice came from outside the door.

Startled, Xiomara turned off her light, shoved the Bible back under the bookcase, and jumped behind Papi Ramon's desk. The doorknob turned, and Aury hurried inside, closing the door behind her. Xiomara held her breath and waited for the lights to be flicked on. The floor was still littered with his awards, and Xiomara worried that Aury would see dusty handprints all over the bookcase.

Years passed. Glass cracked. The light never came on.

"Mierda," Aury grumbled to someone on the phone. "Yeah, I'm still here. No, I just stepped on some glass."

Xiomara slowly let out a breath. Though she wasn't in any danger of being found out, her heart seemed to miss the memo. Aury's voice appeared to move about the room, but came no closer. Perhaps the frames were her saving grace.

"No, I'm saying there's no need. Alluria only produces cruelty-free lines of makeup and skin-care products. Do you know what that means?" Aury hissed. She was close enough that Xiomara could almost hear a murmur on the other side of the phone. "Exactly. And if this issue didn't come up during the testing phases, it shouldn't be coming up now. ¿Oíste?"

Something slid across the floor. Papi Ramon's desk creaked in a way that made Xiomara's pulse jolt. In the window, Xiomara saw Aury's reflection plainly. She leaned against the desk, almost sitting on it. If Aury so much as turned her head, Xiomara would be caught.

Don't look, don't look, don't look. If there was ever a God that cared about Xiomara's family, He could show it now by keeping Xiomara hidden.

"Oh, so you want to tell me how this works? Is that what I'm hearing?" Aury asked. "Official statement, nothing. Did you see the news? Everyone is too busy with my older brother and his mess of a son. We don't have to do anything. And if I hear anything else about this, I will personally hold *you* responsible."

Xiomara watched her aunt hang up the phone. Aury clicked her tongue as she stepped away from the desk. "Unbelievable . . ."

Xiomara didn't move until she heard the click of the door closing once more. Caution made her peer around the desk slow and sure before crawling back to the bookcase for the Bible. She flipped through the pages, keeping an eye out for any markings or hidden messages from Papi Ramon.

She didn't get to search long.

Aury shrieked so loud, Xiomara's heart nearly stopped. But worse was what came after it—Manuel's laughter. Xiomara jumped to her feet and ran toward the sound. Three pairs of footsteps thundered down the steps in a hurry and followed her to the dining room. Wanda stood frozen in place at the entrance, and if it weren't for the rest of the family at Xiomara's heels, she would have careened out of the way. Instead, Xiomara barreled into her cousin just in time to see Manuel picking up Aury by her waist while she clawed out to the television.

"Manito, put her down!" Rafael's voice boomed over Manuel's laugh. The man hardly acknowledged him, overcome with a vicious glee that made Xiomara wonder what exactly was happening. While Rafael and Marisa moved to peel the two apart, Xiomara looked to the TV.

Aury's face looked back. Specifically, a picture of a smiling Aury holding up a sleek bag with her company's logo visible. Xiomara recognized it as one of the main promotional photos she used when selling her skin-care products to other members in her multilevel marketing start-up.

"Aury Abreu comes under fire for allegedly selling chemically harmful face masks that are rumored to cause severe burns when worn too long . . ." the newscaster read. The report came with videos of crying women and blistering red skin.

Xiomara's mouth dropped. Now Aury's hushed phone call made sense. She likely had a subordinate who'd known this information would come to light and wanted to get ahead of it.

The TV suddenly clicked off. Rafael put the remote down. Manuel had let his sister go, and now he and Aury stood on opposite ends of the table, with Marisa standing in front of her and Henry joining his father.

"You were so high and mighty about what I did for my son, but what are you ruining lives for?" Manuel spat.

"You don't know what you're talking about!" Aury yelled. She lifted her half of the table and pushed it into his lower half. Doubling over in pain, Manuel shouted obscenities at her between ragged breaths. Once again, Marisa and Rafael worked to keep the two apart.

"Two scandals in one night?" Yaritza said breathlessly. "I must be living in a telenovela." Her eye darted down. "Why do you have a Bible?"

Xiomara didn't have any words for that. Rafael looked to the remaining grandchildren and waved them away. "Go to your rooms. We'll handle this."

At first, none of them moved. Then Wanda peeled off first, returning to the kitchen. Xiomara began to step away, but Yaritza held her ground. Rafael sent a look to his niece, as if to say, *get your cousin*. She nodded and looped her arm into Yaritza's, pulling her away.

"Come on," Xiomara mumbled. Luckily, Yaritza didn't fight her.

Xiomara's head swam with the newfound scandal. It was bad enough to find out about Henry and Manuel. But Aury? Yaritza was wrong: it wasn't two scandals, it was three.

And when Xiomara looked back, Rafael was still watching them with his arms crossed and a darkened look in his eyes.

Xiomara had a feeling the family's sins were only just beginning to be revealed.

7:02 P.M.

Yaritza paced about the room. It had been over an hour since Aury's scandal hit the news, but energy flowed through her like electricity in a high-voltage power line. She never stood in the same place once, and her eyes hadn't once torn away from her phone as she searched for newly written articles about their family. Like she'd said, the whole situation seemed about as bizarre as a telenovela, sans any romantic tension. She waved a frantic hand to Xiomara and tried to get her attention.

"Oh my God, they're lighting Aury's ass up online!" Yaritza laughed. "Listen to this—'I should have known not to trust Alluria products when I heard it was a pyramid scheme.' Aury would have an aneurysm if she saw that!"

Yaritza's amusement sparked confusion in Xiomara. What was *her* reason for being delighted in the awful news regarding her family? As far as Xiomara could tell, no one had ever spread rumors about Yaritza's mother or been callous enough to suggest Rafael wasn't her father to her face. If anyone should've been reading the comments with astonished glee, it was Xiomara.

Instead, she was sitting on Mami's bed, puzzled by the Bible on her lap. It was light on her thighs and completely brand-new. Black leather shined, the spine hardly bent at all. It was like Papi Ramon had bought this from the nearest Christian bookstore right before he passed.

The weirdest part was that despite being found underneath the bookshelf, the Bible itself had collected no dust. She wondered when it might have been placed there, in the dark of the study, completely out of sight. If it were not for that strange smell, she wouldn't have found it at all.

"What was that . . . ?" Xiomara muttered.

"Did you say something?" Yaritza looked up. Xiomara shook her head and flipped through the Bible. The thin pages felt like they could be torn at the lightest hint of force. She started from the back, allowing gravity to do most of the work as the paper flourished out from her fingertips. Her eyes quickly scanned each page. Was that a highlight she saw? Something underlined? Xiomara would work back to it, only to find she had imagined it.

Eventually, she made her way back to the front cover. Still nothing. This book wasn't just brand-new, it was unmarked completely. Frustration mounting, Xiomara rubbed her eyes and met Yaritza's stare.

"What's with the Bible? Was it in the library?"

"Yeah," she lied.

"Hm." Yaritza looked back to her phone. Xiomara looked down again.

What should I be looking for? That was a tricky question if there ever was one. Xiomara wasn't exactly following clues as much as she was following feelings. Something feeling off led to something else not making sense went to a third thing that didn't match what she knew. It was a single thread that cleaved through her life in an odd pattern, and if she didn't chase it to the very end, she'd be stuck with an itchy dissatisfaction. But now the odd pattern grew cold because what was she supposed to do with a completely unmarked Bible?

Maybe I missed something . . .

Xiomara flipped through the pages again, her vision blurring somewhere around Lamentations. There was something about staring too intensely at tiny letters that stung her eyes. Her chest tightened—oh God. Was she crying? No, no, no—not here. Not in front of Yaritza.

Xiomara shoved the book aside and dashed to the door. "I'll be right back."

She zipped down the stairs, passing Papi Ramon's study, and stopped.

Naomi was likely in the library. Wanda was in the kitchen. From the sound of the TV in the living room, someone was clearly taking up residence there. Xiomara needed to be alone, and the house was now much too stuffy for her.

She turned right, opened the front door, and stepped outside.

The cold was a shock to her bones. Rain and wind whipped through the air so chaotically that even though Xiomara was under the archway, she found her legs growing damp within seconds. Her cheeks became flushed, and her ears burned from the icy weather.

Xiomara welcomed this cold discomfort. It cleared her head, forced her to breathe. She hadn't realized she was coming down with a headache until the wind cooled her temples. Xiomara dropped her shoulders.

Finally, she was calm and could process the last couple of hours. It had been nothing but confusion and frustration and tension—of course she'd become overwhelmed. Of course she'd gotten upset with herself—and Papi Ramon for doing this to her. This shouldn't have been her problem in the first place. Xiomara wasn't his only grandchild, and she most certainly wasn't the last to ever visit. Papi Ramon hadn't thought this through. Xiomara's insides felt scorched by rage, but the high winds and cold rain tempered it.

The door moved behind her.

"Wanda says the sancocho is done," Naomi said. The home aide looked at her blankly, waiting for an answer.

"Thanks." Xiomara sniffled. Whether it was from emotion or the cold, she wasn't sure, but she knew she would blame it on the latter if Naomi asked.

She didn't. Naomi just stared blankly and widened the door.

"Well, all right, then," Naomi said as she walked down the hall. "Whenever you're ready."

Xiomara's stomach grumbled loudly. Hunger had caught her by surprise. She took one step into the doorway—then stopped.

Right below the where the doorknob would meet the door frame, three lines were carved into the wood of the house. Xiomara traced her fingers up and down each one, then stepped out and closed the door. The lines continued across the frame and even into the sidelight. It was a jagged cut, leaving splinters in the wood and cracks in the glass.

And it looked like a claw mark.

Manuel and Henry would not come to the kitchen. Aury stopped by to grab a bowl of sancocho before retiring to her room. The rest of the family sat and ate together in the dining room, unsaid thoughts about the night's developments circling their heads like vultures. Marisa was too loyal to Aury to gossip about her, and Rafael seemed to just want some peace, so he was unlikely to say more than a few words about his brother and nephew.

"They said they'll eat later" was all he said. It was a lie, though, Xiomara knew. As soon as she exited the kitchen with her own sancocho, ceramic bowl practically scorching her fingers, Wanda darted out and flew up the stairs with a tray. Manuel likely texted her to bring up their meals, so they wouldn't have to deal with the family's judgmental eyes.

Naomi didn't join in either. She sat in the kitchen, on a stool pulled up to the counter, while Xiomara's family skirted around the elephant in the room.

Who was next? First was Henry's scandal, which led to Manuel's. Then Aury's scandal hit the news. The anonymous letter sent to the family now appeared to be unspecified on purpose because it wasn't targeting just one of them.

It was targeting all of them.

And if Papi Ramon's letter is related, then someone really isn't who they say they are. Xiomara bit into a plátano. It singed her gums as she chewed, and she quickly washed it down with water. Her tongue may have been burnt, but under the circumstances, it was already difficult for Xiomara to enjoy the food.

It was an awkward meal, to say the least.

At some point during it, though, when they all continued to clutch tact, Yaritza brazenly dropped a bomb.

"They're starting to cancel us online," she said, licking her spoon clean. Her bowl held the discarded oxtail bones, which only solidified the vulture image to Xiomara. Her cousin had picked the bones clean and was now back to what truly interested her—drama.

"They've even got a hashtag going." Yaritza continued, scrolling on her phone. "Hashtag AbandonTheAbreus. Apparently, we're no longer considered the pillar of the Latino community, or whatever that's supposed to mean."

"Enough!" Rafael dropped his spoon into his bowl. "Don't read anything they're saying about us."

"Why not?" It was the first time she'd addressed her father directly all night. Her eyes lit up, and she chuckled as she double-tapped her screen. Xiomara watched Rafael flex his fingers in irritation.

"You think it's funny?" he asked. "Your grandfather was just buried, and now we're being dragged through the mud—and you're laughing about it."

Yaritza made a face. "*I* didn't do anything wrong. If you're so worried about our family reputation, go talk to your siblings."

"Don't talk to your father that way." Marisa scowled. The sudden solidarity between siblings was almost enough to surprise Xiomara.

Almost. As she studied her aunt, she looked for any signs of guilt—shifting eyes, tense shoulders, fidgeting—but none were present. In fact, it wasn't shame or regret Xiomara saw in Marisa's face.

It was relief.

"Oh yeah, take his side." Yaritza rolled her eyes. "But when something about him hits the news, don't say you're surprised."

Marisa snapped to Rafael. "*Is* there something we should know?"

Rafael's face was hardened, and his stare was fixed on Yaritza, who was doing the greatest job at showing how little she cared. She shoved her bowl away from her and leaned back.

"No," he finally answered. "There isn't."

Xiomara wasn't convinced.

Marisa huffed. "There better not be. You said it already—we *just* buried Papi. We don't need any more surprises right now. So—Yaritza, put down the phone. I'm talking to everyone."

Yaritza scoffed but conceded, dropping her phone to her lap instead. It didn't take a genius to know she was still sneaking peeks below the table. Still, Marisa wasn't dissuaded. She pressed both elbows on the table and laced her fingers together, taking on the appearance of a coconspirator.

Marisa took a deep breath and said, "Here's what I think—we should confess."

The phrasing made Xiomara's ears twitch. So Marisa was now the only other person taking the anonymous letter seriously? Xiomara couldn't help but study her aunt, following the hairline where it met her skin and wondering if she was just trying to get ahead of whatever scandal was coming for her. In all her years of knowing Marisa, Xiomara couldn't imagine her aunt being able to hold any secrets—she wasn't even good at being a Secret Santa. Anytime the family attempted it, she found ways to constantly drop hints to the giftee, like the time she suddenly asked Xiomara, "You wear heels, right?"

And she still got the wrong size.

"Um—" Xiomara sheepishly raised her hand.

"Confess what?" Wanda interrupted. She jutted her chin out, defiant, with a look that said, *how dare you*. Xiomara brought her hand back down, waiting to see how this played out.

"Whoever sent that letter knows too much about us." With every syllable, Marisa tapped her finger against the table. "So if we already know what's coming, we can work together, figuring out who's targeting us. Who did we piss off lately?"

"Why, are you going to post about it?" Yaritza muttered.

"Yaritza!" Rafael scolded.

"What?" She crossed her arms. "Do you know how early news channels get their information? It's not like they're being told to wait for a signal or anything. If they already know something about us, there's nothing we can do to stop them from telling the world."

It was a valid point. Why bother confessing to a crime when they were already on their way to the executioner? Who did that really serve?

"What if it's not a person?" Xiomara blurted. The shock of hearing her own voice seemed to spread to everyone. They processed her question in bemused silence and with weary sighs. As if they'd somehow known what Xiomara was going to say and they'd been really hoping she wouldn't. She quickly cast down her eyes, kicking her own impatience.

"I understand your frustration, Xiomara," Rafael said, wiping his face with his hand. "But Papi was old. He wasn't okay mentally. So don't start saying things to cause a fight, because if we start arguing, it'll never end."

The accusation made Xiomara's blood run hot. First, Wanda had accused her of gossip, now Rafael was implying Xiomara liked to stir people up. Who did they think she was?

Rafael continued, turning from one side of the table to the other, "And like Yaritza said, I don't think forcing a confession out of anyone is going to stop this person—whoever they are—from throwing our business out there."

"But if we *know* what's coming, we can get ahead of it. At least get some media training—"

Rafael clicked his tongue. "Here she goes again, with the 'media training' . . ."

"I'm an *influencer*! I have to have media training!"

"Yeah, yeah . . ." He waved her off.

The dismissive tone of his voice curdled Marisa's face. "Why do I feel like you're just saying that because *you* don't want to say what you've done?"

"I haven't *done* anything. Can you say the same?"

"Yes," she hissed and then quickly cast a look to her nieces. "Yaritza? Wanda? Xiomara? What about any of you?"

Wanda's answer was to collect her bowl and go back to the kitchen. She ignored the sneers and every shout for respect. Wanda clearly had none for any of them, and had decided that she was better off elsewhere. Yaritza stifled a laugh as she shook her head.

"Don't look at me!" Yaritza exclaimed. "I've been a perfect angel."

Rafael shook his head, grumbling otherwise.

And that left Xiomara. All eyes were on her once again, seriously taking her in. She willed herself to become transparent, shrink down, or open up a hole in the earth to fall in. This much attention from the people she liked least was taxing, and somehow the tiny prey-like part of her sensed that not only did they know, but that they enjoyed it.

"No one. All right?" she answered steadily as if to appear earnest. "I haven't pissed off anyone or done anything bad. Well, not as bad as what everyone else did . . ." The thought of Marcus made her stumble. "I'm just flawed a normal amount." No part of that sentence sounded normal, and Xiomara wished she could take it back.

"Except for that weird scar you have," Yaritza mumbled again.

Rafael and Marisa shared a look. "What weird scar?"

"Whose side are you on?!" Xiomara shouted, face reddening.

"The back of her head," Yaritza divulged. "It looks like her skin split open, and she *says* she doesn't remember how it happened."

"Because I don't!" Xiomara snapped, hiding the scar behind both hands. With no access to the sight, Rafael and Marisa quickly lost interest.

"It probably just happened when you were a baby," Rafael said, readily dismissing it. Xiomara gritted her teeth. The longer she spent with her extended family, the less they seemed to take her or her concerns seriously. *I have to tell them about it.* It was the best clue she had so far, save for the Bible, and it wasn't one anyone could steal and hide as easily.

"There are claw marks on the front door," she said. Everyone stilled. Xiomara decided to repeat herself. "I saw claw marks on the front door. It's on the bottom corner."

Yaritza was the first one out of her seat, followed by her father and aunt. Xiomara remained seated. She listened intently as an open door allowed the roll of thunder to echo through the house. The sound of rain became more pronounced.

"Ay!" Marisa exclaimed. Xiomara waited until the closing door muffled the storm. When her family returned to the dinner table, they were cold, damp, and muttering between themselves about animals in the area.

"When did that happen?" Rafael scratched his head. Genuine confusion beat out any exhaustion, and instead of sitting back down, he made long strides to the back door behind the dining room. A gust of wind blew into the home, chilling the room quickly.

He came back after shutting the door. "I don't see anything out there. Is it just on the front door?"

"I don't know, but it wasn't there when I got here. I would've remembered that," Marisa said. "You think it was a coyote?"

Yaritza took the seat next to Xiomara, eyes serious and cast down.

"Hey," she said, trying to get Xiomara's attention. "When did you notice that?"

Xiomara stared through her. "When I said I was going to the bathroom earlier, I was actually outside to get some air. I saw it then."

Yaritza was quiet for a moment. Xiomara could tell the gears were turning in her head.

"Why'd you lie?"

Xiomara struggled to come up with a good enough answer. *It didn't seem like a big deal at the time* was not good enough. *I said it without thinking* was also not good enough. It was the truth, though, and the truth was Xiomara's character could also use a bit of work.

"I just wanted to be alone," Xiomara said with a shrug. When Yaritza didn't answer, Xiomara decided to take her leave then, using her bowl as an excuse to escape to the kitchen. She discarded the scraps into the trash bin and looked around for Naomi. The kitchen was empty. Wanda had probably escaped upstairs when she'd gotten a chance. Xiomara went down the hall to the library. The door was locked when she tried it, and a stern voice answered, "Who is it?"

"It's Xiomara."

Naomi unlocked the door. "Sorry," she said. "I have to be careful."

Xiomara didn't blame her. As she closed the door behind her, Naomi took a seat in the corner.

"What's going on out there?" she asked.

"Yaritza's instigating," Xiomara hissed, still in shock over the instant betrayal. Of all people who should've been accused of stirring up trouble, it should've been Yaritza, not Xiomara. Yet somehow, Xiomara had been dumped in the same category as her. "And Marisa wanted all of us to confess to something, I don't know."

"Let me guess, she had nothing to confess herself?" Naomi chuckled. "Sounds like she just wanted to feel better than everyone else."

That was possible. Between an older brother covering up a crime for his son and a younger sister who was responsible for selling unsafe products, Marisa and Rafael were the only ones who seemed to have good heads on their shoulders.

For now. Xiomara still couldn't rule out the possibility that either of them had something to hide. Not to mention Wanda or Yaritza—their relationships with their fathers were something to be studied.

"You just going to hang out here?" Xiomara sat in front of her. She noticed that in Naomi's corner were a blanket and a folded comforter that cushioned the floor. The home aide was going to do more than just hang out here, it seemed. She was ready for bed.

"Where else can I go? The weather is too dangerous for me to go home. And with all of you here, this house is more cramped than usual," Naomi said as she leaned into the wall.

Xiomara glanced around the room. The library was about half as big as Mami's room, and made smaller by the stacked boxes sitting in rows. Even without the bookshelves lining the walls, Xiomara felt this would be a cozy fit for one person, much less two. Still, she could breathe easier here. Maybe it was because Xiomara had never felt afraid in the library, or maybe it was because she wouldn't have to listen to Yaritza cackling the night away at the family's misfortunes.

She turned to Naomi with a question.

"You mind if I camp down here with you?"

Naomi looked at her, then got to her feet. "Sure. I'll grab an extra blanket and pillow."

While she did that, Xiomara remembered she had left Papi Ramon's Bible upstairs.

"I'll be right back," she said, and headed toward the stairs. On the second-floor landing, a tense silence filled the hall. She felt it flush against her skin and thought she needed to hold her breath as she walked by each door. Maybe it would make her lighter, and the floorboards wouldn't creak.

No dice. Each step came with a louder groan, somehow reverberating through the house. This place would not let go of its grudge against Xiomara and made sure she knew it.

She quickened her pace, only hesitating when she thought she heard a sharp inhale of breath. A sniffle? To her left, inside Aury and Marisa's room. It was almost a surprise to think that her aunt may have been crying, even distraught, while her company suffered the consequences of her choices. She didn't think Aury was capable of such emotions. *Regret* was hardly in Aury's vocabulary.

Regret for what you've done is one thing, Xiomara continued on. *Regret for how it comes back to bite you in the ass is another.*

To her right, Papi Ramon's room, now housing Henry and Manuel. Neither of them was speaking, by the sound of it, but Xiomara noted the empty bowls sitting right outside the door. Like they were waiting for Wanda to come by and scoop them up. Either she didn't see it when she went to Aury's room or she blatantly ignored it. Pettiness, in this family, could not be understated.

Xiomara grabbed the Bible from Mami's room and met Naomi back in the library. Her face was twisted in annoyance as she entered with a bundle of blankets in her arms.

She said, "Your uncle is a piece of work."

Xiomara blinked and looked past her to see Rafael at the storage room. He waved at her with a forced smile. She mirrored his smile right back, and let it fall once he disappeared behind the door.

"Something happen?" Xiomara followed Naomi inside. The woman dropped the bundle across her own nest.

"He wouldn't stop looking over my shoulder when I was trying to find you a blanket. And then he starts saying shit like I look just like my mom—does he think I want to hear that? Ugh!" Naomi fell into her corner, seething with a tension that Xiomara could pick up but not name. And half a moment later, she shook it off, sending self-conscious glances to Xiomara as if she was hiding something. "I swear, if it's not your cousin getting on my nerves, it's your uncle. Or your aunt. Or your other aunt. Honestly, your whole family is annoying."

"Sorry," Xiomara said sheepishly. "If it makes you feel any better, I don't like them either."

"Yeah, I can tell." Naomi snickered. "I'm surprised you showed up at all. But I'm glad you did. It's . . . nice to see you again." The last few words came out low, nearly a whisper, but it was enough to make warmth bloom in Xiomara's chest. Bashful, she fidgeted with the Bible, flourishing the pages to make a satisfying *shh* sound.

Naomi's eyes jumped to it, and she snorted. "Is that what you were getting? Did you want read a book above an eighth-grade reading level or something?"

"Yeah. Something like that . . ." Xiomara paused. Should she tell Naomi the truth? What even *was* the truth? "I think Papi Ramon left it for me," she finally admitted, passing it to Naomi.

"Really?" Naomi looked over the cover, as if appraising it. Just like Xiomara, she flipped through it from back to front, hearing the satisfying flap of pages as they fell together.

"Only, I can't figure out what he wants me to do with it. I expected a hidden letter or maybe some highlighted passages . . ." Xiomara's voice died as she watched Naomi flip through it again, albeit slowly and with odd precision. The home aide's fingers crinkled the edges, sometimes picking up entire page chunks and sometimes only flipping a few at a time. Xiomara realized that Naomi was going book by book, from the start of Genesis, all the way to Revelation. Was this strange—for Naomi to not only take Xiomara's concerns seriously, but to diligently help in pursuit of the source? Should it have been strange? Once upon a time, they'd been friends, and Naomi had verbally expressed desire of returning to that time. Other than being better at graciously mending relationships, what reason did Xiomara have to accuse the woman of being duplicitous?

Naomi got to the end of the book quickly and shut it with a sigh, inadvertently dashing Xiomara's hopes in the silence.

"There's a book missing," Naomi said.

"What?" Xiomara dropped to her knees and scrambled next to Naomi. The Bible looked brand-new enough—not a dog-ear in sight. "How do you know?"

"Your grandfather may have been a businessman, but he still made me read the Bible to him daily." She looked up at a confused Xiomara. "His eyesight was constantly failing. Even with glasses, he said he couldn't read the small text without getting a headache. One time, he hassled me to learn the order of all the books." Naomi pointed to the center of the book, where the pages met the spine. It was subtle, but it was there—the tattering of a page, like someone had carefully ripped it out.

"It's not suspicious." She frowned, noting Xiomara's expression. "I swear, there are songs online with mnemonic devices—"

"I'm not suspecting you," Xiomara clarified. "I just didn't expect you to . . ." To help? Know the Bible that well? Neither sounded like anything other than a backhanded comment. Most of her family already looked down on Naomi's role—and heritage—in their home. Did Xiomara want to sound like she did too? She cleared her throat and asked, "Could you show me where?"

"Jude, I think. It goes right before Revelation," Naomi said. "I'm not surprised you didn't notice; it's the shortest book of the Bible and really only takes up one page."

Just one page. Sweat percolated on Xiomara's palms. Was this one of the distractions Papi Ramon had talked about? Coming to his old home, hearing her nickname in the will, getting a threatening letter in the mail, then having scandal after scandal hit the news—she couldn't deny that something was going on there. But to find a pristine Bible in her grandfather's study with exactly one page torn out—when did Papi Ramon get so cryptic?

Was it even Papi Ramon? *Who else would it be?*

Xiomara pulled out her phone and googled, *The Book of Jude.* The first link contained the entirety of it. Naomi was right—it really *was* short.

She scanned the verses in the same way she'd flipped through the physical Bible—quickly at first, and then slowly. It had been years since Xiomara had read any part of the Bible, and she was beginning to feel the strain of an old muscle she hadn't thought she'd ever need again.

It was a lot of what she expected. Talk of eternal damnation, of how to faithfully follow Jesus, etcetera, etcetera. And amen. But if there was one verse that stood out to her, it was the one about ungodly people slipping into the congregation and using God's grace as a license to do more harm. Manuel immediately came to mind. Xiomara wondered if there were other torn-out pages. She went page by page, meticulously looking for other anomalies in the Bible.

But as the rain came down and the wind howled, exhaustion took root in her bones and lulled her to sleep.

8:10 P.M.

"Do you want to know how your mother *really* died?"

Xiomara woke with a start, the smell of rotting sulfur punching her from the dream. Her head and elbow slammed into the wall, pain plucking her humerus like a guitar string. She curled into herself, rubbing the arm until the reverb stopped, and then sat up. Slowly, all her other senses colored in the moment. The constant drumming of rain, an otherwise permeating silence, and her own heart, thumping against her rib cage, all in that order. Xiomara's hands curled into the blanket.

It was just a dream . . . And an unpleasant one, at that. But there was something about it that felt important nonetheless. Her gut feeling was to reach out and grab it, wrench the contents apart in a messy dissection. Yet the more her mind lingered on what the dream was about, the more it slipped through her fingers like silk threads. All she could remember was a single question.

And she refused to answer it.

How long have I been asleep? she thought, swallowing spit. Her throat was so dry, it felt raw. The dark was a curtain, and it obscured everything in the room. Xiomara felt around, hands knocking into the familiar leather of the Bible. Right, that was what she was doing before falling asleep. She decided to blame that for her strange dream and continued on. Eventually, her eyes adjusted and she recognized the vague outlines of the towering boxes—as well as her phone just a few inches away from her face.

It wasn't even 9 p.m. She was barely asleep for an hour. Still, the lights were off, so Naomi must have decided to have an early night. Xiomara checked her phone—it had been charged to full battery before she arrived, but now it was sitting at 78 percent. She imagined the battery would last until morning as long as she didn't waste it scrolling on social media.

I should've brought my charger. She sighed and spared at glance at Naomi's figure on the other side of the room. Xiomara wasn't insensitive enough to wake her for a charger and instead used her phone to light her way to the door.

On top of being thirsty, she realized she also had to pee.

Xiomara shuffled toward the bathroom next to the stairs. Upstairs, her family seemed to be up and about, with such energy that it made her envious. The floor above creaked and whined for every step taken. If Xiomara were fully awake, she might've been able to tell who each pair of feet belonged to. Despite the noise they made, the family had been kind enough to shut off the lights on the first floor. Her eyes thanked them for the consideration.

On the toilet, she thought about the Bible. Checking every single page would be time-consuming and might not even yield any results. What if she was instead meant to find the page? The task wouldn't be any simpler. She would have to search her grandfather's study again, rummage through his desk. Most papers would end up there or in the ottoman.

Or in his bedroom. Xiomara had only gone in there a handful of times, but she specifically remembered a small dresser drawer with bundles of old receipts, junk mail, or notepaper with numbers scribbled on it. All in all she would have to search three places.

Papi Ramon's bedroom was absolutely not an option. Not while Manuel and Henry slept there. She would have to come up with a convincing lie to let her look through his dresser—and even then, they'd watch her closely as she went.

Xiomara flushed and washed her hands. Her best bet was circling back to Papi Ramon's study. While everyone was still secluded in their rooms and avoiding one another, she could slip in and out without anyone knowing. The ottoman, she could get to at any time of day without rousing suspicion.

She killed the faucet when she heard it—the lightest creak just outside the bathroom. It came down the stairs, pausing at the door and continued down the hall, the soft whining of wood flexing under weight. Soon enough, the sound disappeared.

Xiomara cracked the door for a peek, working fast to decipher who had come down. It could've very easily been Marisa hunting for privacy to call her boyfriend, or Yaritza wanting to catch more scandals on the news. Or it could have been Wanda, needing to use the downstairs bathroom because Aury was using the one upstairs.

Or it could be Henry or Manuel . . . Her heart quickened at the possibility.

The light in the kitchen flicked on. Xiomara relaxed. Whoever was down there was not looking to keep their presence a secret. Curious, she found herself moving toward the light. The low rumble of water boiling and splashing against glass and liquid met her halfway. A rich, earthy smell flooded her nose, and she rounded the doorway just as Rafael grabbed a mug and turned to the coffee maker.

"Want some?" he offered.

Xiomara shook her head. The smell was enough to wake her. Instead, she grabbed a water bottle from the stack of cases and watched Rafael pour himself coffee with all the enthusiasm of an overworked high school teacher.

"Fell asleep fast after that sancocho." He chuckled. Xiomara shrugged as she guzzled water. Half was gone by the time Rafael reached for the sugar in the cupboard.

Xiomara expelled air before she said, "It's been a long day."

Rafael's smile faded. "Yeah. It has." He took a sip. Silence hung between them like a tarp, thin and easily punctured. Neither had much to say. Xiomara wondered how much longer her uncle was planning on staying in the kitchen. She hoped the caffeine wouldn't keep him so alert he'd notice her snooping through Papi Ramon's study—

"I still can't believe he's gone," Rafael muttered. Xiomara froze, emotional whiplash catching her by surprise.

"O-oh" was all she managed to say as she fumbled to put the cap back on her water bottle. Her uncle turned away. He rested his mug on the counter as his other hand ran over his face. His shoulders came up in a tense wall, then flexed as they shifted downward. Xiomara noticed how Rafael seemed to stand taller when he relaxed, shaking out the brief grip that grief had on him. He turned with a smile and a seed of shame planted itself square between Xiomara's lungs.

She wasn't the only one who missed Papi Ramon.

"Can I ask you something weird?" Xiomara hesitated. "What was Papi Ramon like as a pastor?" Not exorcist, just pastor. Her family made it clear what they did and didn't remember about Papi Ramon, and Xiomara wasn't eager to start a fight about why *she* was actually right.

Rather, she hoped to find something in his answer, a story about how Papi Ramon went off for days at a time, strengthened only by his Bible and bottle of anointed oil and protected by God. That was how her grandfather had made it seem, at least. He'd always made himself a triumphant hero, something between a David and Samson. Xiomara remembered his gleaming smile, the way he leaned in when he dropped his voice into a conspiratorial whisper. She tried to think—what was it that he said? Did he say a specific prayer? Did he invoke God's name and make the demon jump?

She grasped at the memory, but all that came was that damned question—*do you want to know how your mother* really *died?*

Rafael hacked up a laugh. His eyes glistened, staring into a distant memory before finally answering.

"He was *mean*."

Xiomara was stunned.

Rafael slurped coffee. "You know, I used to be jealous of you and the others when you were little kids. Papi was always so nice to you. Made me wonder what I did wrong that he was so mean when I was a boy." He shook his head as if answering his own question. "But that's just how it is. You have kids and you're hard on them, but then your kids have kids and it's like they're angels . . ."

He spoke like he knew from experience but the last time Xiomara checked, Yaritza was still childless.

A chuckle escaped Rafael's lips, and he stumbled around the table, finding stability on a stool around the counter. Xiomara caught it then—a tinny scent, the kind she was used to smelling late at night when she walked across campus to her dorm and a gaggle of freshmen tried to hide their underage drinking. It was nearly hidden by the coffee, but Rafael's clumsiness confirmed her suspicion—he wasn't just grieving. The man was *drunk*. The coffee was just an attempt to sober up.

Was he drinking all day in the storage room? Xiomara frowned, wondering just how many bottles he had.

She got her answer when Rafael's chuckle turned into a sniffle, which rolled into a barely contained sob. *He's been* drinking *drinking.* Rafael choked back tears and coffee as Xiomara backed out of the kitchen, praying that God would be merciful and not let the damned floor creak in alert. For once, God—and the house—played nice.

Xiomara slinked past the library and to the study. She lingered right outside the door and kicked herself when she turned away from it in favor of the stairs. She was sick of the way no one ever paid her consideration back in kind. And still, and *still*, she climbed the steps, forcing herself forward and refusing to quiet her steps even when the house came alive with its petulant groaning and whines. She entered Mami's room and stood right next to Yaritza until the young woman finally glanced away from her phone.

"What?" she said, in mid-text.

"Your dad is drunk, crying in the kitchen." *And also, I think he implied you were pregnant.* She didn't want to know, so she wouldn't ask.

Yaritza scowled. "So?"

"So go talk to him," Xiomara pleaded. *Exasperation* didn't even begin to describe what she was feeling. Was it too much to ask to want a burden to be shared? Yaritza didn't budge. Staring down at her cousin's phone, Xiomara briefly considered chucking it out of the window.

"Wait . . ." Xiomara squinted and snatched the phone. "Are you talking to a journalist about our *family*?"

"Hey!" Yaritza launched herself off the bed. She all but tackled Xiomara, taking the both of them down.

Xiomara's ass smacked the floor, a flat and dull pain marking the point of contact, and she rolled onto her side to keep away from Yaritza's clawing hands. Yaritza chained her arms around Xiomara's waist and let gravity deliver a second blow. Xiomara spilled onto her side and sprawled on her stomach. She felt the full weight of Yaritza's knee in her back, and she screeched in pain.

"Get off!" She bucked. Unbalanced, her cousin thunked down next to her.

"Give it back!" Yaritza struck her shoulder with the soft underside of her fist. The pain was manageable and light. Xiomara maneuvered to bring her foot against Yaritza's torso and push her away. She held the phone far away in one hand while forcing Yaritza farther with the other. Yaritza, in turn, clawed at Xiomara's shirt and cardigan, stretching it until stitches popped. Her nails were sharp enough that they dug into her skin, leaving a trailing burn down Xiomara's side. Xiomara's arms weakened, and Yaritza gained the advantage. She yanked Xiomara's hair hard, wrenching a scream from her lips.

"What are you two doing?!"

The door flew open. Manuel's red glare made the room grow ten degrees chillier. Though Xiomara froze, Yaritza made for the phone and jumped to her feet.

"What are you doing?" the man snapped once more. "Don't you have any shame, acting like this in your grandfather's house?"

Yaritza and Xiomara shared a look from across the room. A quick calculation being done—if Xiomara revealed that Yaritza was talking to a journalist about the family's scandals, how angry would Manuel be? The answer was neither wanted to find out. Xiomara forced a pout, feigning remorse until their uncle would leave.

"People are trying to sleep!" Manuel continued. "If you're going to fight, take it outside."

And the outside, in response, roared dramatically with thunder.

Manuel turned on his way out, slamming the door behind him.

The silence that followed was as fragile as a cobweb. Not knowing where to start, Xiomara sucked in a deep breath, hoping to collect her thoughts, but before she was able to exhale, Yaritza pounced her with a plea.

"Please don't say anything."

Xiomara looked at her in shock. "Why? You're literally the one spreading everyone's business."

Yaritza quickly shook her head. "No, I'm not! I promise, I had *no* idea about Manuel or Chico or even Aury. Please, you have to believe me."

"Who else could it be?" Xiomara said. "You're the only one who thinks all of this is funny."

"Because it *is* funny," her cousin said. "Don't act like you don't think it is."

Xiomara bristled, feeling a tickle of truth in there. It climbed up her spine and pulled on the corners of her lips.

"Ha!" Yaritza threw a pointed finger at Xiomara. "I saw that smile."

With ironclad will, Xiomara pressed her mouth into a line.

"Sex trafficking isn't my idea of a joke."

"That's not what I meant, and you know it," her cousin said. "Seriously, I would *not* have kept this a secret if I'd actually known what they were doing."

Yaritza's eyes glistened with desperation. It was unnerving to see her like that. Xiomara thought about the situation from all angles. Even if she wanted to snitch, telling *anyone* in the family that Yaritza was talking to journalists would not end well. Marisa would tell Aury, making her promise not to get mad first. Aury would promise—and then immediately break her promise.

Manuel and Henry would hear her screams and join in. It would likely get violent. Xiomara did *not* want to be responsible for that. More importantly, she couldn't see Yaritza being the one that had sold their family out. If she had, why bother showing up to the will reading at all?

"Fine," Xiomara agreed.

Relieved, Yaritza flopped back on the bed. "Thank you!"

"But you still shouldn't be talking to a journalist about it." Xiomara tutted. Maybe Marisa was right—they needed media training. "They'll twist your words around on you."

"I can handle it."

Sensing the conversation was over, Xiomara went to the door. An aura of pain spread through her lower back, and she winced as her fingers softly prodded the edge.

"You didn't need to press your knee into my back."

"And you didn't need to take my phone." Yaritza smirked.

Resting a hand on the doorknob, she was hesitant to ask one final question. "Hey. What do you think about what Papi Ramon said in the will? About there being a demon among us?"

With her back to Yaritza, Xiomara waited. She didn't want to turn around. There was that feeling again—the feeling of the walls reaching out to her, the floor closing in. She wondered why Yaritza didn't feel anything of the sort. Maybe she did and she was just better at ignoring it.

"Why not?" She tossed the answer at Xiomara with the same kind of tone someone would use to order a pizza. "If we're being real, it's not like we don't have worse people in our family."

Xiomara trudged back to the library in a haze. Listlessness was setting in. It was beginning to feel pointless, following vaguely connected clues. Everyone else seemed to be more worried about the scandals and ignored the urgent request in Papi Ramon's will. Worse than that, they couldn't even agree not to fight with one another. Xiomara couldn't argue with her cousin—Yaritza was right, after all. Even if there *was* a demon in the family, that still meant everyone else was horrible *and human*. What was their excuse?

I wish Papi Ramon were still here, Xiomara thought miserably. She wanted to leave the demon stuff to him. *What was he thinking when he wrote the will?* Ironically, only God knew.

Or Naomi. Xiomara had already asked the home aide what Papi Ramon was like in the last days. As a housekeeper and home aide, Naomi had spent more time with Papi Ramon in the last couple of years than anyone else in the family. After Josefina's death, he was near inconsolable. Even Xiomara didn't want to visit for more than a few hours.

But Naomi was always there. Xiomara could ask again, maybe ask different questions, beg and plead for Naomi to tell her something she missed, some odd statements Papi Ramon made when he thought he was alone or a strange new routine he had taken up in his old age. She was exhausted and desperate for something more than just vague hints and flimsy clues.

The library door creaked open, and with her eyes already adjusted to the dark, she searched for Naomi's sleeping figure.

"Hey, Naomi?" Xiomara whispered. The bundle of blankets fooled her into sinking her hand well into the folds. She pulled and flapped the blanket, finding no one underneath it. Xiomara stood up just as the door creaked again.

"What are you doing?" Naomi asked, closing the door behind her. Compared to Xiomara's whispers, there was an accusatory tone in her question. If the lights were on, Naomi might have even glared at her.

"I was looking for you," Xiomara said. "I need to ask you something. About Papi Ramon."

"Oh." There was a frown in her voice. An awkward pause that made it seem like Naomi was now a little self-conscious. Her silhouette wrapped its arms around itself in a hug and leaned against the door frame.

Xiomara softened, all at once realizing that the topic might have actually just been difficult for Naomi to discuss. *I'm not the only one who misses him.* Sure, the home aide worked for him, but wasn't that a kindness in itself? Instead of abandoning her after the loss of Julia, the job was a lifeline to help the freshly turned eighteen-year-old avoid homelessness. What other man would do that?

"What about him?"

"I was wondering if—"

A shriek sounded through the house, carving through the air like a rusted knife. Xiomara and Naomi just about collided trying to open the door and went skidding out into the hall. Rafael nearly crashed into them from behind.

"What was that?" Xiomara asked her uncle. Despite his being previously drunk, he seemed to have sobered up fast and maneuvered around them. He ignored her question, instead sprinting to the end of the hall and stopping at the door of the study. Light spilled out, illuminating Rafael's bloodshot eyes and confused expression.

"Aury?" His voice came out like a mewling cat's, soft and small and vulnerable. Xiomara could easily imagine him as a young boy, fidgeting with the end of his shirt, eyes as wide as the sun.

Something scrambled inside the room, and a figure suddenly emerged from the light, angular in form and scraping against the floor as it crawled out. Tears, fat and inky, streamed down Aury's face as Rafael tried to help her up. She wouldn't have it, though. She pushed against him just as much as she pulled upward to get to her feet.

"No! Get off me!" Her eyes were wild and darted around, unfocused.

"Stop! It's me!" Rafael tried to soften her blows. But the moment she was on her feet again, she barreled straight through him and jumped up the stairs.

"Aury!" Rafael yelled after her. "Aury, ¡espera!"

"What the hell . . . ?" Naomi muttered, frozen. Xiomara listened to the thumping feet upstairs eventually end with the slam of the door. Rafael knocked persistently, begging to be let in.

Xiomara cut through the hall to the study. Her eyes winced with pricks of pain as they adjusted to the harsh light. It was so bright that she swore she could feel it.

But even stronger was the smell. Pungent copper mixed with burnt wood. The undertone of sulfur. Xiomara stepped into the study for the second time that night to discover large claw marks on Papi Ramon's desk.

And they dripped red.

8:32 P.M.

Twenty minutes later, the family coalesced in Marisa and Aury's shared old room. The same size as Josefina's room, made even smaller by two twin-sized beds pressed against opposite walls, and with all the extra bodies, Xiomara might as well have been sitting in a sauna. Warmth swaddled her even as she tried to keep space between her, Yaritza, and Naomi. And it didn't help that the older adults were so much more tense than the younger ones. There was a quiet understanding that if someone spoke out of turn, it would only lead to a major fight.

Aury sat on her bed, hugging her knees to her chest, sniffling intermittently while we waited for her to calm down. Marisa rubbed circles into her back, cooing soft words of consolation. Sitting on the opposite bed, Xiomara's knee jiggled with anxiety, knowing that she had to approach this delicately.

What were you doing in Papi Ramon's study? No, that sounded like an accusation.

What happened? Too broad, but it was a starting point.

What did you see? The *what* possibly being a demon. Xiomara didn't want to bring it up again so soon, but they *had* to see reason now.

"Everything is going to be okay," Marisa murmured. Aury leaned into the crook of her sister's neck, staring blankly at Rafael's feet. Despondent.

Rafael shifted from foot to foot impatiently.

"Can I ask now?" Rafael huffed, throwing a hand up as if waiting for something to fall into it. An answer, perhaps. Marisa sneered at him even as she spoke to Aury.

"You talk when you're ready," she said. Rafael scoffed and turned away. Both Manuel and Henry remained right at the door frame, lingering like a bad cold. Their faces were neutral, but Xiomara caught the way their eyes darted to Aury every single time she so much as hiccupped; they were only feigning disinterest. Despite treating the open door like an invisible barrier, curiosity still got the better of them. Aury's crocodile tears were nowhere to be found. She was truly and utterly shaken, and—worst of all—refusing to speak. The only sound she made was a sharp nasal inhale that forced her snot up into its cavity, rippling like a buzz saw cutting through the room.

From behind, Yaritza leaned over Xiomara's shoulder and whispered, "Is she ever going to say anything or . . . ?"

"Shh!" Marisa hushed her. "If you're just here to gossip, go somewhere else!"

There was that word again—and that accusation. Marisa may have sent a sharp look to Yaritza first, but then it dashed to Xiomara just for a moment before dissipating completely.

Manuel could not hold it in anymore. "This is ridiculous!" he yelled. When Marisa shushed him, he spat back, "No! Why are we all here if she's not going to talk?"

"Then go back to your room, Manuel!" Marisa's voice cracked. Her feet came down on the floor with a loud thud, and she planted both hands on Manuel's chest, pushing him away. "No one asked you to come over here! All of you—get out! All you're doing is stressing her out!" She turned to grab Naomi first and then Yaritza. The two protested against being dragged out.

"I'm not even doing anything!" Yaritza whined.

"I can walk!" Naomi said.

The men grumbled with each other outside the door, and when Xiomara looked back to Aury, she could have sworn she saw her lips move.

And this time she heard something.

"You too, Xiomara!" Marisa's hand circled Xiomara's wrist. She had begun dragging Xiomara out when Xiomara saw Aury's lips move.

". . . saw it . . ."

"Wait!" Xiomara wrung her hand from Marisa's. "She's saying something."

Everyone returned to the room. Aury's shuddering breath felt amplified in the silence of the family.

"I . . . saw it . . ."

"Saw what, Aury?" Marisa sat next to her.

"The thing . . . that clawed Papi's desk." For the first time since the initial scream, Aury's eyes met Marisa's. "I saw it." She gulped.

The world shifted under Xiomara's feet. A high-pitched ringing started in her ears.

"What did it look like?" Xiomara whispered. She pulled against Marisa's grip. The woman let go, only to push Xiomara aside and return to Aury. She took Aury's hands in hers, stroking her thumbs across the curves of her sister's knuckles.

"It was big," Aury answered between sniffles. "Bigger than me. And it had a face like a dog but nastier. And—and it was burnt." Her face contorted into a fearful expression, eyes widened like she was seeing it again for the first time. "It had burnt skin—like concón at the bottom of a pot."

Though Xiomara had a hard time imagining burnt rice as skin, the rest of her family didn't seem to try.

"I don't believe this." Manuel shook his head. He scoffed, turning away, but wouldn't leave the entrance.

"Manuel, *shush*."

"You really want to believe this crap?" he asked. "She's just doing what she always does—making up whatever she wants so we forget about what she did."

"Aury, forget about *him*." Marisa leaned into her sister. But Aury shrugged her off, throwing the blanket down and stepping onto the floor. She closed in on Manuel, a hardened expression on her face as she quietly glided across the floor.

"It was you, wasn't it?" she whispered. "You called the demon."

And there it was. Aury said it outright, and the room was frozen in consideration. The only person who didn't share in their sympathies was her older brother.

Manuel chuckled in a way that seemed more like he was just expelling air. "You're really going to accuse me of calling a demon?" He searched her eyes, smile falling when he realized just how serious she was. "You're crazy. I lead a *church*."

"You *prey* on a church," Aury retorted. "You took their money and used it to cover up el diablo's crimes." She tossed a nasty look to Henry, lips pulled back in a disgusted sneer like he was no more her nephew than he was a congealed pile of shit and vomit. It wasn't missed by Manuel, who flexed his jaw in an act of barely constrained rage. Xiomara held her breath, half expecting the two to continue their physical fight from earlier. Despite Manuel's being about as tall as Aury, the look in his eyes said he was looking down at her. His younger sister was beneath him. In contrast, Aury was calm and certain, staring him through and through like a pin driven into an insect on display.

Manuel's lips parted for a moment, somewhere between a scoff and a laugh.

"Your eyes are really big," he said, so low that Xiomara almost didn't catch it. Confused, she looked to Aury in time to see her face twitch before taking a step back from Manuel.

"What were you doing in Papi's study? Hm?" he asked, louder. "What were you looking for?"

"Get out," Aury said.

"You see?" Manuel looked to Marisa. "Suddenly, she doesn't want to—"

"Get out of my room!" she shrieked, over and over again. "Get out! Get out! Leave! Get out of my room!"

Xiomara couldn't escape the room fast enough. Most of the family clotted the doorway as they struggled to leave, but once Xiomara was out, she took in deep breaths. She had never controlled her breathing so much as to be nearly lightheaded—or was it just because the room ran warm?

The cool hallway welcomed her with calming breezes, and she felt her head clearing immediately.

"Come on." Naomi threw an arm over her shoulder. "Let's get away from all this." They hardly took a step toward the stairs before Yaritza cut them off.

"Hey, Xiomara? Can I talk to you real quick?" She held her phone close to her chest and completely ignored Naomi. The home aide shrugged and left.

"Okay." Xiomara felt awkward, wanting to follow Naomi, but having the decision seemingly made for her. "What do you want to talk about?"

"I don't think it's a good idea for you to stick around you-know-who."

Xiomara furrowed her brow. She followed her cousin's line of sight and immediately regretted it. "Leave Naomi alone. She's going through a hard time too."

"I bet, now that she's out of a job," Yaritza said, so smooth that it almost slid under Xiomara's attention. She rolled her eyes as she changed the subject.

"Hey, do you know why Manuel said that about Aury? That her eyes looked big," she clarified. "And she got this weird look on her face, so I was wondering—"

"*Ooh.* The pills." Yaritza's eyes widened. "Wow, I can't believe she's still doing that. I thought she quit after rehab."

Xiomara's head spun. "Wait, rehab? *Pills?*"

He said eyes *when he meant* pupils.

"But that *does* make sense, now that I think about it." Yaritza looked down at her phone. She tapped the screen a few times, holding it up to Xiomara as she spoke. "It says here that el bacà—"

"Slow down." Xiomara pushed Yaritza's phone aside. "What do you mean about Aury doing pills and going to rehab?" All of this was news to her, and it painted a new picture of Aury that she hadn't seen before.

Yaritza's mouth fell open. "You mean you don't *know*?"

"How am I going to know if no one tells me anything?!" Xiomara said, exasperated. "Are you going to tell me or not?"

"I mean, it's kind of an open secret in the family. At some point—probably around the time Aury started Alluria—she got addicted to some kind of pills. Benzos or whatever it is rich people do."

Xiomara suppressed the urge to point out that they were *all* rich people, and almost none of them did drugs. She waited patiently for Yaritza to explain.

"Papi Ramon made her go to rehab after your mom died," Yaritza said. Xiomara raised both eyebrows, expectant, but Yaritza shook her head. "That's it. That's the whole story."

"So Manuel thinks Aury was popping pills in the study?"

Yaritza cheesed. "More like popping *his* pills in the study," and Xiomara realized she was saying Aury was taking Papi Ramon's medication. Yaritza continued, "I wouldn't be surprised if Naomi didn't finish packing up all of his medication. Oh, right! Look at *this*."

Yaritza turned her phone over. At first glance, Xiomara thought she was looking at a dog—maybe even a wolf. But the thing on Yaritza's phone had no fur. Instead, it looked like a mass of twisted bones and meat standing on all fours. Sunken eyes that attempted to bury pinpricks of fire and a snarling mouth revealed overgrown piercing teeth. They were like overbites, shaved into piercing tusks. And the claws were more like serrated knives, barely softened by black grime. Just one swipe, and a person would be walking away with more than a few scratches.

Yaritza quickly scrolled down her phone and read, "'El bacà is believed to be a *Haitian* spirit, one that only *Haitians* can summon and dismiss.'" She looked up with an eager smile, pride in being the first to come to a solution.

A solution that filled Xiomara with dread and a grim realization. This was what looking for the demon eventually meant—a witch hunt. Family against family until they all united against one common enemy. And Naomi wasn't even family. What a convenient choice. Papi Ramon sent a message in the will, knowing that Naomi would be in the house when it was read. He didn't just say "the demon"—he called it el bacà. All signs pointed to Naomi.

Papi Ramon wouldn't have wanted this. Yet, did that matter? Papi Ramon was not around. Just his kids were. Family that rarely united *for* something as often as they did *against* it, and in this situation, where everyone's dirty laundry was in danger of being aired, the unification could only be swift and deadly.

They wouldn't dare . . . Xiomara wanted to believe her family had their limits. And maybe before this night, believing that would've been easy. But with one cousin being exposed as a sexual abuser, his father a thieving enabler, and an aunt being responsible for chemical burns, the limit for bad decisions appeared nonexistent.

And even more than that, more than the idea of a demon in the house, more than the knowledge that Naomi already held the short end of the stick, was a simple question that made Xiomara sweat: *And then what?* A witch hunt rarely claimed just one victim.

Xiomara swallowed.

"So we already know what to do," Yaritza said, words coming out faster than Xiomara could process. "We have to tie up Naomi and force her to dismiss the demon. And obviously, I'm not, like, pro-torture or anything . . ."

"Whoa!" Xiomara's eyes widened. "Stop before you say something you can't take back."

"I *just said* I'm not pro-torture!" Yaritza huffed. "I'm just stating facts, okay? El bacà is a Haitian spirit. One that can only be controlled *by* Haitians. They use it to protect their property. *Naomi* is Haitian, literally from Haiti, so obviously—"

"*Julia* was *literally* from Haiti. Naomi was born and raised in New Jersey," Xiomara corrected her. "Jesus Christ, how can you hate someone this much and not even know basic facts about them?" She had to stomp this out at the source. Yaritza was a firecracker—once she got started, it was hard to stop her. "Do me a favor and keep all of this to yourself, okay? Otherwise you're going to get someone killed."

Yaritza was silent. Her shoulders formed a straight line, and she gave Xiomara a look that sent chills down her spine.

"Why are you defending her so much? You know we have to stick together, otherwise *all* of us are damned," Yaritza said. "You really want to risk damning all of us for her?"

If it were up to Xiomara, she truly wouldn't care. But as she thought about Papi Ramon, about all the things he did for the Abreus, from immigrating to a new country and bankrolling all of their futures, to his very last message to her—Xiomara curled her hands into fists.

She looked down but said, "I think our family did a lot of the damning on their own."

"Hm. Maybe." Yaritza coldly sidestepped Xiomara as she made her way to the stairs. "By the way, Wanda's in your mom's room. She asked to pray in there while we were all dealing with Aury. I think she's still there, so don't bother her for a bit."

"Thanks for the heads-up," Xiomara said.

"Of course," Yaritza responded. "What are family for?"

Sitting on the floor beside her mother's closed door, Xiomara's ass grew numb waiting for Wanda to emerge. She thought it would only take five or ten minutes, tops, but the young woman seemed to have much to discuss with the Lord. Eventually, she took out her cell phone and scrolled absentmindedly through social media. She wondered if Marcus was doing the same, waiting for her to reach out, out of desperation or maybe sheer boredom. Once or twice, she opened his text messages, thumb hovering over the touch-screen keyboard before swiping away to another app. Her battery had gone down to 62 percent.

Yaritza wasn't lying about the hashtags. A number of posts decried her family's wrongdoings, going so far as to speculate what else the Abreus might have been hiding. After all, three scandals in one afternoon? That was a record. And the people were out for blood. Posts about her family ranged from mild disappointment to outright xenophobia.

It was probably a good idea she kept all of her online profiles private, only allowing close friends to follow and DM her.

Eventually, Xiomara needed to stretch. She stood in front of the door with a budding curiosity as a hushed voice spoke fervently inside.

". . . Perdóname, Señor . . ." Wanda's voice rose just enough for Xiomara to hear short breaks between sentences, a slight wheeze as she pushed through in prayer.

Is she crying? Xiomara pressed her ear against the door. Wanda sounded too muffled to parse, easily drowned out by the desperate downpour and crackling thunder.

And then there was air where the door should have been.

"What?" Wanda snapped, hand still on the doorknob, a subtle message that she would be closing it again once Xiomara was done there.

"Sorry to bother you . . ." Xiomara cleared her throat. "Just wanted to check in and see how you were doing."

A piss-poor attempt to explain away her eavesdropping, Xiomara knew, but it was the only idea she had. Wanda hastily wiped her nose before she answered.

"I'm fine," she said.

"Oh. Okay." Xiomara nodded. As much as she wanted to leave, her body wouldn't move. She felt stuck in front of Wanda, like a reflection of her. The door frame was the mirror. Unless Wanda closed the door, Xiomara wouldn't be able to go.

". . . Did you want your room back?" Wanda asked.

"What? Oh. No, that's okay. You can finish up."

And the door was shut again, freeing Xiomara from her position. She exhaled and made a beeline downstairs.

The kitchen appeared lively with conversation. Rafael, Manuel, and Henry carried on, their shadows merging in the light of the doorway. Xiomara backed into a bathroom, peeking out just enough to see the men go from the kitchen to the dining room. Rafael seemed to have grabbed an extra mug of coffee while Henry chugged a Modelo. The TV clicked on and the sound of a sports game filtered down the hall.

Fuck it. This was her best chance. Xiomara ducked into Papi Ramon's study while the men were still distracted. She closed the door quietly, wrinkling her nose at the acrid smell of burnt wood lightly washed in blood. It didn't mesh with Papi Ramon's cologne at all, instead overpowering it something fierce. It caught in the back of Xiomara's throat, teasing her gag reflex. She pressed her sleeve to her face and crossed the room.

Whipping out her phone, she cast a light onto the claw marks. The blood had all dried, nearly blending in with the splinted dark wood. Where did it come from? Aury didn't appear to be injured, and she also didn't seem like the kind of person to hurt herself, all to garner sympathy. Xiomara carefully traced the marks with a finger, from end to end, imagining each one to be like a toiled field the way they were equally distanced apart.

It's rough, she noted. Like whatever had cut into the wood was mildly blunt, forced into the desk with sheer strength. Xiomara pressed a nail against it, just beside the claw mark. Pressure spiked through her thumb, and she shook her hand when she pulled it away. She didn't even leave a dent.

Not that it mattered. Aury could have spent an entire hour filing a path through the wood, and it still wouldn't have looked like an authentic claw mark. Xiomara doubted Aury could make a single line, let alone three. The desk was made out of an extremely tough wood—that much, she knew. Once her family was calm enough to reason with, she would point this out.

Xiomara's phone buzzed in her hand, screen lighting up with a message from Marcus. She clicked ignore and focused on the scene around the study. Many of the awards and plaques were still face down on the floor, undone and taken apart in search of a clue from her grandfather. But many of them seemed to have been cleared away. Shoved to the side, as if clearing a path for someone to easily walk through. Xiomara followed the path to the other side of the desk. She hadn't gotten a chance to look through it last time, with Aury suddenly intruding for a phone call.

The first drawer opened to a handful of pens, scattered to the side and above a notepad. Several pages were already torn out, and when Xiomara flipped through the rest, she was disappointed to see nothing but notes written to himself and a collection of phone numbers to call about certain bills.

The next drawer below that was largely empty, save for an old glasses case and the cleaning cloth it came with. Xiomara held the hollow vessel in her hand, suddenly overcome with a sense of longing for the glasses. She knew they had buried them with Papi Ramon—it seemed too weird for him not to wear them in his coffin—but she wished she had something of his to hold on to.

Xiomara's phone buzzed again. She ignored it.

In the last drawer, Xiomara found several white caps staring up at her. Pill bottles, each at least half-full, with Papi Ramon's name printed on all of the labels. Some were weekly vitamins to make up for some kind of deficiency—D3, magnesium, iron, omega-3, it went on. Others were medications prescribed to deal largely with Papi Ramon's known heart issues—lisinopril, simvastatin, and something Xiomara had trouble pronouncing but was blue and round and was supposed to be taken at meals. She shook the bottle and listened to the pills smack against plastic. She almost put it away when she noticed one bottle appeared to be open. The cap hadn't locked all the way, and when she picked it up, she could instantly see why.

It was cracked. The rim of the bottle missed a piece, and a line cut down behind the label.

Oh, Aury . . . Was this what she'd taken before the attack? Xiomara scanned the label for a name. Tramadol. Xiomara googled the medication, ignoring the growing number of notifications on her phone from Marcus.

Tramadol—a strong narcotic for moderate to severe pain. Xiomara let out a shuddering breath and fell into the desk seat. Right, now she remembered. It was the medication that Mami was prescribed right after her surgery. She couldn't move very much without it, and even with it, she made sure not to twist, bend, lift, or do much of anything while her lower back healed. It was almost impressive how much a person relied on their lower back functioning painlessly in order to do any amount of movement. If Mami was in a car that hit a bump in the road, it was all she could do not to cry out.

Xiomara closed the bottle and put it back. Her phone vibrated again, an irritating sensation that continued much longer, and Xiomara saw that instead of taking the hint, Marcus was now calling. Her head was on the verge of imploding.

She took a deep breath as she answered.

"*What!*" she whispered angrily. "What? What is it? I'm in the middle of something, and you are—"

"Sorry, sorry, I just . . . Have you seen the news?" Marcus asked.

"I know all about my family, Marcus!" Xiomara hissed into the phone. At the sight of a shadow crossing the light of the door, she ducked down and pressed the phone against her chest. Marcus's voice was muffled as the footsteps faded in the direction of the bathroom.

". . . Wanda?"

Xiomara blinked and put the phone up to her ear. "What? What did you say?"

"Uh . . . how much do you know about Wanda?"

Maybe it was the grief of losing her grandfather, or the stress of trying to decipher his last request, or the fact that Marcus was not understanding boundaries—but all at once, Xiomara's nerves were fizzing, a low flame consuming them fast like the wick of fireworks, and if she did not put out that fire fast, she would not be responsible for her actions.

She chewed on her tongue, but irritation got the better of her. "Are you really asking me what I know about my own cousin?"

"I'm just wondering—"

"Marcus, you have sent me"—she paused to check her notifications—"five text messages, presumably about Wanda, and then called me when I didn't answer once. Is there a point to this phone call besides you being a patronizing fuck, or are you going to just tell me what you assume I already know?"

Her temple throbbed. There was a twinge of guilt almost as soon as Xiomara cursed at Marcus, but it was quickly overshadowed by more anger.

"When you didn't answer, I got worried," he mumbled.

Do I have to answer you immediately all the time? Oh God, he was not making this easy for himself. Or for her. Xiomara hit her head against the desk a few times, testing the strength of the wood. Next time she dated someone this clingy, she would block them.

"Good night, Marcus," she said dryly.

"Wait!"

She hung up and quickly swiped to his texts.

The first two were just messages to ask if she was currently up. The third was about how he couldn't sleep and wanted to know what she was doing.

It was the fourth message that made her jaw drop—a link to an article titled, *Wanda Abreu, Discovered to Be the Assailant of a Cold Hit-and-Run Case.*

The link opened up to a web page before Xiomara realized she'd clicked it. Every second she was forced to X out another ad felt like an eternity, but eventually the article itself was unobstructed.

Two years ago, an odd hit-and-run case captivated the true crime community due to the bizarre nature in which thirty-two-year-old Miley Jones was killed. Jones was a young mother on her way to pick up her child from day care, when a speeding Honda hit her at the intersection of Neely Street and Alwright Avenue. The driver initially stopped to check on Jones and help her up, and the two appeared to get into an altercation. The driver then pushed Jones down, got into their car, and backed up to hit Jones once more before speeding off.

A coroner's report stated that Jones had suffered severe head trauma upon the first impact, and likely did not know she was fighting with the assailant initially. The second hit was what killed her.

Though the driver was partially obscured by a turtleneck and a hoodie they had pulled over their face, and the car's license plate was concealed by roadside greenery, true crime YouTuber JalissaSolvesCrimes was able to make a connection between Jones and Wanda Abreu. The video of the hit-and-run showed a unique rearview mirror hanging decoration in the form of a carved wooden cross. While authorities focused on identifying what could be seen of the assailant's face, the cross had Abreu's initials carved on the back, which could be seen in the video.

JalissaSolvesCrimes was only able to make the connection when trying to solve an unrelated crime that occurred during a protest outside a Planned Parenthood on that same day. A photo showed Abreu leaving the clinic from a side entrance and quickly going to her car, which has the same hanging cross under the rearview mirror.

Xiomara gasped. The implication could not have been clearer if it were a ten-foot-tall neon sign. Were people already talking about this? The article was from a lesser-known news outlet, practically the tabloids. Maybe no one in her family had seen it yet.

"YOOOOO—" Yaritza was cut off by a sudden thud.

"Everything's fine!" Marisa yelled. No one went rushing upstairs. No one seemed to find anything suspicious. That was fine, because Xiomara could already imagine what was happening in Marisa's room, and it was only a matter of time before it spread like wildfire.

Xiomara peeked outside of the study before speeding out. Behind Marisa's door, there were not-so-subtle signs of a struggle. One of her aunts hushing Yaritza, another not-so-subtle cry of pain, and the gentle thrash of a body against a bed. Xiomara waited until they quieted down.

"Hey . . ." She knocked. "It's me, Xiomara."

Aury cracked the door an inch. Her eyes darted from Xiomara to the hallway, quickly scanning for any threats. Meanwhile, Marisa had her full body weight on Yaritza, both legs pinning her arms to her side and a hand holding a pair of socks in the loud cousin's mouth. Yaritza's own legs continued to thrash, and she wriggled to get out of Marisa's grasp.

The sight alone would've been hilarious to Xiomara if not for the fact that this was *her* family.

"Hurry up and get in!" Marisa yelled. Aury pulled her in, gripping her arm so quick, she was certain it would leave a bruise.

"What is going on here?" she asked.

"We're trying to keep this little *snitch* from yelling your cousin's business everywhere," Aury explained. She gestured to Yaritza like she was backslapping the air. Though her makeup was still a mess, the younger aunt seemed to have pulled herself together for one purpose—to keep Manuel from finding out about his daughter's supposed scandal.

We don't even really know if that's her. Xiomara thought of anything that would provide plausible deniability. Those initials could belong to anyone, could mean anything. Wallace Adams. Wendy Abbott. Will Armstrong. Willow Austin. The WA combinations were endless. Wanda was not the only person in the world who drove a Honda with a wooden cross hanging from the mirror.

Xiomara watched Aury angrily mutter warnings to Yaritza.

"What is your problem? You want Manuel to kill your cousin? Is that it?" Aury ripped the socks out of Yaritza's mouth.

"He's not going to do *shit* to her—he didn't even do anything to Henry!" Yaritza whispered back. "How do we know he doesn't already *know* about the abortion?"

"If he knows, then you don't need to go yelling about it." Marisa shifted, letting Yaritza sit up. The two older women stared her down, an unspoken threat hanging between them. Yaritza rolled her eyes but sheepishly looked away. "But if you think Manuel doesn't think differently about Wanda and Henry, then you've never met a Domincan man."

"Fine, I won't say anything. Can I get my phone back?" She held her hand out and Marisa retrieved it from her back pocket.

"Who was it even with?" Aury asked the room. "Wanda doesn't have a boyfriend."

The three women formed a circle, discussing intimate details of Wanda's hypothetical personal life. Was it the young man that she was always in pictures with? What was his name—Eric? Did Manuel ever talk about someone like him? How well did he know Eric? Wasn't it funny how much Wanda liked to pretend she was above all the drama?

Their comments became like chirps, like singing, the way they discussed the cheap cliché.

The pastor's daughter, it's always the pastor's daughter. Obviously, neither of the aunts would ever get an abortion, they wouldn't need to, they were always *careful*, unlike church girls. This was karma, wasn't it? A punishment from God, really. God didn't like ugly, and Wanda was hiding her own ugliness underneath that ankle-length skirt.

The topic of Miley Jones never even registered in the conversation, not as an actual person really, just as evidence, *proof* of Christian hypocrisy, because they all knew what Manuel would think, what he would say. He'd make a vaguely neutral statement like he hoped that the woman (she wouldn't have a name, not to Manuel) was capital-*S Saved*. Spared the fires of hell for daring to exist at a crosswalk at the wrong time. Wasn't it kind of funny, they giggled, that Manuel's entire family was caught up in crime, one way or another? Imagine that.

Go gossip with Yaritza like you always do.

Xiomara would've heard the knocking if it wasn't for the high-pitched ringing that bounced around in her ears. Instead, she watched her aunts and cousin turn like deer to the door, alert and sensitive to any sign of danger. They continued their conversation when Naomi slowly entered.

She gave a cursory glance to the chatty women huddled on the bed before approaching Xiomara. With alarms still sounding in her head, Xiomara focused on reading Naomi's lips, then handed the woman her cell phone. According to the brief look of gratitude, Xiomara figured that seemed to be what she'd wanted, and she watched the home aide leave while trying to figure out what was so funny about her cousin orphaning a four-year-old.

9:48 P.M.

There were two broken chairs, an overturned table, a displaced ottoman (hinges bent sideways), a slew of curses thrown like bombs in Spanish, and one inconsolable Wanda when her father finally found out. Xiomara's back throbbed from being thrown into a wall, Yaritza pinched her bloody nose, and both their aunts yelled back in Spanish, defending the same niece whose inevitable demise they were reveling in not too long ago.

"She's a grown woman!" Aury shouted. "She's allowed to make her own decisions!"

"*How could you do this to me!*" screamed Manuel. It was a torpedo of anguish, the way he struggled against his brother and son. Rafael locked his arms under Manuel's armpits, keeping him from swinging out against Henry, who picked both legs up and pinned them to his sides. The image alone could have fooled Xiomara into thinking he was the *real* victim of this scenario.

Chaos had bloomed and was flourishing in the house of the Abreus. Maybe it was the concussion she likely sustained, but Xiomara wondered, how did they get here? Her mind was foggy as she thought back to how it all started.

She was in Aury and Marisa's room, watching the two of them and Yaritza take turns in their chisme session. They wondered aloud, the kind of thoughts that were going through Wanda's mind when she did it, the in-hindsight hints that clued them in to the act (the sudden illnesses that had befallen her—didn't she have to rain check from a family friend's baby shower that one time?), and finally, *what would Manuel do*? Of course, he'd wail and yell about why she had committed such a grave sin (still the abortion, not the hit-and-run), but beyond that, would he disown her? As much as a man can disown his grown daughter, perhaps. She would be disciplined in the church for sure—unable to take part in any service and forced to sit in the very front row, as close to God (and the pastor) as one can be. For religious Latinos, this was the physical act of wearing a scarlet *A* on one's chest.

Never mind the fact Wanda's rash act had taken the life of another mother—no, the church was more concerned about the "life" of the unborn.

At some point, Naomi returned Xiomara's cell phone, and she learned then that she had to borrow it because her own phone was dead and she needed to let her roommate know she would not return home until morning. That was fine, Xiomara concluded, and closed the door behind the home aide.

She sat on the other bed, leaning so purposefully against the wall as though her spine were trying to dig through it. She scoured the internet for more news about Wanda. Which news channels were weighing in? How bad was the public reception? For half a second, Xiomara believed that maybe Marisa was right to call for a confessional. Despite how slowly she breathed, in the presence of her gossiping female relatives, pressure built up in her lungs.

I should be looking for the demon, she thought. *Not doing damage control.*

"I'm going to go to the bathroom," Xiomara announced, going to the door. The announcement went fully ignored, and once she had left, she dove right down a rabbit hole.

When Papi Ramon had mentioned being damned, Xiomara thought he meant the biblical kind, not having her family's name dragged through the mud. *Maybe he was being poetic.* Maybe Papi Ramon knew, in detail, all of his children's shortcomings and that they were coming to bite them in the ass.

No. Xiomara chewed the inside of her cheek. If that were the case, Papi Ramon wouldn't have needed to specify the demon by name—el bacà. This was a real demon. And publicly exposing her family felt like a pretty human thing to do. Only someone with a long-standing grudge would bother to destroy Xiomara's family, one by one. The only problem was, the Abreus seemed to have a lot of enemies.

Xiomara looked down the length of the hallway, all the way down to the glued window. She still couldn't remember the story behind its permanent closure, couldn't grasp it fully, but it beckoned her forward, tingling the space between the edge of her hair and the back of her neck. The mysterious scar. Her father still hadn't responded with the story behind it. Xiomara checked her phone again—57 percent. Her battery would need a charge soon. Meanwhile, the window waited as if promising to answer all her burning questions. Xiomara itched to get closer, finally allowing her feet to reunite her with her reflection.

Outside, the storm continued. A drastic change from the moment of her arrival, where the rain only formed beads—but now those beads formed sheets. It reminded Xiomara of a car wash, the kind where she could stay in the car as it rolled through an automatic washer. The darkness outside made her reflection sharper, and she stared into her own eyes with a disquieted expression.

Do you want to fly? The voice was like a memory, a mimic of one she'd heard before. There was an ominous cloud over that memory. Every inch of her body tensed to remember, and when it released—she fell. Dropped harder than a stone, the sudden free fall ending with a pop at the base of her skull.

She was pretty sure her head had split. Xiomara wouldn't move—couldn't move, couldn't talk, couldn't *feel* beyond the gravity holding her down. Something sticky was pooling around her. She had one more jolt of fear as everything went black.

The world came back on the heels of smoke. Xiomara was still standing, body locked in front of the same window that she remembered opening.

Did I . . . die?

She weakly fell to her knees. Before she could steady herself, she heard trampling feet rumbling up the steps, followed by pleas for calm and mercy.

"Wait, Manuel, just calm down." Rafael put a half-hearted grip on his brother's shoulder.

Manuel threw it off with a snarl. "I don't *need* to calm down."

"Papi, *chill.*" Henry jumped in front of him. It was strange to hear him with so much concern in his voice.

Aury's door flew open. Marisa's and Yaritza's heads poked out, crowding the door and watching Manuel push his son out of the way.

On the other end, Mami's bedroom door opened and Wanda tentatively stepped out. The whites of her eyes were a subtle pink. She looked from Xiomara to the rest of the family with alarm, mouth hanging open, with the realization that it was much too late.

"Papi?" Wanda said.

It all went red. In seconds, Manuel rushed forward, slowed only by the men pulling him back and the women clearing the doorway to get in his way.

"Hold on, Manuel, let's just talk about this," Aury said, holding her hands out defensively.

"You have to remember, she's a grown woman, Manito—" Marisa added.

"She is my *daughter.*" Manuel pulled his arm against Rafael's grip. It almost went flying out, fist just an inch short of hitting Marisa across the temple.

"Hey!" she snapped. "Watch yourself!"

The older adults focused on keeping Manuel away from Wanda while Yaritza scurried to her side. Xiomara followed just as quickly, hoping to shield her cousin from the worst of it. She found it easier to grapple with her family drama now that she was sure she had once met death and somehow come back. *Does the demon have something to do with it?*

Xiomara wasn't sure she wanted to know the answer to that question, so she focused on Wanda. "Come on, let's go downstairs."

Wanda looked like she couldn't breathe.

It continued like that for a while: Manuel yelling for everyone to let go of him and let him deal with his child, Yaritza coaxing Wanda toward the stairs, Xiomara somehow becoming the wall between the parties. Yaritza looked to her for help because there was only one set of stairs to the first floor and Manuel was blocking it.

For fuck's sake.

"Take Manuel to Papi Ramon's room," Xiomara muttered to Aury, sidestepping to catch her eye. By some miracle, Aury heard her niece and repeated the order like an announcement.

"Let's all go to Papi's room!"

"You all go to Papi's room!" Manuel mimicked. But even he seemed to be running out of steam. The combined forces of Rafael and Henry managed to inch him closer to Papi Ramon's room. Marisa pushed the door open and ushered him inside while Xiomara helped keep part of the hallway clear for Wanda's passage. Her cousin was already wheezing, snot bubbling out of her nose while she tried to keep her tears from spilling out. All they needed to do was get her to the stairs while the others sequestered Manuel until he calmed down.

"We're almost there, okay, Wanda, just don't look at him, just keep walking and look at me, you're going to be fine. Just breathe in and out and we'll be downstairs soon." Yaritza chatted endlessly, a line of *just do this, just do that,* one right after another, like every *just* would make her take another step forward. It couldn't be helped, with Wanda walking like her feet were made of concrete. Xiomara had always heard of the freeze response in fight-or-flight, but she had never actually seen it happen before.

Wanda was hesitant, shaking with every step, but once Manuel was in Papi Ramon's room, she seemed to move much faster, giving more validity to Yaritza's insistence on not looking at him.

"There we go, just keep going."

Xiomara stood in front of Papi Ramon's door. Marisa was still too much in the way to be able to close it, but at least she was also blocking Manuel from leaving. Xiomara kept her eyes on Wanda and Yaritza. They managed to cross the hall rather quickly and were just a few steps from the stairs.

But something prickled the back of Wanda's neck. A great sense of foreboding and calamity, the strength of which matched what she imagined God's judgment would be like. She couldn't help it—Wanda looked. Her eyes darted inside Papi Ramon's room, and in the brief moment that Manuel caught her stare, he threw his shoulders down and let his siblings turn him away from the door.

They sighed with relief, removing their hands and taking half a step back, but still circling him warily. That was fine, he decided. It was just enough space for him to burst past them and shove Xiomara into the wall. Her back radiated with pain before she realized Wanda was screaming. Adrenaline finally kicked her cousin's freeze response to flight, and she sprinted down the stairs, followed closely by Yaritza and less closely by Manuel and the three other adults.

Xiomara took her time going downstairs. Stiff discomfort made it hard for her to roll her shoulder blades, and even though she heard the sound of furniture being thrown into walls, alarmed shouting, and on several occasions, a cry of anguish, she was in no hurry to join the chaos below.

In hindsight, it was silly to pray at all. If God cared even a little bit, Xiomara wouldn't be in this mess. Papi Ramon wouldn't have left her such a confusing message, the storm wouldn't have caged them in, and whoever had left that letter wouldn't have been targeting the family to such a degree.

And yet, there they were, family split to gendered sides. Henry and Rafael still holding Manuel back. Aury and Marisa huddling around Wanda. Yaritza sitting next to her cousin, wracked by choking sobs. Xiomara was sure she would eventually hear the story of how Yaritza got a bloody nose. She wondered if it had to do with the furniture, or maybe she was pushed into the wall too. At some point in the debacle, two holes had been drilled into the wall shared by the dining room and the pantry. Paint chipped, curving outward from the depressions like spiderwebs.

"Are you done?" Aury shouted. Her lips curled back to reveal bright pink gums. "Look at what you did!"

"What *I* did? What about what *she* did?" He pointed an accusatory finger to Wanda. "Do you know what people are going to say about her? The pastor's daughter, committing a big sin like that?"

"Which sin—the abortion or the manslaughter?" Yaritza muttered in a nasally voice. Xiomara sent a jab into her side. She shot Xiomara a dirty look in return.

"You want to know what they're going to say? They're going to say, wow, what an amazing family. The brother's a rapist, the father's a thief, and the daughter killed someone!"

"I didn't know . . . !" Wanda cried. She swallowed big gulps of air and hiccupped before she continued. "I didn't know she was dead. When I came out of the car"—*hiccup*—"and, and she came at me, I thought she was just pretending to be hit so she could rob me!"

Xiomara rubbed her fingers against her temples. A headache bloomed faster than she could mitigate it.

"First of all, I didn't rape anyone. Those women made their own decisions—" Henry's defense was quickly drowned out by everyone's groans. He threw his hands up. "I'm just saying! But you don't wanna hear my mouth? Fine. Deal with this yourself."

"Henry, don't," Rafael said, but it was too late. Henry was already backing out of the room, leaving Rafael to deal with the full force of Manuel's rage.

"I should beat you like I did when you were small—that's what you need!" Manuel started, gaining an extra step toward Wanda. Rafael gritted his teeth as he pushed back. Wanda curled into herself and sobbed.

Xiomara took her chance to leave, desperately needing to be away from all the noise if she was going to find Papi Ramon's next clue. Her stomach grumbled, reminding her that fear burned a lot of calories just as well as working out. She decided to go to the kitchen.

Was that a trick of the demon? Xiomara wondered about that free-fall memory. She couldn't tell. It was an interesting coincidence that the memory ended right when the smell of smoke did. Like a thumbprint, the demon's mark. It made her wonder if this was a true memory, one that brain damage hid away. *Can the demon plant false memories? Or just manipulate the ones already there?*

Xiomara sat with Naomi at the kitchen counter, sharing a bag of plantain chips. They crunched, salt dissolving on her tongue and easing her troubled stomach.

"Do you want to talk about it?" Naomi asked. Xiomara didn't have the energy to look up.

"Talk about what?" she murmured between bites.

Naomi swallowed before she answered. "Whatever's got you all twisted up."

Xiomara closed her eyes. If Yaritza didn't know the story about the scar, then she wouldn't have known there was an accident—a *death*. Hers. What were the chances of Naomi knowing exactly what happened?

Fuck it—she wanted to find out. "I have this . . . scar on the back of my head, and I don't remember what happened." Anticipation soaring, Xiomara held her breath.

"Hm. I heard you had a nasty fall once, but the next time I saw you, you seemed fine," Naomi admitted. "So I thought everyone was just exaggerating."

"Exaggerating how?"

"Like . . . you died."

Xiomara felt herself hollow. Was she right? Did she actually die? Or did the demon plant a false memory to make her think she did?

Why is it always Naomi that remembers? None of her family members remembered the same things she did, and they were *actually* related to her. She hadn't spoken to Naomi in years! What made her special?

Xiomara let out a long breath. Well, at least she had one person that could fill in the gaps.

"Remember how I told you Papi Ramon left me the Bible?" Xiomara's eyes darted to the kitchen doorway. She could still hear her relatives through the adjoining wall, switching from English to Spanish and back while they discussed what to do. It was mostly Rafael and her aunts. Xiomara imagined that Yaritza was back on her phone, scouring the web for more Abreu-centered scandals. Wanda seemed to have stopped crying. At the very least, they were too engrossed in their conversation to eavesdrop on Xiomara's.

Still, she dropped her voice to a whisper. "I think it's because he wants me to find the demon."

Naomi gave Xiomara such a blank stare that she wondered if she heard her at all. The home aide continued to snack, each chip cracking audibly between her teeth.

"You're serious. You're serious? You're serious." Naomi said it in such quick succession, going from realizing the insanity of the statement, to questioning it (because she didn't know if she heard that right), and then accepting it all in the same second. And just for added measure, she ended the statement with "Huh."

"Is that all you have to say?"

"Well, you don't have a cousin named Jude, so you rule that out."

"I know you don't believe me." Xiomara crossed her arms.

"Has that ever been my job?" Naomi asked pointedly. "The only reason anyone in your family talks to me is so they can get me to do something for them, anyway. Or to pretend like they haven't avoided me the last couple of years."

Xiomara's shoulders dropped. "I . . . I'm sorry. I didn't know how to . . ." She looked down at her hands, squirrelly and fidgeting, but the truth was hard enough without trying to put words to it. "I'm sorry. I shouldn't have . . . I'm sorry," Xiomara repeated, squeezing her eyes tight like she was wishing on a star. With what's been happening so far, she wasn't above it. "But please—I need your help. And it's not because of your job or anything—I need someone on my side."

"Your family isn't on your side?" Naomi raised an eyebrow.

"My family can't even—"

Her skin nearly ran off when an abrupt howl and crunching wood shook the house. The family yelped in surprise as the ceiling thumped repeatedly above them, lights flickering and storm raging; a crack of lightning snapped them to attention, and a grip on Xiomara's arm made her realize Naomi had jumped out of her seat.

But the howling didn't stop. Instead, Rafael and Manuel ran up the stairs.

"That's Henry!"

It sank in thirty seconds later.

That wasn't howling. That was Henry screaming.

Xiomara and Naomi went running, nearly tripping over themselves on the steps. By the time they got to the second floor, Manuel's thunderous voice filled the hall.

"Call an ambulance!" he repeated, throat getting hoarse with every shout. "Someone call an ambulance!"

Xiomara was inside Papi Ramon's room before the smell hit her. Burning wood, a putrid sulfur undertone—more of the same stench from the study, but with a layer of rotten pus-filled flesh. She retched until bile touched the back of her throat. Her eyes stung and vision blurred, but even she recognized Manuel, who had dropped to his knees and spread his hands over a misshapen lump that shifted and groaned painfully with every touch.

"Call an ambulance!" he shouted once more.

Rafael snapped at him with a phone to his ear, "I'm calling already, shut up! Hello—we need an ambulance. We don't know what happened, but my nephew is bleeding and . . ."

Bleeding? Xiomara's vision cleared. Manuel's hands were covered in a sleeve of slick crimson. Henry slumped in his arms, barely speaking and barely coherent. Half his face had already swelled, and his shirt looked like it had been run through a shredder, held together by the coagulation of his own blood.

Xiomara could only imagine how upset Henry would be when he came to. If there was anything he was particular about, it was his clothes, how expensive they were and how recognizable the brand name would be.

It's not even recognizable as a shirt, she thought as Naomi pushed pass her.

"Move!" the home aide said. She was fast, kneeling beside Manuel and analyzing Henry's body. "We have to stop the bleeding, first. Get me more towels. Manuel, you have to let go of him. Go get towels. Go!"

"Aah!" Aury's voice rang like a bell. "What happened to Henry?"

Chaos painted the room, and all the colors blurred into one another. Xiomara pressed her hands against her ears, blocking out as much of the screaming as she could. Then she waited. Xiomara waited until the yelling had stopped, until the blood stopped running—until everyone evacuated the room, afraid that whatever had happened to Henry would happen again to someone else. Henry was stabilized, thank God, but the storm made it difficult for any ambulance to make it through the roads. It was either they drive him to an ER or they wait out the storm.

Like Xiomara, they all decided to wait. Henry was moved to Rafael's old room, where Naomi monitored him as best as she could. He was wounded on his chest and arms—but the worst of it was his left arm. Naomi turned an old T-shirt into a makeshift tourniquet and tied it just above his elbow to stop the persistent bleeding.

"He'll be okay for about two hours," she said, "but we should really take him to an actual ER as soon as we can."

As if with mocking laughter, thunder shook the house.

While most of the family had split to various corners of the house—Rafael in the storage room, Manuel and Aury in the dining room, Wanda and Yaritza together in Marisa's room, and Naomi with Henry—Xiomara returned to Papi Ramon's room. She hadn't fully taken stock of the entire room while it was still filled with bodies and noise, pumping her full of adrenaline and vibrations from her head to her fingertips. It was a wonder how she remembered to breathe.

Naomi caught Xiomara before she opened Papi Ramon's door.

"What are you doing?"

"I'm trying to find the demon," Xiomara blurted. "The one from Papi Ramon's will. I know you probably don't believe me—I wouldn't either if I were you, but look—first Aury was attacked, now Henry. I don't think these attacks will be stopping anytime soon, so I really need you to have my back, because at least with you, I know you'll *actually have my back*."

Xiomara hoped her earnest tone came across as that—earnest, and not desperate. (And to be fair, she *was* desperate, but it was more important to her that she was received as earnest.)

"I . . ." Naomi's lips remained parted, as she searched for words. On failure, she shook her head. "I'll keep watch," she instead offered meekly.

Xiomara nodded. It was a start. The knob turned easily in her hand, allowing her entrance into the room. Everywhere she looked, there were claw marks and scorched lines carving through floor and wall and bed and clothes. Mattress foam had been exposed, and broken glass glittered over the floor around the dresser mirror. A great force had split the dresser in two, but that's not what caught her attention. Out of the five drawers it contained, only one was overturned on the floor.

Old watches spilled out when Xiomara picked it up. Most seemed broken from the struggle—there was no shortage of cracked glass and bent hands curling outward. A pile of gold and silver watches stared up at her, and Xiomara sniffled when she remembered the way they'd hung on Papi Ramon's bony wrists. He'd been buried with one of his favorites, that much she knew. But unlike glasses, which he wore only out of necessity, his set of watches were a collection. Xiomara wondered who might have gotten them in the will. It was likely Henry, knowing how much he adored luxury wear.

Xiomara put the loose drawer aside—and stopped. A wisp of white poked out behind it, and when she turned it around, adrenaline jumpstarted her heart. She didn't need to open the taped paper to know what it was—she could already read the Bible verses folded over themselves in a square.

The Book of Jude.

And there was a weight to it. Just light enough that Scotch tape fastened the package to the drawer. Xiomara carefully removed it and unwrapped the delicately packaged cassette tape. She stared at the label for a long time, feeling slapped not by Papi Ramon's familiar handwriting but by what he had written.

Because for some reason, Papi Ramon had labeled the tape *Josefina 4/6*.

10:02 P.M.

Do you want to know how your mother really *died?*

The question was more pronounced, and suddenly, Xiomara remembered. Not the entire content of that unpleasant dream–slash–possible nightmare, but she remembered how it ended—with that question. The person asking it had a deep and raspy voice, like his vocal cords were made of wood and had themselves been clawed through and through by some devilish creature.

But she remembered who it was. The voice belonged to Papi Ramon.

Why would he ask me that, though?

Tears fell onto the Bible page, still curling around the cassette tape. Xiomara reached backward, trying to smooth the end of the dream that faded toward the center, like unraveling a scroll. But the act of recollection fought her, dimming the light on her memories until she was left in the dark and grasping at nothing.

Xiomara stared down at the tape labeled with her dead mother's name. What was on it? What would she do if it were her mother's voice? After Mami passed and Xiomara thought she had processed it, she made the mistake of accidentally happening upon an Instagram Reel of her mother a few days before she went into surgery. Sometimes Instagram did that, showed people things completely out of order; something from way back months ago could pop up the next day as if it had just happened—Xiomara knew that her feed was not necessarily chronological, but she hadn't expected to be haunted by her mother's online permanence while she was waiting for her next class to start.

In the reel, Mami was reading. Her eyes were lightly sunken from the chronic pain she always experienced. She seemed to be unaware that she was being watched, until her eyes flitted upward, meeting the camera and then whoever was behind it.

"What are you doing?" She laughed, so light and carefree that for a moment, Xiomara almost thought she was still alive. What a tremendously heartbreaking truth to experience twice. Grief attacked her like a wolf clamping its snarling mouth around her throat. She had fully broken down in that moment, sobbing with the force of entire tropical storms while her classmates ran for the counselor's help.

And now, here was Xiomara with this cassette tape.

Do you want to know how your mother really *died?*

Did she?

"Xiomara?"

Mami's death had caught her off guard, of course, but she didn't want to imagine, for one second, that it *wasn't* purely accidental. The tired truck driver had hit her mother fast and hard. Xiomara had read the coroner's report—severe internal bleeding, head trauma, it was unlikely Mami was alive for five minutes after that initial hit. Best-case scenario was that she was so out of it, that she didn't even realize she was dying, much less that she would be dead soon. Xiomara hoped the painkillers dulled her mother's senses until the moment she was gone.

"Xiomara!" Naomi shouted, shaking her back to the present. "What are you doing? Get up! You said you wouldn't be in here long."

Xiomara was dragged to her feet and then out of the room. Naomi closed the door with a huff, curious eyes darting to what Xiomara held in her hands.

"What's that?" the home aide asked.

"It's . . ." Xiomara didn't get a chance to explain before Naomi cocked her head to the side, reading the label. "Yeah . . ."

"Wow." Naomi's eyes widened. "Is that *from* your mom, or . . . ?"

"I don't know." She swallowed. "But I don't have anything to play it on anyway, so . . ." Xiomara turned the cassette over in her hands, noticed how glossy new the plastic appeared. *When did Papi Ramon make this?*

In a strange, roundabout way, Xiomara finally felt herself stumble over a glimmer of hope. This had to be the next clue, she was sure of it. Look, it was wrapped in the same page torn out of the brand-new Bible from Papi Ramon's study. What the hell else could it be?

At the same time, Xiomara tried not to bask in that hope. Hope was just a precursor to disappointment. "Did Papi Ramon keep anything that could play cassette tapes?" Even as she asked the question, she felt silly. Why else keep tapes if he had nothing to play them on—no, if he had nothing to *record* them on?

"I don't know? Maybe?" Naomi's face furrowed. As she delved into thought, she leaned against the wall and looked past Xiomara. "I remember putting a box of electronics down in storage. I think it was mostly HDMI wires and old chargers, though."

Xiomara quickly turned heel and sped down the stairs as she pocketed the tape. She could feel Naomi at her back, footsteps both raining down behind her and propelling her forward.

"Who is—Xiomara? What are you—?"

Xiomara pushed through the door and through Rafael.

The storage room was similar to the library in that it was a tower of boxes—but because it was much longer, the room was also a *grid* of boxes. Large and small, each row seemed to differ in size, and it wasn't until Rafael jumped in front of Xiomara that she stopped dumping the third load of clothes mixed with books.

"Whoa, at least put things back!" Rafael organized the mess at Xiomara's feet. He threw sweaters into a lazy fold before dumping them into a cardboard box, hiding his frustration when the top wouldn't close over cotton and tweed.

"Sorry." Naomi tried to catch her breath. "I think she's trying to find something that . . ." The home aide's voice faded as Xiomara continued on. She worked through piles of sweaters and blouses, trousers, shorts, and underpants before she came upon boxes labeled *tech nonsense*. That seemed like Papi Ramon. If there was something he didn't understand, it would be labeled *nonsense*.

Xiomara turned over the box and let wires spill out. They were all tangled, with one end leading to actual earbuds and the other end with a stereo plug. She growled under her breath, aggravated by the knotted plastic that obscured her goal. She threw them aside and tried again with a new box.

Unlike the others, this box felt heavy.

"She's making a mess!" Rafael shouted before grabbing Xiomara's upper arms. She threw her full force against him, bringing down her weight as she kicked her feet. She wasn't done searching.

"Get off me!" she yelled.

"What's going on?" Aury asked, suddenly at the door. "Rafael, what are you doing?!"

The shout of frustration was paired with an extra set of arms, trying to pry the two apart. Xiomara welcomed it, her knees finally hitting the floor with a pained thud, just a few feet away from the next box she had yet to search. Her hands went for it without a second thought.

"She's just trying to look for something!" Naomi explained. "A tape player."

"What for?"

". . . She found a tape. With Josefina's name on it." Naomi's voice faded in the background while Xiomara tore through the box. More wires, both black and white, some chewed through enough to expose thin copper threads braided over one another. Xiomara tossed them out quickly, searching for something rectangular and yellow.

At the very bottom of the box sat an old DVD player. Xiomara pushed it aside and went for the next box.

"You see!" Rafael's voice cut through her frantic emotions. When she looked up, she realized all the other women in the family had come to the door, each at varying levels of interest and concern. Aury was at the forefront of the group, focusing intently on Rafael, disapproval puckering her face until he was too annoyed to look back. Frustration wafted off his frame like fumes, thickening closely around him in such a way that Marisa and Yaritza seemed to steer clear of him. Instead, Marisa's eyes skirted between him and Xiomara, as if still deciding who was more of a threat to the other.

"Jesus, was Papi Ramon a hoarder or something?" Yaritza glanced around the room, taking in every square foot and box and mess with mild disgust. She wriggled in through the door behind Marisa and ignored the way her father made a sound between a groan and a scoff.

Xiomara looked up, eyeing Rafael with a question that was more like a demand.

"While you were in here," she began, "did you see a yellow Walkman?"

His answer came in the form of a blank look.

"Did you?" she pressed, desperation clawing at her.

"Watch who you're yelling at," he scolded. "And no, I haven't seen one."

Xiomara went back to searching. There were two boxes left in the tower of tech nonsense, and she would be damned if she didn't thoroughly investigate them.

"Just leave her," Aury murmured softly. From the corner of her eye, Xiomara could see Rafael taking a few steps toward her. If he thought he could grab her again, she was going to do something much worse than kicking. But instead, he stopped next to her and held a hand out.

"Can I see it?" He was frowning, and something in his eyes deepened. It was like they went from emotionless marble to an ocean of unsaid feelings. "The cassette tape. The one with Josefina's name on it."

Xiomara steeled herself. She made no movement to get the tape—she didn't want him to know where it was, and even if he knew, she would fight Rafael if he tried to wrest the tape from her.

"Please?" he asked, softening his voice. It stirred up a tornado of emotions in her, and before she knew it, she slowly retrieved the tape from her pocket and placed it in his palm.

He studied it, tracing a finger around the Scotch tape and pursing his lips in a line.

"April sixth . . . ?" His face wrinkled. Rafael's finger lingered on *4/6*.

At the door, Xiomara's aunts chatted.

"Do you think there's more?" Marisa asked. "Like more tapes with our names on them?"

Xiomara blinked back tears. A new kind of clarity hit her like a wall.

Why did she think there was only one tape? Just because there was only one torn Bible page? What if it was just to lead her to the next set of clues? She wanted to deny it, assume that there was just the one tape and eschew the idea of there being any others. But then she looked to her aunts and uncle. The pit in her stomach deepened, making room for doubt even when the tape was shared with Aury.

Her aunt held it in her hands the way someone held a menu. She flipped it over quickly until she saw the name. She held it back to Xiomara, as if trying to get rid of it before it stained her fingers.

"Xiomara, where did you find this?"

Xiomara tried not to bristle from the action.

"It was in Papi Ramon's room." She sniffled, holding the tape to her chest. "I found it after Henry was attacked."

Yaritza gasped. Marisa and Aury shared a look.

"You shouldn't have gone into that room," Rafael said gravely.

"Even if we find more tapes . . ." Xiomara said. "They're useless until we find something to play them on."

That seemed to get them. Marisa came to Xiomara's side and squinted over the open boxes. "So is there something we can use here? Something that can play cassettes?"

Rafael ran a hand over his hair. "Can we at least not make a mess while we search?"

"Wait, Naomi . . ." Marisa turned to the home aide. She stopped her immediately with a raised palm.

"I already told Xiomara, Ramon had me box up everything he owned in this room."

"But clearly not everything," Xiomara said, eyes widening when something dawned on her. "Because I still found a drawer of his watches upstairs. This tape behind it."

The same realization rolled over the room, starting with Yaritza and ending with Rafael. If not every little thing could be packed and placed in a storage room (and really, how could it be?), then that mean the rest of the house would still have to be meticulously searched to find not only something as small as a tape but the Walkman with it.

For a moment, the house once again felt as large to Xiomara now as it had been when she'd been small enough to sit on her grandfather's lap. It loomed around her, breathing and groaning, with a mocking air about it.

But Xiomara was no longer a child—and even more than that, there were four other people in that very room with an interest in searching with her. Whatever they were personally dealing with would have to be pushed aside if they were going to figure this out quickly. Bickering, after all, only produced wasted time. Static zipped between them, strengthening when they looked to one another. It was an agreement, then.

Rafael was the first one to respond. He let out a grievous sigh and rubbed his eyes. "I'll search the rest of this room for a tape or a tape recorder—"

"A Walkman," Xiomara said. "It's yellow."

"I'll go talk to Manuel." Aury walked to the door. "Maybe he or Chico saw it somewhere inside Papi's room."

Marisa looked thoughtful for a moment, then announced she would be searching the bathrooms. "Honestly, it could be anywhere . . ." she mumbled as she left. Xiomara and Yaritza went to the living room, splitting to each half of the room. Though Xiomara had already opened the ottoman once for the remote, she wondered if she had completely missed another tape the first time. Her mother's tape burned in her hand, as if desperate to be played.

"Xiomara, I'm going back upstairs," Naomi shouted from the stairs. Xiomara's head snapped back, unaware that the home aide hadn't followed them. "I need to check on Henry."

"Oh, okay," Xiomara answered, trying to drown her disappointment in understanding. Naomi was the most qualified among the family to look over the wounded—she couldn't let the sting of urgency blind her to that fact.

When her cousin made a noise that sounded like she'd stepped in dog shit, Xiomara shot a look over her shoulder. Yaritza seemed fine, and seemed to have only been reacting to the sound of Naomi's voice. What the hell was her problem with the home aide? The question almost came out until Yaritza pulled a cushion up from the couch.

The same urgency then pushed Xiomara to say, "We already looked through there before, remember?"

"No, we were checking *between* the cushions." Yaritza turned it on its side to reveal a zipper. "But what if there's something *inside* a cushion?"

That was something Xiomara hadn't considered. Her eyebrows twitched, telling her cousin so, and she watched as Yaritza fished into the cushion with a gleam in her eye. That gleam dimmed and the smirk on her face flattened into a line when she retrieved nothing short of loose lint and foam.

"Well, that was a bust. I'm bored." Yaritza dropped the cushion and fell into the couch behind her. She propped her feet up into the empty slot where the other cushion was removed.

"You barely looked!" Xiomara said, incensed. She watched Yaritza happily pull out her phone and begin texting. The woman looked so carefree, unbothered by the chaos that enveloped their family. It almost made Xiomara envious.

The corners of Yaritza's lips twitched. "What?" she asked, with a tone that seemed to sour and slightly downturned eyebrows. She wasn't even looking at Xiomara, and Xiomara still felt like that expression was for her. "I can feel you staring at me."

Xiomara had to be sure. She asked, "Are you sure you're not the one pulling the strings?"

"We've already been over this." Yaritza didn't bother looking up from her phone. Whatever other conversation she was engaged in seemed to demand more attention. "I'm not smart enough to pull something like that off."

"I never said that." Xiomara frowned.

"You know it's true, though. It's why I failed out of college." She muttered that last part, though her fingers texted faster, as if she was trying to outrun the truth of her words.

Xiomara gawked at her. "You *failed* out of college?"

Yaritza scowled and finally looked up, first sending daggers to her cousin and then softening. "You didn't know?"

"How was I supposed to know? When did this happen?" It sank in then—the downside of being purposefully distant with her family was that she would be fully blindsided by any old news that came her way.

"Like a month ago. It's why Papi's acting like it's the end of the world," she said, finally answering Xiomara's unasked question.

No wonder the two were fighting at Papi Ramon's funeral. She had failed out recently.

"Honestly, I'm surprised you didn't know. I thought the whole family knew already." Yaritza seemed to relax, or at least sink into the couch and shift to make herself more comfortable.

Xiomara made a half twist back to her search, but a newly formed question forced her to turn again.

"Wait, you're older than me."

"Yeah, I took a gap year before college." Yaritza's eyes fluttered. Try as she might, she couldn't hide the way embarrassment tinged her cheeks pink.

"You're *two years* older than me," Xiomara pointed out, less to her cousin and more to herself.

"Oh my God!" Yaritza jumped off the couch, curving around the dining table and escaping down the hall. "If you're going to keep making me feel bad about myself, you can look for the damn tapes yourself."

"Wait!"

Yaritza did not turn back. Xiomara let out a regretful sigh and shuffled over to fix the couch while thinking about how much she'd missed out in the last few years. How was she supposed to know that Yaritza failed out of college? Was that something the family talked about at length in the group chats? No, Xiomara couldn't imagine that. If anything, the truth of Yaritza's failing spread through the family like a parasitic vine, eager to twist and tangle from hand to hand, wrapping around wrists to elbows until it crawled up to the ear and whispered, *did you hear about Yaritza?*

Yeah, that seemed more like the Abreus' style. No one was supposed to know about it, yet everyone knew anyway. Xiomara pressed the cushion into the couch. She wandered around the dining room, checking under the table and each chair (no matter how broken), inside and under and around the ottoman, and even behind the mounted television. It was all incredibly devoid of not just extra tapes but also a Walkman.

Xiomara gripped her mother's cassette.

Is this worse? she thought miserably. *Or is it better that I don't hear Mami's voice?*

If she really wanted to, she could pull up Mami's old Instagram account and click on any on of the dozens of Reels her mother had posted. That was the good thing about the internet being forever—it extended to people as well.

Xiomara rubbed the tears out of her eyes and continued searching. If Papi Ramon had hidden a bunch of tapes around the house, where would he have hidden the one thing they needed to listen to the tapes?

Where would I *hide the Walkman?* she wondered, trailing down the hallway to the study. A huge part of Xiomara doubted she would find it there—she had already been there twice earlier and found nothing but a Bible and a drawer full of pills. But the only person who had ever used the Walkman was her—so where did *she* last put it? Yaritza mentioned Xiomara being scared of Papi Ramon's stories. She remembered being afraid of the entire second floor. One of the very few good memories she had was of playing with the Walkman's buttons, clicking them without any concern for what action it took.

Xiomara's left hand curled as she imagined it again, the feel of plastic against her palm and rubber against her fingertips. One finger coiled inward.

Click! It stayed down. Then the next. *Clack!* She turned away from the study, muscle memory guiding her with each imaginary press of a button. *Click! Clack! Click!*

She found herself beside the staircase. Not quite on it, just next to where the stairs began. With the next curling finger, Xiomara bent down and pressed her other hand against the base. The floorboard leaned inward, and she narrowed her eyes at the glistening screw. It looked fairly brand-new. Xiomara stood up, thinking about where Papi Ramon kept his toolbox. She found herself going into the kitchen, straight to the back, where the door of the pantry stood. She frowned as she slid the doors open and picked up the toolbox underneath the lowest shelf.

Why would he put it there? Xiomara wondered before returning to the bottom of the steps. She pulled out a screwdriver and got to work. At first, the screw wouldn't budge. The screwdriver slipped over a handful of times, making Xiomara's forehead bead with sweat.

After, it finally caught, and she used a lot more force to work the screw loose. She repeated the process on the other side, then switched to the hammer. Digging the claw into the floorboard, she pulled it halfway up, just enough to stick her hand in and rummage through what felt like tufts of torn sheets of paper and fiberglass before her fingertips scraped against something smooth. Xiomara forced herself farther to grab it. The moment it came out, her eyes widened.

Take the first step.

Written into the will was the exact thing he wanted her to do to find the yellow Walkman. It had been hidden right inside the first step. Xiomara sucked in a deep breath, just as she heard a hurricane of footsteps running down the hall to the stairs. Panicking, she kicked the toolbox aside and covered the loose floorboard with her leg. She quickly shoved the Walkman into her other cardigan pocket, half a second before Yaritza appeared, skidding to a stop at the bottom of the steps.

"Xiomara!" She doubled over as she wheezed from excitement. "There's more! Marisa found *three more tapes*!"

10:27 P.M.

Yaritza pulled Xiomara into Rafael's old bedroom. Henry lay peacefully asleep, his injured arm propped up on several pillows. Black and red ballooned through the towels that wrapped his wounds, but at the very least, it was no longer spreading. Manuel and Aury faced each other, both wielding sour expressions that matched so well they might have been identical.

Xiomara felt the weight of the Walkman in her pocket. Every time someone looked at her, her heart sped up. To keep herself from jumping, she watched Henry's chest rise and fall by centimeters. He was thankfully still alive, but just barely hanging on. Xiomara felt a pinch of desperation for the storm to let up—the sooner it did, the sooner an ambulance could reach them.

But then everyone would leave. And the chances of her figuring out who was the supposed demon would drop tremendously. The truth of it settled in the back of Xiomara's mouth like bitter medicine. She swallowed it, accepting that the storm was both an opportunity and a barrier. She would just have to work faster.

"Should we really be doing this here?" Aury asked, with a careful glance over to her nephew, as if her eyes alone would collapse his lungs. "We should let him rest."

"But what if he gets worse?" Manuel asked.

"I can stay," Xiomara blurted, itching to listen to Josefina's tape.

Her uncle shook his head. "No, it's fine. An earthquake couldn't wake that boy, anyway."

Manuel took off his glasses and massaged his face. The man had only untucked his shirt, and yet the change in style made him look disheveled. Or maybe it was just seeing him in the context of the night—being exposed and accused and then fighting with his siblings. The man no longer appeared to have it all together.

"Someone go get Wanda." He gestured to the door nonchalantly. Not so much forgetting about his earlier outburst due to her secret, as he was completely skirting over it.

Xiomara turned to go. "I'll—"

"I already tried," Yaritza said. She sat on the floor next to an outlet as her phone charged. "She doesn't want to come."

Manuel tsked audibly.

"Fine, just leave her," he said, washing his hands of it.

Xiomara subtly clenched her jaw. She considered leaving anyway, making up an excuse to be alone even for five minutes. Impatience turned her into a ticking bomb. If she didn't listen to the tape within the next twenty minutes, she was sure to explode.

The door creaked open, and in came Naomi with a few bottles of water and a fresh hand towel. Xiomara stepped out of her way and watched her cut across the room to Henry's side. Quickly, she dropped the water bottles on the bed and carefully lifted the edge of the bloody towel. Naomi pursed her lips and went straight to work, dousing the fresh towel with water and slowly cleaning his arm from the elbow up. Xiomara turned away, unable to keep nausea from roiling her stomach. Instead, she looked down at Yaritza, who looked quite comfortable for someone whose minidress was riding up her thighs.

"Hey." Xiomara nudged her. "Where's Rafael?" She had expected him to be in the room when Yaritza yelled about Marisa finding three tapes. "And where's Marisa? I thought you said she found more tapes."

"Papi's still looking for the Walkman, and Marisa is looking for the rest."

Xiomara blinked. "The rest? The rest of what?"

"The rest of the tapes," Yaritza said.

"How many more can there be?" Xiomara muttered, willing the jitters in her body to calm down.

"You good, cuz? You look sick."

"I . . . think I just need to—"

"Use the bathroom?" Yaritza raised an eyebrow, speaking the lie before Xiomara could.

To sell the act this time, Xiomara pressed a hand around her torso. "Might have been the sancocho."

"Sure it was."

As soon as she was out of the room, Xiomara booked it to the end of the hall and slipped into the bathroom. The door was hardly shut behind her before she tore out the Walkman and jammed in the tape.

Xiomara plugged in her wired earbuds.

The rubber button clicked as she hit play.

The first thing she heard was sniffling.

"Xiomara . . . Xiomara, I'm so sorry . . ." Papi Ramon's voice cracked. *"It's my fault . . . it's all my fault . . . Josefina is dead because of me . . ."*

She paused it. Stared at the Walkman in her hand. Tried to feel it, really feel it, but all feeling had slipped away. She wasn't sure what she'd expected, but it wasn't that. Xiomara breathed in slow and deep and flexed her fingers once again.

She pressed play.

For several minutes, Papi Ramon let out shuddering breaths. Glass clinked and liquid filled a container. It sounded like he was drinking. In the recording, there was a soft knock at the door. Plastic scraped and clattered against wood, and the sound all but became muffled. Was he hiding the Walkman?

"Come in." In his drunkenness, he seemed to have forgotten he could pause the recording. Someone entered the scene, hesitant and slow. Xiomara almost didn't catch the words, but she felt them on her lips.

"Are you okay?"

It was her. Xiomara was in the recording. She realized exactly when this tape had been recorded and why Papi Ramon sounded emotionally and completely in shambles.

It was right after Josefina's funeral.

"I'm fine, mija. Don't worry about me. You go to bed."

Xiomara's past self said nothing and slowly left the room. Xiomara barely remembered that. Nearly every day after the funeral, Papi Ramon remained in his study, inebriated and slurring his words so much that Xiomara stopped listening. There was one day she had to help him up the stairs.

"Do you know how your mother *really* died?" he had asked. The question perturbed her so much, she made up her mind—she didn't want to be there anymore. Xiomara left that same week.

That's what I dreamed about, Xiomara realized. It was that exact memory.

Papi Ramon had retrieved a recorder from its hiding place.

> "If you're hearing this now . . . it's because you deserve to know. You should know the car accident . . . wasn't an accident. It was because of me. Because I couldn't stop them . . . I just didn't think they would do that to their own sister . . . I'm sorry . . . I'm so sorry, Xiomara . . ."

The tape ended. And Xiomara's blood went ice-cold. Did her aunts and uncles band together to kill her mom? Perhaps it was just a pair—Xiomara could imagine a collaborative effort between Aury and Marisa, though she wouldn't rule out Manuel either. Was Rafael in on it as well? And if Papi Ramon knew, why didn't he say anything?

Xiomara ejected the tape. She turned it over and stared at the fraction. *Not a date.*

Four out of six.

There *were* more tapes. And if she was going to find out who was responsible for her mother's death, she would have to listen to all of them.

By the time Xiomara went back to Rafael's room, he was already there.

"Sorry, Xiomara." He awkwardly patted her shoulder. She studied him with newfound suspicion. Like Manuel, there was a ragged air about him, as if he was moments away from falling apart at the seams. His shirt revealed moisture collecting under his armpits, and he wiped beads of sweat from his forehead.

"I checked every box," he announced to the room, lightly shaking his head. "Couldn't find it anywhere."

"Then what are we supposed to do with these?" Manuel held up the tapes in his hand. Each had that same brand-new sheen to them like Josefina's tape did. Xiomara squinted and came forward, squeezing between the older siblings to pick up the tapes. She turned them over in her palm, tracing the labels as she read them.

Aury 3/6

Marisa 2/6

Manito 1/6

With her other hand, Xiomara gripped the hidden Walkman in her pocket. What would it take to slip away a tape one at a time? She could swap the labels—but that would be too conspicuous.

"And you didn't find anything else that can play cassettes?" Manuel asked, an accusatory tone lacing his voice.

"I tried. Okay?" Rafael snapped. "Did *you* find something, or did you leave Marisa to do all the work?"

Yaritza failed to hold back a snort, slapping a hand over a wry smile while her eyes widened both in disbelief and amusement. Manuel squared his shoulders when he stood up, and Aury quickly stepped between them.

"Calm down."

But Manuel was already throwing a finger in Rafael's face. "Watch who you're talking to . . ."

Xiomara tuned them out. Instead, she held her mother's tape against the others and studied the similar curvature of Papi Ramon's letters on the labels. There was no question about it—it was his handwriting.

Josefina 4/6

One. Two. Three. Four.

"We're missing five and six," she said, interrupting the hostility broiling between her uncles. They ambled over to her, curiosity just barely stifling their tension.

"Look at that," Aury mused, picking up her tape. She flipped it over, holding it with her pointer finger and thumb as if it were a delicate relic. Uncertainty crossed her face. "It looks brand-new. When did he make this?"

Manuel retrieved his own but with less grace. He held it so tight, Xiomara was sure she heard the light squeak of splintering plastic.

"I don't know," he grumbled, sharing Aury's expression. They looked at their respective tapes with frowns and hints of trepidation in the corners of their eyes.

It was odd, Xiomara thought as she studied their reactions. Though they handled their tapes differently, it was like they were not at all pleased at their existence. Something about the tapes put them ill at ease. Was it because they knew the tapes were clues they could not unlock without a cassette player?

Or was it because they were afraid of what was on them?

Xiomara quietly slipped her mother's tape into her pocket.

"All right, so where's mine?" Rafael asked. He looked at the other tape Xiomara held and lost interest when he saw Marisa's name instead.

"Marisa's still looking."

And how did she find three tapes so easily?

"Oh my God—Naomi, can you go get Marisa?" Rafael gestured to the door.

Naomi looked down at her hands, stained with blood after cleaning up Henry. "Sure. It's not like I was doing anything important." Sarcasm dripped from her voice.

"I'll do it," Xiomara volunteered. The air in the room was already getting stale, cemented by Henry's sanguine fluid sinking into the sheets.

Xiomara wrinkled her nose like it wasn't already coated on the inside of her lungs, and she could no more stomach that than the possibility she would never find out what was on these tapes.

The hallway seemed dimmer in the night. Not quite completely dark, but dark enough that even though the hall was completely barren, decorative shelves and portraits removed, she thought she sensed something there. Faces made out of scuffed wallpaper leered at her; figures in the shadows laughed at her.

Steeling herself, Xiomara started toward Marisa's room.

"Marisa, we're all in the . . ." Xiomara stopped. The room was empty, save for Wanda's curled body in the corner of the bed. Obscured by a blanket, she stirred until two eyes stared out of a rough opening. Her eyes were red.

"Oh." Xiomara shook off the secondhand awkwardness she felt. "Sorry. Where's Marisa?" she asked.

Wanda's eyes disappeared immediately as she dissolved back into bed. It took Xiomara another ten seconds before she registered her cousin had said anything at all— a mumble of a reply only further muffled by fabric and the space between them.

"The bathroom," she'd said. And with that, Xiomara closed the door.

She first checked both bathrooms on the second floor. Each on opposite sides of the hall, both doors were wide open, with lights off. She headed downstairs.

The very first bathroom across the study was locked. Xiomara knocked and pressed her ear against the door. She heard a hiccup.

"Marisa?" Xiomara called. The sink hissed water behind the door.

"I'm coming!"

Her voice sounded strange. Narrowing her eyes, Xiomara jiggled the knob.

"Is everything—" The door swung open before she could finish her question. Marisa stared down at her, the skin around her eyes pulled back tight. Her smile was strained.

"Sorry, did you need to use it?" Marisa skipped around Xiomara, not waiting for an answer. Xiomara watched her aunt stomp up the stairs, like each step up was heavier than the last. The house didn't groan as much as it screamed under her violent pace.

Upstairs, the family was finally assembled. Even Wanda sat in the corner of the room with a blanket draped over her and turned away from her father—but she was still there. Manuel clearly didn't see the point in taking the high road; he turned away from her too.

Strangely enough, Marisa was a little too quiet.

"All right, now that we're all here," Aury began, sweeping her gaze around the room and attempting to lock eyes with every single person, "we need to discuss these tapes. Does anyone know what these are and why Papi made one for each of us?"

Xiomara clenched her mouth shut.

It would take too long to listen to the tapes alone, she thought. *I need to narrow it down sooner.*

She looked between her aunts and uncles, searching for suspicious behavior. A nervous tic, an unnecessary stammer, hand-wringing where didn't make sense to be—but nothing so far screamed *murderer.*

"Each of *y'all,*" Yaritza interrupted. "It says it's out of six. That's clearly just meant for his kids."

"There's only five of us." Rafael pinched the bridge of his nose.

"Really?" Yaritza leaned forward, quickly counting each of the older adults. Manuel, Marisa, Aury, Rafael—and Josefina made five. Her eyebrows shot up. "Huh. Could've sworn it was six."

Xiomara's eyes shot to her cousin. Had she really thought there were six—or was it another memory trick by the demon?

"No, but how can it be for us?" Manuel looked to his siblings. "Josefina died years ago. This looks brand-new."

"So he took really good care of it," Rafael mused.

"Hey, Marisa," Xiomara spoke up. "Where did you find the other three tapes?"

Her aunt bristled. "In Papi's hiding places."

The family balked. Xiomara gritted her teeth. "What hiding places? Where?"

"In our rooms. Under our mattresses."

Everyone's eyes went to Henry, lying injured atop Rafael's old bed.

"Don't—" Manuel began to protest, until Rafael interrupted.

"We're not going to move him." Rafael placed a hand on his shoulder. "We're going to lift the mattress at the same time. Henry can stay where he's at. Everyone, pick a corner."

Aury and Marisa mirrored each other, crossing their arms.

"Who is *we*?" Marisa raised her brow. "Aury and I can't lift the bed with Henry on it. He needs to move."

Xiomara watched the argument unfold. Rafael unsuccessfully argued that it would be easier if his sisters helped, and his sisters refused. Manuel would have none of it.

"We are not moving my son!" he growled.

The compromise they settled on was not a compromise at all. Naomi and Xiomara would be taking the older woman's place, while Yaritza's sole role was to look under the mattress when lifted.

"Okay . . . lift!" Rafael dictated.

Xiomara felt all the blood rush to her arms and head. The few seconds the mattress was up in the air were more than she could stand, and once they were over, she leaned against the wall for strength.

"Nope, nothing!" Yaritza announced.

"Are you sure?" Rafael asked in disbelief.

Naomi groaned audibly. "I'm not doing that again!"

Yaritza snickered to herself, and Wanda rose to her feet, making a line for the door before Aury called out for her not to leave.

Xiomara massaged her temples, a spark of irritation threatening to blind her if she didn't calm down. She stepped over to the window. It was cracked an inch, a wise decision considering how sharply the wind whipped through the air. Just standing next to it, Xiomara felt like she was being stabbed multiple times with icy knives—but she refused to close it, preferring the way it allowed her to breathe to the sweltering heat of the room, which felt suffocating.

A low rumbling groan from Henry shut everyone up immediately. His face pinched as he tried lifting the injured arm, but Naomi held it down with little force.

"Don't move," she said. "If you move, it'll increase blood circulation, and you cannot afford to lose more blood. Just rest."

As if not hearing her, Manuel jumped to his son's side and shook Henry's other shoulder. "Henry, who did this to you? Huh? You have to tell us—"

"Don't shake him like that!" Naomi snapped at him.

"You shut up! Henry, come on," he continued. "Don't go back to sleep until you—"

Henry let out a pained groan, and Manuel pulled his hand back with the quickness of a young child touching a hot stove for the first time. Naomi didn't try to hide her *I told you so* face and stepped back, gathering the dirtied towels before leaving the room.

The family was more than quiet—everyone had stopped breathing and would've gone as far as stopping their own heartbeats if it meant they could hear Henry speak. Manuel towered over Henry. He leaned down so far, Xiomara was sure he could probably feel Henry's breath on his ear.

One Mississippi. Two Mississippi. Xiomara counted the seconds while something like a scratch sounded in the air.

It was when Henry moved his lips that Xiomara knew the sound was coming from him.

"Hot . . . s'hot . . ." Henry complained. His lips moved a few more times, then stilled as his head lopped to the side. Manuel slowly straightened himself. His slackened jaw and dazed eyes filled the room with unease.

"What?" Aury grabbed his arm, trying to shake him out of his stupor. "What did he say?"

"Nothing," Manuel answered. "Just that it's hot."

Wanda silently left the room. Xiomara could tell it was only a matter of time before everyone dispersed again, each to their own corner of the house. She saw it in the way they were regarding the tapes—Aury had a doubtful frown, and Manuel dropped his on the bed. The family's interest in them was waning without a cassette player. Tapes were useless without one. Xiomara prayed they would leave their tapes behind when they left.

"Oh!" Yaritza clamped a hand over her mouth. "Um . . . so don't look now, but it looks like someone's bank account was hacked . . ."

Ironically, it felt like the floor fell out from under her. Xiomara's aunts and uncles reacted similarly as they processed those words.

First came the disbelief.

"What?"

"What did she say?"

"A bank account . . . ?"

Then came the shock. They rushed toward Yaritza, trying to squeeze between the wall and a nightstand to look over her shoulder. Marisa shoved Aury, who knocked into Manuel, who reacted just about as strong as a brick wall. Yaritza bounded to her feet, unprepared for the sudden attention.

"Someone's bank statement was leaked online—wait, hold on! I'll just send it to the group chat!" Yaritza shouted. Xiomara's phone buzzed.

"Whose account is this?" Manuel stared at his screen. It was hard for Xiomara to tell if his eyes were narrowed in anger or if he was just having a hard time reading small text.

"It's not mine," Aury said, trying to mask her sigh of relief.

Rafael shook his head. "It's not mine either."

With a quick look, Xiomara knew it wasn't hers—she didn't even share the same bank as the rest of the family. Still, she zoomed in on the charges. She could probably tell who it belonged to by the expenses alone.

Luckily, there was only one.

International Wire Transfer . . . $50,000? Xiomara's jaw met the floor. *To who?*

The statement said it was sent to an overseas LLC she had never heard of. Xiomara quickly ruled out Henry—everything he bought had to be a recognizable brand. The same could be said of Aury, so she was ruled out as well.

"I don't see a name on this. How do we even know it's one of ours?" Aury wondered aloud.

Xiomara searched the document herself. Most of the identifiable information was redacted, save for the last name.

"They're tagging it with our name." Yaritza shrugged.

"We're not the only Abreus in the entire world," Xiomara said, a bit of relief sinking into her bones. Then she looked to Marisa.

She was staring at—no, *through* her phone, color leeching out of her skin like she had been splashed with bleach.

"Marisa . . . ?" Aury tentatively tapped Marisa's shoulder. She did not react and the tension in the room became very brittle glass. No one wanted to say a word or else risk shattering it. Just watching her aunt sweat, Xiomara was sure this was yet another scandal unfolding.

"Tía Marisa?" Xiomara hesitated. "Is this . . . yours?"

Marisa's answer was to break into a sprint. She nearly stomped on Yaritza's foot on her way out, grabbing the door frame for stability as she whirled around it. Within seconds, the bathroom was locked and Aury was begging Marisa to let her in.

Fifth one today, Xiomara thought. How many scandals could possibly exist within one family? Maybe Papi Ramon's death was a mercy, buried before the stories went out.

"What was she spending so much money on?" Manuel sneered, taking another look at the account statement. He muttered disapproval under his voice while Rafael took to pacing up and down the room. He cut a glance to Yaritza every time he crossed in front of her, wringing his hands like they would go flying if he didn't keep them busy. Xiomara's core tightened with every look, until finally he stopped.

"You need to stop doing this shit," Rafael said, crouching as he pointed a finger at Yaritza. "You got a problem with me? Fine, but stop putting everyone's business out there."

Yaritza made a face. "I didn't even *do* anything."

"You're the one who keeps bringing up everything that goes on online." He fixed her with a look. "I bet you've already been talking to people about us too."

Yaritza put down her cell phone and looked her father in the eyes. She jutted out her chin, a false bravado if Xiomara had ever seen one because her cousin's shoulders were curling around her in shame.

Rafael gave a slow nod, as if to say, *is that so?*

"Xiomara," he called to her. "Has Yaritza been talking to anyone outside this family *about* this family?"

Xiomara felt turned to stone. She didn't move in either direction, or so much as blink, but Rafael took that as an answer itself and gave another slow nod before he stood up and left the room. The feeling of brittle glass was present again, only extending between her and Yaritza.

Her cousin slowly exhaled. "Wow," she said. "Thanks for fucking snitching."

"Wha—" Xiomara watched Yaritza pull herself to her feet and disappear out the door.

And then there were three. She looked between Manuel and Henry. Slim pickings for conversation. The elder sat back in his seat, arms crossed and a grim expression as he watched his son.

"Xiomara." Aury came to the door. "I need to speak to you."

She followed her aunt out. A few steps away from Rafael's room, Aury hit her with an absurd question.

"Did you have something to do with that?"

Xiomara blinked. "With . . . what?" What was she asking?

"Okay, don't tell anyone else, but Marisa just got pulled into a group chat with other women that are victims of a scam, all right, they're saying that the guy isn't real. It was all AI-generated."

Xiomara hated everything about that sentence.

"She's really upset about it and asked them to keep that part quiet, but I know her. She's going to snap sooner or later, and I'd rather know everything before I try helping. So if you did that—"

"I didn't!" She shook her head vigorously. A computer science degree did *not* make her an AI genius.

Aury rubbed her face. Exhaustion ate at her, aging the aunt by years. Xiomara could almost see her grandmother in Aury's downturned lips.

"All right, but just for tonight, give Marisa space, okay?"

"She doesn't blame me, does she?" Xiomara's face paled.

"No . . . I wouldn't say that."

11:13 P.M.

Marisa was glaring from down the hall. Xiomara could make out those aggrieved eyes, shooting daggers and accusations without ever saying a word. Marisa didn't even look away when Aury came back to her, placing two hands on her shoulders like she was trying to divert her attention.

Whatever she said to Marisa worked, because Marisa's face seemed to soften for a split second before crumpling all at once. She threw herself into Aury's arms, face buried into the crook of her neck, and sobbed quietly. Xiomara watched Aury rub her back and slowly turn toward the bathroom. The light of the bathroom briefly exposed Marisa's ugly crying, the sharpness of her expression, and the snot that ran down to her chin. Before Aury went in, she gave Xiomara another look that said, *remember that we're in here*. Or maybe it was, *remember not to come over here*. She had to give her aunt space, after all.

Xiomara's stomach clenched. She had managed to go so long without being blamed for one thing or another in the family, but it seemed like her mother's curse followed her.

Xiomara returned to Rafael's room and came face-to-face with Manuel.

"I'm going to the bathroom. Watch Chico for me," he said, not waiting for an answer. He ducked out immediately, and Xiomara's eyes fell on Henry.

And then there were two. She walked over to his sleeping frame. He slept so peacefully for someone who hadn't even endured half of the night awake with the family. Injury or no injury, Xiomara was envious of that. She looked him over and saw that his breathing even seemed a little deeper. She wondered if his body had already replaced some of the blood he'd lost.

At Henry's feet were two tapes left behind by the family: Aury's and Manuel's. Marisa's tape was the only one missing. Her suspicions seemed to be proven more and more right. Of all the siblings, Marisa was the only one keeping her tape close to the chest.

Still, Xiomara reached over and plucked Manuel's tape from the bed. Papi Ramon had made six tapes for a reason. While she still had time, she should make a point to listen to each of them. Xiomara watched the door as she connected her earbuds and slid in the tape.

Papi Ramon's voice was a lot calmer and more collected than in his earlier tape.

"Manuel is my first child," he began. *"The only child of mine who decided to follow in my footsteps . . . To this day, I don't know why he decided to become a pastor. Sometimes I think it's because he wants to be like me. He used to follow me around all the time, when he was little. No matter where I went, he wanted to be there. I could be in the bathroom, and he'd cry against the door. He never wanted to be alone. It used to bother me. I think that's the reason why we decided to have more kids. Just so he would have someone else to follow."*

Xiomara frowned. Papi Ramon talked about Manuel like he was discussing a colleague. Or perhaps he was half-asleep. It was hard to tell. She glanced to the door again, making sure no one came back through as the tape went on.

"Out of all the kids . . . I don't think he liked Josefina."

Xiomara's guts twisted at the sound of her mother's name. Papi Ramon barely sounded affected, and she wondered how long after the funeral this tape had been made.

"I don't think he liked any of them, actually. He's okay with Rafael and goes a long time without talking to Marisa or Aury. But Josefina always upset him one way or another. I think maybe . . . he knew that she was better than him."

The tape ended there. Baffled, Xiomara rewound the tape and played it again. Nothing in the words changed. Papi Ramon's voice didn't suddenly fill with energy. But the second time she listened, there was one thing Xiomara caught that didn't make sense to her.

Apathy.

Papi Ramon was completely apathetic to Manuel, his firstborn son. Xiomara unplugged her headphones and sat in quiet concern. The grandfather she had grown up with had been full of love for all of his children.

Had he? Xiomara's mind creeped with doubt. Had she ever actually seen him interact with Manuel outside of funerals?

Henry shifted in his sleep with a low groan that nearly sent Xiomara through the roof. She fumbled when ejecting the tape, hiding the Walkman back in the pocket of her cardigan and throwing the tape onto the bed beside Henry.

The slits of his eyes opened on Xiomara's face.

"Henry?" she breathed. She looked back to the door, still open. If anyone walking by peeked in, they might not even notice he was awake, but she didn't want to chance it. Xiomara mimicked Manuel in the way she leaned over, hoping that Henry was more awake now than he had been earlier.

"Xio . . . mara?" He grimaced, trying to sit up. She stopped him quick.

"Don't. Don't move," she whispered, looking over her shoulder. She was frantic now. Any moment now, Manuel was going to walk through the door, and if he saw that his son was awake, Xiomara would not get any answers at all. "The thing that attacked you. What was it?"

"S'hot . . ." Henry complained again, crinkling his nose like he smelled something foul.

"I'll open the window wider, but you have to tell me what it looked like." She pleaded, "*Please.* What was it?"

". . . was hot . . ."

That's when it clicked. He wasn't saying *it's hot*, he was saying the thing that attacked him *was* hot.

"It was hot?" she asked.

"Burning . . . claws . . ." Henry's body settled down. "Watch . . ."

"Watch what?" Xiomara repeated. "Henry, watch what?"

His only reply came from his injured arm. He raised it slightly, letting out a pained yell that summoned Manuel immediately.

"What's going on?" His father practically flew into the room. "Is he awake? Henry? Henry!"

No matter how much Manuel shouted and shook Henry, he didn't stir with more than a faint moan. Cursing his luck, Manuel stomped right back out, as if he couldn't bear to see his son in a horrible state. Xiomara stared at Henry's arm intently. Was he trying to point at something?

Watch.

It wasn't a verb. It was a noun.

Henry wore a watch on his injured arm. Xiomara took a closer look. It was golden, expensive, and more importantly—all in one piece. She carefully undid the clasp and slipped it off. Underneath the case, right next to the crown, was an engraving—*RA.*

This was Papi Ramon's watch.

"This isn't his." She didn't see him come in with it, and wondered if he'd taken it.

El bacà protects its owner's properties. Yaritza's brief Google search surprisingly had come in handy. Henry had taken Papi Ramon's watch, and Aury had taken his pills. What were better shows of ownership than a prescription and an engraving?

Before Manuel could return, Xiomara made her way back to Papi Ramon's room. The pile of watches had been left exactly as it was, half-covered by the broken drawer ripped out of the dresser. As she sifted through them, a careful finger nudging each metal band away from crystal pieces, one stood out to her. It was a Cartier—one of Papi Ramon's favorites. Absent-mindedly, she picked it up, her thumb and index finger feeling guided to the crown like a puppet being pulled by strings.

You have to be careful, though, Papi Ramon had said. The memory resurfaced through the murky waters of her mind. *Because sometimes when you think you found something that could help you, it's just another trick he left behind for you.*

"But why would he do that?" Xiomara's lips moved on their own. Muscle memory sparking without warning.

Papi Ramon's voice answered, *Because he likes to play.*

Sulfur tickled Xiomara's nose just as an earsplitting scream threw her on her back. She felt the floor beneath her shake, the sound of a tornado tearing through the house. Then more screaming mixed with a thunderous roar. Xiomara's heart nearly popped with fear. She scrambled to her feet, every cell in her body desperate to *go go go*, throwing the door open and slamming into Manuel just as she escaped the room. He pushed her off just as fast and sped to the stairs.

The cacophony below had dulled but not ended. Booming thuds replaced the screams, and Xiomara stood petrified in place. Marisa's room opened, and Yaritza tentatively peeked out.

"What the hell was that?" All color had drained from her cousin's face. Betrayal instantly forgotten, she looked to Xiomara for answers. All Xiomara could do was shake her head, to say, *I don't know.*

"AURY!"

Confusion cut into the core of Xiomara's being. *Isn't Aury up here?* She looked back toward the bathroom at the end of the hall. Marisa stood frozen in place as though she was waiting for reality to come back to her.

"Naomi! We need more help!" Rafael shouted. That jolted Marisa to action, and she sprinted past them on her way downstairs. Yaritza soon ran after. Once her legs felt solid, Xiomara ambled downstairs.

Yaritza pressed her back against the wall across from the storage room. She plastered her hands over her mouth, barely moving when Xiomara approached. Panicked voices shouted at one another, clawing the walls like an animal trying to escape containment.

"Why isn't she waking up?"

"Step back and shut up! I can't hear anything with you shouting in my ear!"

"What happened to her?"

"Yes, there's been another attack—"

Xiomara stepped through the door and immediately felt her blood pool at her feet. The scene was worse than Papi Ramon's room. So many boxes were overturned and emptied, a hoard of clothes, decorations, and knickknacks littering the floor. Two of the walls had punctures the size of a bowling ball, drywall giving way to wood, and wood splintering from sheer force.

There was heat in the air. Not quite smoke, just the feeling of warmth, thick but fading. Xiomara tried to pick apart the mass of bodies with her eyes. There was Naomi again, being hounded by Marisa and Manuel to do more, hurry up, answer their questions, help Aury, why isn't she moving faster? The three were like a wall, huddled over what Xiomara assumed was her aunt. She stared at the floor beneath their feet.

No blood. She tried to take heart until she got a good look at her aunt. Just because she didn't see any blood, didn't mean her aunt wasn't gravely injured. Xiomara wondered what she'd tried to take this time to warrant a more serious attack.

"What do you *mean* you can't send anyone?" Rafael growled into the phone. Among the mess, he had cleared a path for himself to pace, like it was the only thing he could do to keep from exploding. The stress and fear inside him turned his more leisurely walk into something brisk and forceful. "We have someone *stalking* us and so far there have been two attacks and—yes, I'm aware of the storm, I'm fucking stuck in this house *because* of the storm—"

"Xiomara, move out of the way," Naomi said. She had turned aside, allowing Manuel to hook his arms under Aury's shoulders and legs and pick her up, though not without his knees half buckling under the weight.

Aury wasn't bleeding half as much as Henry had, but rows of red lines carved through her skin all over her body, and she was unconscious just the same. Claw marks dug into the floor right around her like she'd been circled.

"You're going to drop her!" Marisa panicked.

"No, I'm not!" Manuel gritted his teeth as he shifted Aury more comfortably in his arms. Xiomara stepped out of the doorway and let him carry Aury out while Marisa demanded he bring her to their room.

"No, put her in the same room as Henry," Naomi argued, voice fading as she followed them upstairs. "It'll be easier for me to look over both of them . . ."

Xiomara stepped into the room. Like Rafael, she had to clear a path for her to walk, nudging blankets and bent hangers aside to find solid ground cleaved in rows of four over and over again. If she were to trace over them with her hands, her fingers would need to be splayed to follow the path of each groove. Xiomara hadn't thought about it before—the fact that whatever made these markings would have to be big.

Big but stealthy. How was it that the creature had struck so many times but no one outside of the victims had come across it? The house had only two floors and a single staircase connecting the two. Ignoring the damage done to the front door, there had now been three attacks—the first being Aury, then Henry, and back to Aury again. Was the first attack supposed to have been a warning for her?

The first time, she was going through Papi Ramon's medicine drawer. She remembered that there was an open pill bottle in that last drawer. Then Henry was attacked while going through Papi Ramon's watches.

What was Aury doing down here? Xiomara scanned the room as she followed the claw marks, imagining the path the creature had taken in pursuing Aury. The fact that the lines weren't continuous, a long break between one and another, told her that it likely jumped from one end of the room to the other. Where it landed, there was a skirmish of singed crosshatches surrounded by crushed boxes.

Xiomara couldn't be sure where the marks started or ended—she wasn't an expert in tracking known animals, much less supernatural creatures—

but she could hazard a guess at what Aury did in response. Her aunt likely threw what she could. That was why so many of the boxes were overturned, contents spilled all over the path. She didn't have Henry's strength or boldness—so she did her best in keeping her distance and using whatever was around her to escape.

Unfortunately, she wasn't able to escape for long. Xiomara circled right back to where Aury's body had lain. She crouched over empty Tupperware containers, most snapped into pieces.

Sulfur. Xiomara froze as if afraid she were going to startle the scent into fleeing. She inhaled slowly through her nose, until the subtle sting of heat and rot had touched the back of her throat. The smell was weak but steady. She chased it to her left, where her aunt's cassette tape glinted in the light. Aury must have dropped it during the attack. Xiomara picked it up. The tape was somehow in pristine condition.

Outside the room, Yaritza hadn't moved an inch from the wall. Shock had rooted her to the spot.

Maybe it was Yaritza's usual devil-may-care attitude or the immediate danger that awaited them in the shadows. Whatever the reason, Xiomara felt herself grasping for sympathy and found it shaved down to a nub. She asked, "You going to talk about this online?"

And Yaritza shook her head, eyes glazed over as she stared into the middle distance. Xiomara sighed and held out her hand.

"Come on," she said. "At this point, no one in our family should be left alone for even a moment."

They went upstairs. The door to Rafael's room was wide open, with a constant stream of pissed Spanish and accented English rushing over one another like water molecules in a river.

"Don't *touch* me!" Aury's voice kicked up, sobbing. "Why was it me again? What did I do?"

"You took something." Xiomara explained, entering behind Yaritza. "Yaritza told me earlier that el bacà protects its owner's properties. You took Papi Ramon's pills the first time, and Henry took his watch. Look, you can see his initials on the book. So what did you try to take?"

Yaritza beamed at her cousin. "You *do* listen to me."

Xiomara didn't look away from her aunts. Marisa was trying to get Aury to lie down next to Henry. Manuel stood on the other side, massaging his forehead like he was trying to scoop out his frontal cortex. Wanda sat facing the corner of the room, wrapped in one of the thinner bedsheets, eyes closed like she was in the middle of a prayer.

"I didn't take anything!" Aury screamed, nose flaring. "I was just organizing his stuff!"

"Until that lawyer gets back with the will, none of us own any of Papi Ramon's things. So don't try to take anything in this house." Xiomara realized the timing of the storm on such a day was too perfect. What if the lawyer never came back? Why hadn't Papi Ramon just given them their inheritances along with the message in the first will? It seemed he'd been keen on keeping his wealth and assets away from the family.

"She's fine!" Naomi scoffed, pushing past Marisa. "She's awake and breathing. She doesn't need my help."

Marisa gasped. "What if she has a concussion?"

"The fuck am I supposed to do about that?"

Rafael rolled his eyes and dug his fingers into the back of the armchair as he swiveled it around. "Everyone sit down," he said. "We need to talk."

Yaritza hesitated but then obeyed.

Xiomara closed the door. "Are we finally going to talk about the will?" It was beyond time that they kept that in mind. They'd read the will about eight hours ago, leaving them with four hours to find the demon and remove it from the family.

The energy in the room heightened with every look exchanged. Rafael rolled his lips over each other, casting his eyes down in muted shame. "Yes. I think we should talk about Papi's will."

A weight fell off Xiomara's shoulders. *Finally.* The first step to solving a problem was acknowledging it. How were they going to extract a demon they didn't believe was there?

Marisa sent a nervous smile around the room. "We don't have to worry about that. Remember—the lawyer is getting the—"

"I'm not talking about some other will!" Rafael snapped, and turned his attention to Manuel. "I'm talking about the one we all heard today. Come on, let's read this again," he pleaded with a steady voice and wrapped an arm over his brother's shoulders; with his other hand, he waved the document out of his pocket.

Manuel could not move away fast enough—he planted his feet and shoved Rafael's arm off. "Papi did not deal with demons!" Manuel shouted. "He was a man of God."

Rafael tried again with a soothing tone. "Even men of God make mistakes—"

"Not Papi!" Manuel shook his head vigorously. "So stop talking bad about him."

"Okay, then," Xiomara cut in. Her family members turned with such bewilderment, it made her wonder if they'd forgotten she was there. "Let's just . . . all go around and say where we were when Aury was attacked." The fastest way to determine who did the attacking.

"I was with Xiomara," Yaritza said quickly.

Bewildered, Xiomara shook her head. "No, you weren't."

"Then who else were you with?"

"I was with . . ." The truth arrived in a single thought. *No one.* Xiomara was told to wait for Manuel to return and she didn't. In an impulsive bid for safety, she said, "Oh. You're right. You and I were together."

Xiomara kicked herself for not risking it and turned away from her cousin immediately.

"Then I ran into Manuel on my way down here," Yaritza added. Manuel confirmed it.

"And I ran past you two to get down here," Marisa declared, giving Yaritza a look.

"Yeah, I remember that." The niece nodded with half-hearted enthusiasm.

Aury sniffled through an accusatory "Where were *you*?"

Rafael balked. "*Me?* I was trying to get to *your ass*, but you had the door locked!"

"I didn't lock the door!" Aury shouted. Tears were still falling down her face, trailing mascara while droplets of blood pricked through her skin.

"Well, it *was* locked, okay?" Rafael said. His lips were pulled back into a snarl, and he squared his shoulders the same way Henry did when he got defensive. It seemed that stance ran in the family.

Aury stared at Rafael in silence as she struggled to regulate her breathing.

"Wh-wh-why are you lying?" she hiccupped.

Rafael exploded. "Oh, *I'm* lying?"

"Yes, you are!"

"Okay, stop!" Manuel shouted, getting in between them. "Aury, I saw Rafael trying to open the door."

"Mm." Aury looked at Manuel up and down. "And? Am I supposed to believe you after everything *you* did?"

"This is not the same as that!"

"Ha! Why's that?" Spittle flew when Aury laughed. "Because we're supposed to be family?" The bed shifted under her as she swung her legs over the side. "Tell me, who am I supposed to trust in this family?"

"You can trust me," Marisa whimpered. Aury laughed once more.

"You? A year ago, you asked me to borrow money. I sent you ten thousand dollars—that you *still* haven't paid me back—but I find out that you sent your little boyfriend fifty?"

Stunned, Marisa took a step back, tears coming faster than she could wipe them away.

Rafael snapped. "Why are you accusing Marisa?" he said. "She's the only one here who was crying over you. God only knows why. You're probably the demon the way you're always trying to drag people to hell with you."

Aury turned to the rest of the family. "Isn't it suspicious that all this stuff came out about me and my company and Manuel and his kids . . . but there's nothing in the news about Rafael? Or Yaritza?"

Panicked, Yaritza threw out an accusation. "What about Naomi? Where was she?"

Naomi chuckled in response. "Bet you were holding that in for a *while*."

Yaritza held her gaze, steady and hostile, as she raised her phone before passing it on to Marisa. Xiomara paled immediately as she watched her aunts' expressions change. "I did some research on someone's *background*."

Naomi lengthened her back and squared her shoulders. "Yeah? And what did you find out?"

Xiomara's pulse quickened—she could feel the fire ignite, making her warm, *so* warm; how could a room rise in temperature so quickly? *Calm down*, she told herself. *Don't get hot now.*

"Don't listen to Yaritza—she's just making things up," Xiomara muttered.

"We need to send her out already," Yaritza argued. "What are we still waiting for? For Aury to *die*?"

"Don't say that!" Marisa rebuked.

"I'm just being honest!" Yaritza clicked her tongue. "It's either her or us."

Naomi threw up her hands. "I don't know anything about a demon, *dumbass*."

"Everyone, shut up!" Manuel roared. Once the accusations faded to silence, he looked about the room. "Papi never dealt with a demon. Don't even say that. Whatever is going on here is because someone wants something from this family. That's it."

"But I *saw*—" Aury jumped up.

Manuel stomped, shaking the room. "I don't care what you saw!"

Xiomara massaged her temples. Being around her family was beginning to impede her investigation, not make it easier. Without another word, she made her way to the door, not caring if anyone had anything to say about it.

"Where are you going? The *bathroom*?" Aury mocked. With one foot already out the door, Xiomara simply turned with stoic determination.

"We still haven't found a cassette player," she lied, and held up Josefina's tape. "And I need to listen to this."

Do you want to know how your mother really *died?*

11:32 P.M.

Why did you stop?"

If there was ever a burning question Xiomara had during Papi Ramon's exorcism stories, it was that one. A simple one that could lead to a simple answer—not that it ever did.

At the end of every exciting tale, when Papi Ramon would beam with self-satisfaction, and pride would pour out of his skin like light, Xiomara would ask him the question. In fact, he gave no answer at all. The only acknowledgment Xiomara's question was given came in the form of a hard flinch.

If it had only happened one time, maybe the flinch wouldn't have registered so violently in Xiomara's head. It wouldn't press at the forefront of her memories or followed her as closely. But it was exactly the fact that it had occurred so often that it stuck with her like a stubborn popcorn kernel between her teeth.

It happened every single time.

And it would happen so fast, Xiomara's brain could only process it as a flicker, a momentary lapse in her grandfather's luminescence. Papi Ramon would swiftly change the subject, decide that he needed a bathroom break, or suddenly remember he needed to call someone.

After a while, Xiomara learned to stop asking. As she got older, she started making excuses for him. She thought, maybe Papi Ramon misheard her, misunderstood her, mistook her question for something else and reacted accordingly. But then came the next question—*every time?* He misheard her *every time*, misunderstood her *every time*, so on and so forth, every *single* time she had asked the question—was that right?

What an amazing coincidence that would be. Maybe it was her that was misremembering. Maybe she didn't really ask after *every* single story—what kind of kid would do that? But no, the conviction would punch her in the stomach: she *knew* she asked every time. She remembered it *specifically* because it was such an odd thing to do and she did it.

And it was because of those memories that Xiomara now found herself in Papi Ramon's personal bathroom. She sat on cool porcelain, with the Walkman on her lap and Aury's tape inserted but not played. Not yet. Every time she listened to Papi Ramon's voice, she'd imagine his face, and along with it, that flinch.

This is where he went? She took a cursory look around the bathroom. It had been stripped of towels and floor mats and shower curtains, leaving behind stark white tiles smelling vaguely of Clorox and Fabuloso. Naomi was very thorough in her cleaning.

It spun a certain kind of grief in her chest. Bathrooms are, by nature, very intimate settings. So are bedrooms; so are entire homes. To have much of the house cleared of Papi Ramon's belongings felt like he was being erased.

Or it should have. Instead, it reflected an unflinching truth. That for all that Xiomara adored her grandfather, for all that Papi Ramon fawned over his granddaughter, was accused of favoring her above all else, he didn't really tell her anything she needed to know.

And perhaps the blame was partially hers. Maybe she had been too young to learn everything, and once she got older Mami's death parted them harshly. Xiomara moved to the other side of the country. She hardly visited, hardly reached out. Papi Ramon seemed to respect her space.

Now that she was here, in *his* space, in the same bathroom he'd claimed to run to whenever she'd asked a simple question, she realized something. Papi Ramon only ever told her stories in his study, on the first floor. There was a bathroom just across the hall, right next to the stairs. Yet he would always climb the steps instead. If she had asked him about that, would he have told her the truth?

Had he ever?

Xiomara's heart jumped when a door slammed through the wall. She could hear someone stomping down the hall as they shouted aggressively.

"I don't want to be in the same room as you!" It sounded like Marisa. The floor creaked as others left her alone. Finally, silence. Sighing to herself, Xiomara slipped in her earbuds and pressed play. The tape began with a light buzz of static in the background.

> "Out of all my children, I think Aury takes after me the most. She's sharp, capable, she knows what she's doing with her business. I don't worry about her as much as I worry about Marisa. But that's only when she isn't making the same mistakes she always does. I don't understand why she does it. The pills aren't good for her. Her mother and I didn't raise her to be that way either. I don't know who taught her. I keep thinking it must've been those friends at school, maybe one of her boyfriends . . . but she's single now and she's still doing it. I know she is, even if she tries to hide it. I can tell, I can always tell. Whenever Aury lies about something, she opens her nose like she's not getting enough air. I don't think she knows she does it, and I don't tell her. I think part of the reason why her business does so well is because she's good at lying, at hiding things. She's so good at it that sometimes I think she might be the demon, [REDACTED]."

Xiomara paused the tape. There it was again—the distortion. She rewound and played it again.

> "I think she might be the demon, [REDACTED]."

Pause. Rewind. Play.

> "—the demon, [REDACTED]."

Pause. Xiomara gripped the Walkman, if only to keep herself from chucking it at the wall. The distortion was keeping her from hearing the demon's name.

Is he doing this on purpose? No, she didn't think so. Papi Ramon wasn't tech savvy enough for that. The censoring happened for the same reason that the smell of sulfur still lingered after every attack.

Certainty gripped her by the throat. The demon knew about the tapes. It knew and had distorted them so any information about it was unrecoverable. The way that sentence was going, Xiomara knew the distortion had to be a name.

But then why leave the tapes where they were hidden? Why not just destroy them altogether?

Because demons liked to play. That's what Papi Ramon said all those years ago. A person might think they've outsmarted a demon but really they've played according to the script.

Though she didn't smell sulfur, Xiomara imagined the demon circling her. If she didn't figure this out quick, what would happen? Would she be attacked like Aury and Henry? Would the demon rend her flesh from bone? Papi Ramon had said the entire family would be damned if the demon wasn't caught and expelled—but he didn't say anything about how to expel the demon even if they *did* find it. Or did the demon erase those words from his will too?

Xiomara squeezed her eyes tight enough to see stars. She should've expected this—she had always been told that demons were crafty. Why had she thought she could find and expel one in just one night, especially when she hadn't stepped a foot in a church since Mami's funeral? Xiomara was far out of her depth.

Yet, for some reason, Papi Ramon had believed she could.

She opened her eyes.

"Then again . . . I don't know if I should blame her for lying or hiding things. When she was little, she always told me she felt like she was constantly being watched.

Manuel later told me that she believed it was me secretly watching them through the walls, and that I was lying when I said I didn't. But she's always had a strong conviction. So maybe she learned how to lie from me. I never told her she was right—what else could I do?"

There was a long stretch of silence. Xiomara wondered if this was the end of the tape, or if he was just gathering his thoughts. She shifted forward on the toilet seat as if trying to lean into Papi Ramon's space. All she could hear was the static of a TV in the background.

"Regardless, Aury is one that I want to believe she's not my daughter just as much as I feel she is. How can I not? How can I look at each of my children and believe they might be a demon? I remember when every one of them was born. I was there, I was . . . but I know [REDACTED] and I know how good he is at manipulating memories. And my memory isn't the way it used to be. I just—"

"Xiomara!" Yaritza pounded on the door. "Are you in here?"

Xiomara fumbled with the Walkman, jolted by the sudden interruption. She wondered if Yaritza would leave if she stayed silent, but not knowing the definition of privacy, Yaritza turned the doorknob. The lock stopped her from getting any farther.

"Hey, unlock the door!"

Frantic, Xiomara shoved the Walkman back into her pocket. "Give me a second!"

She cursed her cousin under her breath and flushed the toilet. Hopefully, Yaritza would take the bait and leave her alone. After a second of silence, the door shook again.

"Stop pretending like you're actually using the bathroom!"

Xiomara quickly undid the lock. It swung open, hitting the arm that held the Walkman in her pocket. Xiomara was surprised to see that Yaritza wasn't alone.

Marisa pushed past the both of them and marched into the bathroom. Behind her, Aury pinched the bridge of her nose, walking the fine line between looking exhausted and annoyed.

"Okay, where is it?" Marisa demanded to know.

"Marisa, tranquila," Aury said. It was rare that Marisa could get so angry. Just an hour ago, the woman had been utterly heartbroken and a little suspicious of Xiomara. She flipped the switch on her emotions so fast that it gave Xiomara whiplash, and she tried backing away from all three of the women without giving them even more reason to be suspicious.

"What's going on?" Xiomara asked. She felt her face twitch and thought back to how Papi Ramon had praised Aury's ability to lie. Hopefully, Xiomara was as talented as her.

"What were you doing in here?" Yaritza asked.

"I can't be alone for five minutes?"

Yaritza narrowed her eyes. "Weren't you the one who told me earlier that no one should be alone even for a moment?"

Heat spread from cheek to cheek as Marisa quietly seethed. The woman made a sharp turn and backed Xiomara into the door frame.

"In Papi's bathroom? With the door locked?" Marisa's eyes pinned her to the spot.

"Am I not allowed to be in here?" Xiomara's voice struggled to climb above a mumble.

"Give it back," Marisa demanded. "Aury's tape."

Beads of sweat gathered behind her ears. The tape was still in the Walkman she was hiding.

"I . . . don't have it?" Xiomara said.

Marisa narrowed her eyes, a woman scorned and believed the scorning was done by her niece. "Yaritza, check her pockets."

"Don't you—"

Immediately, her cousin was on her. A dull throbbing pain bloomed at the back of her head. Even though Xiomara had thought she was flush against the wall, Yaritza had slammed into her with so much force that she was still knocked into it. Heavy pressure kept her there while several pairs of hands pulled at her arms. Xiomara struggled against them by trying to curl into a ball—only to be met with an elbow to her nose. Sudden numbness gave way to sparks of pain that pulled tears from her eyes as her nose began to drip.

"Stop!" someone yelled. "She's bleeding!"

Xiomara blinked her tears away to see Aury joining the fray, doing her best to peel Yaritza off her.

"Just show us what's in your pockets!" her cousin screeched. She pulled at Xiomara's cardigan until it was stretched past the limit, popping more stitches and digging a finger-sized hole in the shoulder area.

Eventually, Marisa's impatience won out. She took hold of Xiomara's other arm and pulled until her hand swung out, and the Walkman with it.

"Give it to us!"

The Walkman clattered across the tiles, shards of plastic breaking off and scattering behind the toilet. The four of them froze as they stared in confusion, heavy breathing replacing their previous shouts and demands. Marisa dropped Xiomara's arm as Aury slowly retrieved the broken Walkman.

"What is this . . . ?" She held it up and looked to Xiomara. "You were hiding this from us?"

Xiomara tasted blood. It rolled down her tongue as she pinched her nose. She held Aury's stare unapologetically, shoulders squared in defense like she was waiting for another elbow.

"I had to." She swallowed. "I needed to know which one of you it was."

"Xiomara . . ." Yaritza let go of the cardigan sleeves nonchalantly. "I already *said* who summoned it . . ."

"No, I'm not talking about that." Blood coated Xiomara's throat as she spoke. It was all she could do not to choke on it. "Papi Ramon said something in Mami's tape . . . about how he knew that none of you ever liked her. And maybe it was because you thought she was his favorite—"

"She was." Marisa snapped then rolled her eyes when Aury let out a small gasp. "Oh, don't act like you didn't know. We *all* knew. Josefina was Papi's favorite. That's just how it was. So what?"

"He knew." Xiomara nodded. "Just like he knew at least one of you killed her."

All of the women froze. One by one, they looked to one another, brows knit together in confusion, until Yaritza blurted, "What?"

Her cousin laughed nervously, the way she always did when trying to downplay something or lighten the mood. It was never genuine. She just stretched her lips out wide until her teeth resembled a billboard and forced out a few puffs of air.

"You're serious?" Yaritza asked. Her smile fell, emotion replaced with pseudo-concern that hardened her stare. "Xiomara, no one killed your mom. It was a car accident—you know that, right?"

"Am I supposed to believe you? When none of you even remember the time I split my head open?"

Yaritza's jaw dropped. "When was that?!" she demanded.

Xiomara was sure of it now—she couldn't trust her family any more than she could trust her own memory.

Do you want to know how your mother really *died?*

Her aunts looked at her with contempt. "Fix your faces," she said, sidestepping to the sink. She let the water run for a few seconds, pinched one nostril, and blew out a bright red globule, sticky and surrounded by a splatter of blood that hadn't yet coagulated. It all ran down the sink, the globule getting smaller until the last drop slipped through the strainer.

"I cannot *believe* you would say something so cruel." Aury's voice shook. "I don't understand what your problem is. Ever since you were a child, you never liked being around any of us. You never liked your family. You were always trying to stay away from us. And after Josefina died, there was your excuse. You didn't come back, didn't visit. Papi wouldn't stop talking about you, how proud he was of everything you were doing, but did you ever call? No. And now he's dead and you show up, acting like we owe you the world because your mother is dead. Do you see Yaritza acting like that?" She whipped her arm out to point at Yaritza, whose widened eyes made it apparent that she wasn't used to being the shining example of the Dead Mom Club.

"No, you don't." Aury sniffled. "You should know that before Josefina was your mother, she was *our* sister. And we would give *anything* to have her back." Turning on her heel, Aury stomped out of the bathroom. Marisa tossed a glare over her shoulder as she followed.

"That was so . . ." Yaritza made a face to finish her sentence. Like always, her emotions were superficial at best, and once her hand found the doorknob, she dragged it behind her, leaving Xiomara with her own reflection to contend with.

Instead, Xiomara thought back to Aury. Not her words, not the way she talked about missing Josefina. But her face. Aury had tried to hide it in the sniffle, but Xiomara could tell—her nose had flared, just like Papi Ramon had said.

It took another ten minutes for her nose to stop bleeding. Xiomara scrubbed her hands raw and dried them with her cardigan. Her fingertips knocked against Josefina's tape—she had almost forgotten about it. It was lucky the tape was in her other pocket or it might have gone flying with the Walkman.

Inside Papi Ramon's room, she listened for any movement in the home. The roaring thunder and crashing rain had been pushed to the background, nothing more than white noise that tried to dull Xiomara's nerves.

She heard people walking and felt them when they passed in front of the door. She waited until all the walking had gone down the hall, away from the stairs, before making her move.

"Took you long enough," said Yaritza. She sat on the floor just outside of the door, one leg crossed over the other while scrolling her cell phone. She stood up in the time it took Xiomara to calm her startled heart.

"Why were you sitting there?"

"To make sure you're not alone." Yaritza yawned as she lazily put away her phone.

"Right, because you're concerned about *my* safety." Xiomara rolled her eyes and turned to the stairs. Yaritza grabbed her by the elbow.

"Where are you going?" Her grip was firm and Xiomara got flashes of past skirmishes with her cousin. In the study, in the dining room—one time even in the bathroom. Yaritza was always getting the drop on her, wasn't she? Xiomara considered learning a new fighting technique.

For now, she would remain calm.

"Downstairs." She tried not to look down at Yaritza's hand on her arm. "Don't think anyone wants to be around me right now."

Yaritza let go only to cross her arms. "I mean . . . yeah, but we still don't want you to be alone. Well, no, not alone, just not so far."

They think I'm suspicious. Xiomara saw most of the adults milling about in front of Rafael's room. Aury leaned against the door frame with Marisa to her right. The older aunt was glowering in her direction. Manuel came from the other side of the hall, meeting her with a stern expression.

"Oh." Xiomara blinked. *Wow.* She hadn't expected this—her family taking a stand against her when she had been right from the beginning. Why did they demand to fight her every step of the way? She crossed her arms. "Fine. I'll stay up here."

Silent sighs and shoulders dropping. They all seemed to relax a bit until they noticed that she noticed and all together, they straightened their faces and nearly stumbled over one another to get back in the room. Marisa was the last to go, looking Xiomara up and down with puckered lips.

Yaritza shrugged. "Sorry, cuz."

No, you're not.

"Can I at least stay in Mami's room?" Xiomara asked.

"Oh yeah, don't worry about it. I am *not* sleeping in that room." Yaritza's snicker hit her like a smack.

Then she was alone, in Mami's room, with someone guarding from the hall. She turned out the light, making it easier to see shadows cut across the lit hallway from under the door. They just stood there, waiting silently, and Xiomara wondered what their plan was. Were they just going to isolate her until morning? Or find a way to torture her and get her to confess? Then what? Did they think the demon would grant them wishes if they found out who it was, a fucked-up game for a fucked-up family?

Ill at ease, Xiomara chewed the inside of her cheek as she paced. If she was being honest with herself, what did *she* think she was going to do when she found the demon? The creature had shifted her memories and that of the entire family. It had even touched the tapes that Papi Ramon had made and left them for her to find. It had painted her as the demon, and now whatever Xiomara had *thought* she was going to do to it would be done to her.

She thought back to Papi Ramon's first message of the night.

Find the demon—and get rid of it.

12:02 A.M.

Xiomara was sitting silently on Mami's old bed, engaged in the mindless doomscroll that plagued her generation (and drained her battery to 40 percent), when the lights suddenly went out and she lost all bars. There was a shout in the other room, proof that the family had been caught off guard just as much as she was. She heard footsteps scrambling, a door opening, and someone shouting for Naomi to find a flashlight.

"Yeah, yeah, I'll *try*," she said. Her footsteps disappeared down the hall, going so slowly that Xiomara was certain the home aide was going to take her time searching. When the family quieted down, Xiomara flicked on the flashlight app. A ring of light came alive at her feet again, and Xiomara pointed it to the bed just as she smelled it—a pungent whiff of flaming sewage.

It—el bacà—was here, somewhere in the room, watching her from the corners, mocking her from the shadows, daring her to do something from the confines of the room. Goose bumps spread over her skin like a rash, and Xiomara felt herself swelling with anxiety. Her breath became shorter and shorter, fear compounding until she was overtaken by a strong desperation to break down the door, run to her relatives, and sob like a child needing immediate comfort. She imagined it as well—throwing herself into the arms of her uncle or aunt or cousin (whoever was closest, really) and telling them the demon was *there*, in Mami's room, and it was going to attack her next if they didn't do something.

But a laugh from the hall jolted her. She stood in place, listening to Rafael sputter and muffle himself while being shushed. A second shadow under the door fused with the first, blocking out most of the light filtering into the room. Xiomara's lungs struggled to fill themselves.

They won't believe me. The truth lodged itself in her throat. She was on her own.

Go to the window, the demon said, in a voice like static. It sizzled out toward the end, soft enough Xiomara wondered if she'd imagined it. If she pretended that it was all in her head, would the demon go away? She wiped away trailing snot—when did she start crying?—and didn't take another step. The sliver of light became her air, and it was thinning.

Go, it growled, and Xiomara's feet hurried to the window. Her flashlight flickered on and off—then settled on off, and Xiomara was completely swaddled by the dark. The window in front of her was still mildly reflective, and the longer she stared into the abyss, the more she saw a strange figure standing there.

Right behind her.

Xiomara's phone clattered to the ground. Her eyes felt glued to the creature, unable to look away. The edges of its silhouette blended nearly perfectly with the dark around it, and what she could make of the outline wriggled like snakes.

Then there were the eyes. Torches of lava swirling with an eternity of agony—screams of torment coming through like a phone call. She smelled the burning flesh, felt her body pour with sweat as though she were the only source of hydration for miles.

Do you want to know how your mother really *died?* el bacà asked, in a voice that sounded like a mix of Papi Ramon and a room full of hissing roaches. Xiomara's skin itched with revulsion.

El bacà stepped closer. Xiomara shut her eyes tight, whimpering as the heat closing in singed the back of her neck. Too afraid to speak, she curled into herself, praying silently.

Dear God, I'm sorry, I'm sorry, I'm sorry, I'm sorry, please save me, I can't do this. I need Papi Ramon, I need Mami, I want Mami, I'm scared, someone help mehelpmeHELPME—

She felt those eyes spidering up her spine, and the noxious smell hung over her shoulders like a scarf. Even without sound, she felt the demon laughing at her now, amusement digging under her skin like worms. Xiomara wanted to tear it off, claw at herself until bone was exposed. Yet she was petrified—the only movement came from her lips. She let out a prayer in a choked whisper. "Please help me . . ."

As if an answer, the heat dissipated, leaving a soft clack behind her. Xiomara's flashlight app flicked back on. She wiped the snot from her nose as she used the light to look behind her.

On the floor was a tape.

Marisa 2/6

Xiomara swallowed. Without a cassette player, there was nothing to play it on. She had listened to the tapes belonging to Mami, Aury, and Manuel. Now she had Marisa's, but Rafael's tape still hadn't been found.

And time was ticking. How long until her family grew desperate? Until the next scandal hit the news? Would they descend upon her as she slept, sneaking into the room with a pillow—or would they enter with a hammer?

Xiomara pocketed the tape and looked back to the window. There was a minor possibility she could survive a second-story drop—but a leg fracture would be enough to make her a sitting duck, making her family's decision easier. She looked at her mother's bedsheets—could she realistically make a rope out of them to climb down?

And did she even want to? The storm outside remained as ferocious as it had begun. If the weather made it too difficult for ambulances, she had little hope to get somewhere safe. *I don't need to get home,* she told herself. *I just need to get away.* She was not above spending the night at a gas station, if it meant her family could not get to her. That would have to be the plan—get out and get somewhere else.

There's a trellis outside Papi Ramon's window. It would only take her a couple of steps to cross the hallway and enter his room, and then she was as good as home free.

Except someone was out in the hall, guarding her. Options dwindling, Xiomara quickly went to Mami's closet, hoping there would be something she could use to escape.

Xiomara drew the sliding doors apart and froze.

The closet was bare. That couldn't be right. Everything else in the room had been untouched, down to the very same mattress Mami had slept on. When had the closet been exhumed? Above her was a single shelf over the hanging rod. Even on her toes, Xiomara couldn't reach the back of the shelf, but she spread her arm out in a wide circle, risking small jumps to search with her eyes.

"Xiomara?" Naomi knocked on the door. Startled, Xiomara jumped into the closet and listened as footsteps approached. Naomi peeked inside. "What are you doing in the closet?"

Xiomara answered her with her own question. "What's going on out there?"

"Nothing interesting, if I'm being honest." She shrugged. "They sent me over here to check on you. Make sure you haven't gone anywhere."

Xiomara slowly emerged, glancing out behind Naomi. The door to Rafael's room was decidedly closed, a reminder of how the family had separated themselves from her.

"Where else am I supposed to go?" Xiomara looked at her, incredulous. The weather outside was still raging, and Xiomara hadn't arrived in her own car. She grabbed ahold of Naomi, forcing her to *really* look at her. "Hey, what are they planning? Like, what are they going to do to me?"

The home aide's reaction was sobering. The corners of her eyes pinched together, trying to hide their concern and she looked away as she gently unwrapped Xiomara's hand from her arm.

"Listen, I don't know what they're planning. They sent me out here so they could talk about it among themselves. I'm just doing my job."

"*That you're not getting paid for*," Xiomara emphasized. "Papi Ramon's dead. Without him, you don't have a job anymore." The words came out quick and vicious, popping Naomi's worry. Her face fell and then slowly formed a sneer.

"Wow," She breathed. "*Wow.* Really thought you were different." Naomi turned away from her, and Xiomara instantly wanted to take it back.

"Wait, I'm sorry—" she tried. Naomi laughed at the attempt.

"What for?" She stepped up to Xiomara, body stiff with tension. "You're right, I don't have a job anymore. You know what I also don't have? Prospects. I didn't go to college, because I was taking care of *your* grandfather the whole time. Do you think I can afford to go *now*? With no parents, no safety net, just my last paycheck and a prayer? Do you have *any* idea what it's like to be me?"

Xiomara's mouth was dry. "They'll kill me. You know that."

"You Abreus are so dramatic." Naomi scoffed, looking to the window. Xiomara wondered if she was going to see it, the demon that had appeared in that very same spot just earlier—but if Naomi saw it, she had a hell of a poker face. "They're not going to kill you. You're one of them," she said.

"What if they've already done it before?" Xiomara thought about Josefina's tape. "I listened to Mami's cassette. He said he knew they were responsible for Josephina's death. You've heard how they talked about my mom. They didn't like her . . .

"And I'm pretty sure they did it," Xiomara admitted. The certainty had hardened inside of her, tucked between her lungs, and if she didn't get confirmation, she would choke on it for the rest of her life.

Time ticked on. For a while, Naomi said nothing, but her expression was hardened, and Xiomara couldn't tell if it meant she would help her or not. She took a deep breath.

"Your mom was killed in a car accident. And no offense, but none of your relatives are smart enough to really plan and get away with murder," she said, paraphrasing Yaritza's earlier excuse.

"Maybe not." Xiomara gripped the bedsheets. "But they have the money. They could have paid someone."

"Xiomara . . ." She sighed. "I don't know if—"

"If it were your mom?" Xiomara asked. If Julia's death had been planned, if the break-in wasn't just a tragedy, if someone in the family harbored so much hatred for her that they paid off someone to do the unthinkable, if, if, if . . . *If it were your mom, wouldn't you do anything to find out?*

"If it were my mom, trust that I would be doing something much worse," Naomi said, calmly and with a deadly focus. She had the look of someone with nothing to lose—which, in this case, seemed about right. At the same time, there was also Julia in Naomi's face. Skin like mahogany wood, a heart-shaped face, the way her clear eyes looked like marbles. There were signs of Julia in every pore, a signature passed down from mother to daughter.

A dull sense of loss cut into Xiomara. She wondered if, just like her, Naomi had a hard time looking in the mirror. The home aide looked away from her but didn't move. She rubbed the back of her neck, mumbling under her breath, ". . . must be losing it . . ." Finally, Naomi sighed. "All right. What do you want me to do?"

"Something that no one sees coming."

Xiomara didn't have to wait very long. The moment Naomi closed the door on her way out, the plan began to unfold. Sitting in the closet, Xiomara pressed her ear to the wall, listening to the home aide's footsteps fade toward the stairs when Rafael called out to her.

"Naomi, where are you going?"

Naomi's voice hardly traveled. All Xiomara could make out was something about the dining room. She slowly closed the closet doors, encasing herself in darkness.

"What?" Yaritza shouted. Her footsteps were next, following after Naomi quickly until Xiomara could no longer hear either of them. She gripped Josefina's tape, praying that this plan would work. Her heart skipped a beat at the sound of creaking floorboards. Someone crossed the hallway to just outside the room.

Don't come in, she begged. *Not yet.* Not until Naomi did her part. Xiomara counted the seconds until she hit forty-five. That's when she heard it—a high pitched bloodcurdling scream cutting through what sounded like a series of shots.

Rafael shouted for his daughter and ran. Most of the family followed suit, clambering down the steps so loudly that Xiomara almost didn't hear the doorknob turning. Whoever it was opened the door gradually, putting one foot forward as if they only intended to peek inside. Xiomara tried to imagine it: what it must have looked like opening the door to an empty room that should have harbored the demon while chaos reigned downstairs. The person would be tempted to search the room from top to bottom, and find Xiomara hiding in the closet, but Yaritza's cries of pain forced them to consider the impossible rather quickly.

"She's not here!" Marisa yelled, running out of the room. *"She's not here!"*

Now.

Xiomara pushed the closet doors open and moved with haste to Papi Ramon's bedroom. It would be a while before any of them would muster the courage to check it, but that was fine, because she would hopefully be long gone by then.

On the other side of the window was the metal trellis, still intact and hopefully sturdy. Xiomara quickly undid the lock and pushed herself halfway out into the storm. The wind and rain flattened her hair against her scalp in seconds as she hooked her hands onto one of the rusted poles. Xiomara maneuvered closer, one foot dangling out the window and trying to catch hold, but the rain made it difficult for her not to slip.

"Xiomara?" someone shouted. Adrenaline spiking, Xiomara pulled herself out. She swung to the left, feet scrambling against the trellis while she steeled her arms. Finally, she wedged a foot into a metal corner and shifted her weight to test its strength. It held.

Xiomara scrambled down the trellis. The house had insulated sound so well that she hadn't realized how deafening the weather was outside. She couldn't tell where the family was or where they were going, but she could guess that they were frantically trying to locate her.

The ground squelched under Xiomara's feet. The storm had turned much of the dirt into mud, with an inch of standing rainwater still slowly sinking into the earth. Xiomara already felt like she was swimming in it. Her shoes were already drenched, underwater and lapping up at her ankles as she maneuvered along the side of the house.

She ducked under nearby windows, careful to avoid being seen in case someone happened to look outdoors. In a few steps, she was finally behind the wall of the bathroom right next to the stairs. The small room had a tiny window, so small that not even her younger self could have cleared it. But that was fine, because all she needed was a hand.

Xiomara peered up, blinking away the rush of water as it pelted her. The night was black as pitch. The only thing that gave the dark any shape was the soft glow of light from the second-floor windows. It made the house feel like it was completely submerged in a void, flooded by the constant white noise of the sky. Behind her, the house shuddered, and for a moment it did not feel like an omen, but rather the pathetic whimper of a sick animal. Xiomara shared that shudder, a bitter cold cutting to the bone before she had time to register the feeling on her skin. She wondered how long it would take to develop hypothermia in this kind of weather. She couldn't imagine lasting ten minutes.

The bathroom window squeaked open. Xiomara was tempted to scramble through it, but she forced herself to remain still—anyone could have been on the other side of that window. A hand shot out. The silver glint of a key caught her eye immediately. It dangled on a metal ring that hooked into the fob remote. Xiomara had never felt so much relief.

Naomi's hand shook the dangling key, and Xiomara grabbed it.

"Thanks!" she hissed.

"Just hurry up and get out of here. I'll try to keep them busy," Naomi whispered. Then she was gone. Xiomara shook as she bent around the corner of the house. If she was right, no one would think to check on their car keys until they saw that the car was already gone. Hopefully, by then, she would already be miles away.

If there was any indication that the family were considering taking a look outside, Xiomara didn't see any. None of the windows moved, and no one dared to pop their head out in the storm, not when lightning was flashing. A couple hundred feet away, Xiomara heard the snapping of a tree and the subsequent thud on the ground. No one would come looking for her outdoors.

She pushed herself forward, carefully settling one foot in the muck before dragging the other in front. In just another few strides, she would be at the front of the house and the back of someone's car. She guessed it was Rafael's since he'd arrived first.

But his was not the car she intended to steal.

When everything gets chaotic, go get Manuel's car keys. Unlink them from his house keys first, though.

From the security video, she knew exactly the order the family members had arrived in. Rafael had arrived first, parking his car farther into the driveway. Then Naomi arrived, by Uber. After were Marisa and Aury in a coral Bentley that Xiomara guessed belonged to Aury. She always did enjoy luxurious vehicles that she could customize.

And last were Manuel and his kids, in a large black SUV. Yaritza later arrived via a rideshare just like Xiomara and Naomi.

Another perk of the Dead Mom Club, she thought wryly, just as her foot slipped. Both hands and a knee hit the pavement first, and once the firecracker pain had dulled to a low sizzle, she collected herself and crawled next to the large car. Her hands trembled as she slipped the key into the car lock—using the fob would risk the headlights springing to life and calling for attention.

The key did its job flawlessly. Xiomara opened the door and scrambled inside. She flopped forward onto the dry passenger seat, pulling herself into the driver's seat and shivering in the dark for a few seconds. The inside of the car was not any warmer than the outside, but at the very least, it was dry, and she would not have water sapping every degree of body heat from her.

Now it was time for the harder part—turning on the car. The headlights would flash no matter what, but she hoped her family would assume it was just another lightning strike and avoid the windows. Down the road, the glow of another car's headlights grew larger as it approached. If Xiomara was lucky, it would be Mark, coming back from his office with the previous will sitting dry in his briefcase.

But she was rarely lucky, and this car didn't even have the same make or model as the one she had seen him drive earlier. She decided to wait for it to pass instead, and rubbed her hands together for warmth. It surprised her to feel how numb they'd become in the span of time it took her to enact this plan. Once she was safely down the road, she planned to crank the heat to high.

The car did not pass. It slowed, stopping on the side of the road and killing the lights before Xiomara could see who it was. The door popped open, a cheap umbrella pointed against the direction of the wind as the person struggled to keep it straight while dashing to the front door.

Xiomara couldn't help but freeze, struck dumb by the lanky legs that moved quickly for the safety of the archway. She couldn't imagine what stranger would risk life and limb in this weather to get to the family. Maybe it was whoever had left that threatening letter about confessing sins. Once the umbrella came down, Xiomara's eyes widened at the familiar frame.

What the hell was Marcus doing here?

Her head started buzzing with adrenaline. She had two choices—she could stick to her plan and drive off, leaving Marcus to deal with whatever ensuing craziness her family would think up. Or she could grab Marcus and risk getting caught.

If I leave, they'll assume Marcus is the demon and kill him.

"Xiomara?" Marcus called, his voice muffled by the distance and rain. His fist pounded against the door as he peered into the sidelight. "Xiomara! I'm here!"

Shit, shit, shit. Distressed, Xiomara fumbled with the keys, dropping them somewhere between her feet on the car floor. She dove for them, feeling around the rug with her heart caught in her throat, jerking up only when Marcus said something that filled her with confusion.

"I brought the tape player you wanted!" He pinched the umbrella under his armpit and held up something small and square. He went over to the window in the study. The curtains billowed, as if someone were pushing them aside. "Xiomara, are you in there?"

Someone stood on the other side of the window. Xiomara could see them no clearer than she could see Marcus, from several feet away. They had a smaller frame wrapped in an identical cardigan to hers and rapped a hand against the glass. Marcus leaned in. Xiomara couldn't tell what he was seeing, but she had the sickening feeling that whatever it was, it wore her face.

"Can you let me in?" he asked, a free hand pulling at the window.

El bacà protects its owner's properties.

The figure ballooned. The cardigan melted into flesh, becoming veiny and muscular. Xiomara jolted out of her stupor and threw the car door open.

"Marcus, get away from there!"

Marcus turned, fortunate enough to miss how the thing in Papi Ramon's study smiled—but not fortunate enough to miss what happened next. The window exploded. Xiomara hadn't taken two steps before she was thrown back, her head slamming against pavement and darkening her vision while rain battered down.

Pools of pain radiated down her back. Her hands found the ground, but vertigo kept a strong grip. She crawled along blindly until her vision returned, pushing herself up against a tire and peering over the top of Aury's car to find where Marcus had gone. Unlike Xiomara, Marcus didn't appear to have been blown away in the attack. His crumpled body lay not too far from the window, surrounded by a growing puddle of blood, diluted only by the rainwater that carried the crimson fluid in streaks toward Xiomara.

She didn't have to check if he was still alive. The spine at the base of his neck was visible enough.

12:17 A.M.

Xiomara fell to her knees, and just in time, it seemed. The front door slowly peeled open as Naomi's head poked out, followed by Yaritza's nosy expression. The pile of gore once known as Marcus immediately shocked them back. Naomi fell into the open door frame, sliding down on her ass with both hands pressing into her mouth. Yaritza went running, screaming something that might have been actual words had Xiomara not been too stunned to process them.

She felt herself leave her body. Xiomara watched herself sit in the cold and unforgiving weather, while Aury and Manuel were next to peer out of the door. Aury shouted in surprise, and Manuel did the same. The two delved into some kind of argument while Xiomara wondered what had taken them so long to open the door? They had all run down to the first floor in seconds when they'd thought she had escaped, but when Marcus stood at the front door for several minutes, knocking and yelling for Xiomara, it was like none of them had heard him, or even bothered to check.

Marisa was at the door next, for just a few seconds before Aury waved her back. The family disappeared into the house, leaving Naomi in a horrified state, still transfixed by the corpse. Xiomara watched her, focusing on the way the home aide's shoulders rose up and fell quickly. The panic attack was enough reminder for Xiomara to breathe. She came back to her body, exhausted and wracked with agony, then steadied herself by leaning against the Bentley. Xiomara hooked her elbow over the hood as she came to her feet. She immediately noticed a large crack in the windshield, splintering from the top right corner to the bottom middle—and resting right at the base was the cassette player.

Tentatively, Xiomara reached for it, only to be whipped around and pulled to the ground.

"What are you *doing*?" Naomi gripped her arm tight. Her voice came out strained, like she was trying to keep herself from crying but only succeeding in not choking on her tears. "I thought you said were leaving!"

Xiomara opened her mouth. "Marcus . . . he . . ." She swallowed the words before she could scream it.

Naomi stilled. She didn't blink or turn, yet she looked at the body from the corner of her eye in a way that said she was very aware of where it was. "That was your . . . ?"

Xiomara swallowed again. All the water in the world could've drowned her then, and it still wouldn't have been enough for her dry throat.

"Okay, but . . . you still have to go," Naomi whispered. "Go, get out of here. You still have the car keys, right?"

Xiomara turned to the SUV. "I dropped them somewhere in there."

Somehow, despite having blatantly left the car door open, Xiomara found it shut. Without another word, Naomi went over to the SUV and pulled at the handles. The doors wouldn't budge, already locked from intruders. Was this the demon's doing?

"Naomi!" someone called.

"I'm coming!" she yelled, then pressed the tape player into Xiomara's chest. The numbing cold made it so she could only feel a light pressure when the corners were probably digging into her skin. "Listen, at this point, you're better off just making a run for it. Better yet . . ." Naomi searched the dark for moment. She pointed out toward the road. "Is that his car? Grab his keys and go. I don't care which direction you go in, just *go*."

And then she was alone again. Naomi ran off, yelling into the house about needing a towel. It was unclear whether it was for her or to cover the body. Regardless, Xiomara sat in a half trance while clutching the player.

Her back was bruised, and she was sure she was very concussed, still feeling a light touch of vertigo even while planted on the ground. The study window had been utterly shattered, and the creature had slashed through enough meat and bone to nearly decapitate Marcus. Yet despite it being thrown with enough force to crack a windshield, the tape player was in perfect condition.

How did Marcus know I needed a tape player? She hadn't even spoken to him since she'd told him off. And with the cell tower being down, there was no way for him to contact her either. Yet somehow he had this address.

Xiomara curled over the tape player. Was this the demon's way of getting her to stay? Did it *want* her to find the last two tapes? Xiomara wondered what the demon stood to gain from that. If there was a lesson her grandfather tried to ingrain in her, it was to always fight against demons. Do the opposite of what they told you. If they went right, you went left. If they walked into the ocean, you walked off a cliff. If they offered you a glass of water, you were better off self-immolating. Xiomara considered taking Naomi's advice and driving off in Marcus's car. That would be playing it safe, for sure. She would be able to get farther and faster.

Just as she stood up, a stray scent rooted her to the ground. *No.* She held her breath, denying her recognition. *That's not possible.* And she was right—it wasn't possible, not in the endless rain and wind, for *any* smell to stand out. But it did. Against all logic, when she breathed, it was there. Not the smell of blood or the inherent gore of exposed muscle and bone. Not even sulfurous rot.

An earthy musk with an underlying sweetness, too refined to ever be attributed to nature. It was the unmistakable smell of sandalwood—her father's favorite scent.

And a threat.

Insssiiide, the rain hissed.

Xiomara looked away from Marcus's body. She stood on two shaky legs and made her way to the back entrance. If the demon was capable of luring

Marcus—a true outsider of the family—just to kill him, then her father was no safer. She had to deal with it here and now.

It was great luck that no one was on the first floor. Xiomara slipped in through the back entrance, shuffling into the long narrow hallway that led to the dining room. The lights were all off, and hardly any movement could be heard from the second floor. Xiomara guessed that they were too afraid of the thing that had killed Marcus and thought it might've still been prowling. Whatever the reasoning, it worked in her favor. She sat in the farthest corner from the stairs, hoping to remain out of sight as the warmth of the home gently enveloped her.

Welcome back, it said. Xiomara could only shiver in response. She stared at the player, turning it over and studying it. Unlike her childhood Walkman, this was sleek and black with smaller buttons and sharper corners. It was like someone had wanted to modernize a vintage piece of technology only in style but not in function. It was even lighter in weight. Xiomara slid the back compartment open, revealing an emptiness where a set of AA batteries should have been.

Xiomara stifled a groan.

"Even when he tries to help, he's . . ." She left the sentence unfinished. Marcus was dead. There was no need to deal more blows to his character. Xiomara searched the dining room in silence for the remote and found it underneath the couch. She placed it on a cushion once she removed the batteries and returned to her hidden spot. The player blinked on, awaiting a cassette tape. Xiomara slipped in Marisa's tape and connected her earbuds.

"*Marisa was supposed to drive*," Papi Ramon whispered conspiratorially. *"I know this now because I listened to the voicemail. Josefina called me that day, upset because she knew Aury had taken more of her pills—the painkillers she needed, and that Marisa had promised she would drive to get her more but she'd canceled. She was supposed to drive."* He repeated himself, sounding more crazed with each sentence. *"She was supposed to drive. Aury wasn't supposed to take her pills. And Rafael . . . did he do something to her car? I think he said he tried to fix something. I know something is weird. If I could just remember—"*

There was scratching in the background, like a dull pencil against paper. The tape cut off. She stared blankly at the cassette player. Despite the cold, she burned with indignation.

Did Rafael do something to Mami's car?

"Where is the last one?" Her throat was raw. She imagined the demon was still watching her now. "I know there's one more. Give me Rafael's tape."

There was a hum that moved through the walls, a vibration that mimicked the pitter-patter of the rain outside. It carried into her skin, and Xiomara became all too aware of the movement in the room above.

That's Rafael's room, she thought, envisioning her family huddled around the bed in various states of plotting. Wanda, as silent as ever, only speaking when spoken to. Henry, likely still unconscious while Naomi ran back and forth between checking on him and carrying out orders from Aury. Marisa arguing with Manuel, while Rafael refereed: the two oldest kids fighting for dominance while the youngest attempted to placate both.

Yaritza's probably bored without a cell phone signal.

All of this, Xiomara envisioned in her mind's eye until she heard something move. It was subtle, like the feeling of a plate being slid across a wooden table. She stiffened, pressing her back into the wall as if that would strengthen the signal. Then she realized, something was *actually* moving behind her, until it dropped off, shattering into pieces. Xiomara's eyes snapped open and she zipped toward the dining room.

There was good reason why she could feel something so vividly through the wall—it was shared with the pantry, a small closet space where Papi Ramon stocked cans of Roman beans, mixed vegetables, and a large container of rice, among other nonperishables. Large enough for a person to stand in, which was good because Xiomara was pretty sure someone was coming to investigate the noise. The ceiling creaked toward the stairs. For her own sake, she hoped it was just Naomi.

Quickly parting the pantry double doors, Xiomara searched for the sound of the crash. The pantry appeared mostly bare, with only a few cans left on the top shelf, and the large container of rice in the corner. Broken glass was sprayed around it with the round bottom of a cup that normally would never have been placed in the pantry in the first place. Xiomara's eyes flitted up to a blue tin can. The Royal Dansk cookie label was barely visible, hanging halfway over the shelf. Xiomara grabbed it just as the first creak hit the stairs. She panicked and climbed into the pantry. The one good thing about it was that the tiled floor didn't make any noise. She forced herself into a ball, tucking her head under the lowest shelf. The horizontal panels in the double doors were spaced apart by millimeters, giving her the narrowest view of the kitchen. If anyone were to walk in, Xiomara would see them.

It was only after the footsteps had completely descended that Xiomara thought about the trail of water she likely left after coming in from the pouring rain. It may not have been noticeable in the dark unless someone stepped in it themselves.

She prayed they wouldn't.

Footsteps approached from down the hall, so cautiously slow that a splintering pain formed in Xiomara's neck. Eventually, they stopped at the dining room and turned back, feet picking up speed and jumping up the stairs, running to the safety of Rafael's room.

Xiomara pushed herself out of her hiding place, and crawled into the kitchen. The Royal Dansk cookie tin felt warm in her hands as she wrestled with the top. It came off with a soft pop and a light puff of air that smelled of rotten eggs. Inside was exactly what she'd thought she would find—not cookies, but rather an entire sewing kit. Needles poked out of a palm-sized tomato plush, surrounded by tiny spools of cheap thread.

The tin can had belonged to her grandmother, a surly woman who had very clear expectations of all of her children and grandchildren and didn't hide it. Xiomara thought it was strange to find her grandmother's kit in the pantry. She was sure that everything that had even remotely belonged to that woman was packed up in a storage container elsewhere.

Xiomara fingered through the can, digging out spools one by one and quietly placing them aside. She hissed when a stray needle caught her finger, pricking it hard enough to produce a single drop of blood, then fought the impulsive urge to stick her finger in her mouth. The rain might have washed away Marcus's blood, but Xiomara still felt it on her hands.

She flicked the needle aside and continued unpacking the can.

Her breath hitched when she saw it—another cassette tape. Xiomara flipped it over to read the label: *Rafael 5/6*.

"Okay," she whispered to herself, sniffling. "Okay."

Fishing her headphones out of her pocket, Xiomara slipped the tape into the player and pressed play.

"Rafael is . . . probably one of my best kids. He is always trying to get his siblings to get along, doesn't ask for anything, and doesn't cry about anything. Because of that, his mother would give him anything he wanted. And when his siblings complained, he shared it with them. Food, toys—whatever he got, he shared. Even with Josefina."

There was a long pause. Xiomara heard a few muted gulps and a satisfied *aah*. She imagined he was drinking a Malta when he recorded this. When he continued, his tone of voice changed. It had lowered to a near whisper and she had to strain to hear his words.

"I don't think he messed up Josefina's car on purpose. I think he thought he was doing a good job. He's never been as smart as Aury, or as driven as Manuel. But he liked cars enough. So he tried to fix something in her engine, I think."

Another long pause. And what was this nonchalant tone? He'd gone from sobbing in his last couple of tapes to placid and well-adjusted. Xiomara's finger lingered on the fast-forward button.

"I just didn't think he'd find my gun. I didn't think he'd do that to—"

The audio ended.

So. That's it. Xiomara focused on her breathing. In and out. Process what she'd just heard. Negligence? That's the best her grandfather could come up with? Her mother had died because of *negligence*? Aury swiped her pills, Marisa refused to drive her, Rafael tinkered with her car, Manuel was unbearable to contend with—a hodgepodge collection of her family's poor traits leading to her mother's death—and what, she was supposed to be *okay* with that?

And a gun. She couldn't forget about the gun.

Xiomara sucked in a deep breath until her head rattled with pain.

"Tell me," she whispered. "Where is the last one?"

She waited. And waited. Xiomara strained her ears, tried to imagine any lingering vibrations pointing to any location. She waited for the smell of burning sulfur to guide her to the last hiding place. But all she heard was the sound of thunder, crashing into the stubborn house. The demon said—and did—nothing.

Desperation folded into resentment as Xiomara stared at the tiles on the floor, imagining what it would feel like to tear it up one by one, piece by piece. She'd claw at the floorboards, too, tear away the ugly floral wallpaper just to get at the walls. Then she'd use the wooden panels as a crowbar or shovel, dig into the foundation of her grandfather's home, curse the ground it was built on, and scream until even God couldn't ignore her anymore.

She wanted to do all of this and more—but she didn't. Xiomara only sat there, eyes watering while her lips pulled back into a sneer.

Leaving the cassette player in place, she turned out of the dining room. The house groaned and wailed with every step, alerting anyone who was quiet enough to listen, but they would not get to her in time. She threw open the front door and left it open behind her as she approached Marcus's body. The constant rain had all but washed away the smell of gore, not to mention the color in his skin. He was paler now, with lips tinted bluer than red.

And then there were his eyes. He hadn't been dead long, and yet they had the look of peeled grapes, veiny and moist to the touch. She wished they would flash with playfulness like they always did, the corners crinkling in encouraging optimism. He had always been a glass-half-full kind of guy. Now, Marcus wasn't anything.

Only death stared back.

Xiomara reached for a jagged piece of glass two inches from his face. She stretched her cardigan sleeve over her palm as she gripped it tight then turned to the study window, which was still lined with craggy edges of glass, like the open maw of a voracious creature. She broke through its teeth with her sleeve-covered fist and climbed through.

The study no longer smelled like Papi Ramon. It no longer retained any semblance of warmth. The room had been excavated of all that had brought Xiomara happiness. Now it was empty and cold, less a maw and more a lifeless grave. Fitting, considering she was out for the blood of her blood. She stayed by the door, waiting until she heard it—the sound of footsteps cautiously descending the steps. Her hand gripped the doorknob, slowly turning once the steps had passed in the direction of the wind howling through the open front door.

Xiomara peered out, confirming that it was Wanda they had sent. Her arm was raised up at her side, gripping a claw hammer. Once she turned the corner, Xiomara pounced, tackling the woman into the downpour and knocking the hammer out of her hand. They both hit the wet ground with a sharp smack, and before Wanda gathered her senses to scream for help, Xiomara curled her arm around her cousin's neck and pulled tight.

"Listen, this doesn't have to—" was all she could get out when an elbow suddenly drilled into her side. Xiomara's grip weakened just enough for her to hear Wanda wheeze while reaching for the hammer a foot away. She brought the pointed end of the glass to her cousin's temple. The struggle between them slowed at once. Xiomara took the chance to explain.

"I'm not going to kill you," she blurted. "I just need you to know—there's a gun. And I think Rafael knows where it is—"

"Let *go* of me!"

"Just listen!" Xiomara said. "I listened to almost all the tapes. Papi Ramon said something about Rafael and a gun. Think about it—why was Rafael in the storage room all day? I think he was looking for it."

Wanda's body slackened underneath Xiomara. She could feel her cousin struggling to breathe from the extra weight and shifted to plant a knee into the ground.

". . . your father . . ."

"What?" Xiomara strained to hear her over the plummeting rain. First, all she saw was the back of Wanda's head—then she saw stars. Her face went from numb to sudden agony, gathering at the nose and splintering out over her cheeks and over her eyes. Wanda bucked until Xiomara rolled onto the ground. She wasn't sure if she was even holding the glass shard anymore.

"You are of your father, the devil!" Wanda shrieked, kicking up mud beside Xiomara's head. "And your will is to do your father's desires!"

Xiomara grabbed her ankle, attempting to pull her back down, but by then, Wanda had already gotten to the hammer. She swung it back, blunt end on the bone of Xiomara's wrist.

The pain was exquisite.

Xiomara howled, rolling in the other direction, split between wanting to cradle her hand and wanting to disconnect her arm from her body entirely. But her cousin was not done.

Wanda sat on her stomach, stopping her from moving away and pinning her down. Whatever mercy Xiomara extended her was not reflected back—Wanda did not give her room to comfortably breathe, and Xiomara battled both insufficient oxygen and the excruciating ache now radiating in her wrist. Facing the sky, she now felt like she was being drowned by the rain.

"He was a murderer from the beginning, and does not stand in the truth." Wanda spewed the Bible verse with rage-filled self-righteousness. "Because there is no truth in him."

Unable to sit up, Xiomara rocked from side to side and clawed at Wanda's shirt, yanking her collar to unseat her. Her cousin retaliated with the hammer again, striking the side of Xiomara's arm. Though it didn't connect directly to the bone, the blow was not any less painful, and the resulting ache ricocheted up and down her humerus. Her arm dropped weakly to the ground.

"When he lies, he speaks out of his own character, for he is a liar and the father of lies." Wanda raised the hammer high. In the seconds that followed, Xiomara thought about her mother again. She had always been told that Mami was probably looking down at her, proud that her daughter was growing into such a respectable young woman.

Xiomara hoped that her mother wasn't looking down at her now. God, how embarrassing that would be to meet her again for the first time in a long time, and it's because the rest of the family sent her?

Xiomara closed her eyes and waited to feel the blow that would welcome her into death. But while listening to the roll and echo of thunder sounding in the dark, all she felt was her cousin jolt in place. And then a splash in the mud beside her. Xiomara opened one eye. Her cousin appeared frozen, and on the ground was the hammer.

Xiomara coughed up the water that filled her nose. She shivered. The only good thing about the cold now was that it partially numbed all her throbbing aches and pains.

"Wanda?"

Her cousin didn't answer. She only followed the hammer.

Xiomara winced as she sat up. Wanda was utterly silent and motionless, while scarlet trailed out of her back. Xiomara flipped her over, and found the source—a puncture tearing through her clothes and down into her shoulder blade.

Someone had Papi Ramon's gun.

12:58 A.M.

Blood pooled around Xiomara, lapping at her knees and sinking into her pants while simultaneously being washed away. Despite having already flipped her cousin over, she couldn't bear to touch her again. Xiomara's hands hovered over her, shaking fearfully as if contact would cause Wanda to deflate immediately.

"*Wanda!*" Manuel bellowed, suddenly at the door. He tossed Xiomara aside and fell beside his daughter. "Mija. Mija, wake up." He propped her head over his knees. "Wanda, you have to wake up." He muttered prayers and promises under his breath. Bargains with God that if He didn't take Wanda, Manuel would really give his life to the church, return all the money he stole, go to prison if he must. When that didn't work, the pastor turned to curses and threats. If God didn't bend to *his* will, embezzlement would be the least of his sins.

Manuel stroked his daughter's cheek, speaking as fast as the rain came down. The threats became promises, the curses bent back to prayers. And when all was said and done, his words became silence. Manuel simply sat there, quietly cradling his daughter.

Xiomara's stomach churned, and she thought of the sancocho Wanda made for dinner. The last thing she had ever given her cousin, save for the new wounds that throbbed until she saw stars. Suddenly, Xiomara was being lifted up. Her body was removed from the ground momentarily before she was hurled back down, shoulder hitting the softened ground first. The perpetrator wrapped their hand into Xiomara's hair, tightening at the root and using the leverage to slam her head repeatedly.

Xiomara's vision knocked back and forth between the sky and the ground. When lightning struck with just enough light, she miraculously caught sight of Marisa's contorted expression of anger and hatred.

"Marisa, dejale!" Aury screeched. But whether she simply yelled it or could not stop Marisa, the attacks did not cease, and Xiomara knew this much:

Her aunt meant to kill her.

That knowledge forced her into a second wind. Xiomara fought back, thrashing against her aunt, hooking her fingers into the side of the woman's face and rearing back for a powerful kick. Marisa's grip released her hair immediately. Xiomara ragdolled for a moment, then she scrambled backward, nearly as far Marcus's body.

Aury helped Marisa to her feet, and the two faced their niece.

"Your own cousin . . . ?" one of them muttered. Xiomara couldn't ascertain who when the ground still felt like it was swaying underneath her.

"How could you kill your own cousin with Papi's gun?" It sounded like Marisa. Xiomara looked in the direction of the silhouette most shaped like her and uncorked her rage.

"She attacked me with a hammer!" she screamed. "She tried to *kill* me! All of you are!" What else was there to say? Xiomara didn't want to die. She had already died once and come back miraculously—was that such a sin? Was this entire night now an exercise in repenting? What an Old Testament consequence for the crime of wanting to live.

Xiomara's family met her anguished cries with uncaring silence. The only sound, other than the merciless weather, came from Manuel's slopping loafers. He slid an arm underneath Wanda's legs but could barely lift her more than an inch before sinking in the muck. Death weighed extra.

"Help me bring her inside . . ." He choked, then screamed when his sisters did not move. *"Help me!"*

This jolted them out of their stupor. Aury and Marisa crowded around

Wanda, lifting her on all sides and shuffling indoors. Xiomara watched them, still shivering and drenched to the bone, with aches that proved to be more than what the biting cold could numb.

"*Bring her inside!*" Manuel's voice boomed from indoors. A moment later, a figure emerged from the door. Xiomara could tell instantly from the lanky frame that it was Rafael. He stepped out under the arch and faced her, but said nothing. He only kept his distance, while stewing in contemplation.

"I d-d-didn't sh-shoot her." Xiomara's teeth chattered. But Rafael had to know that already. After all, he was the one who'd spent all day rummaging around the storage room, hiding his actions from anyone who might have peeked in on him. He'd used the gun once—Papi Ramon had said it himself. Rafael knew where it was and had found it at the last second.

And then he shot Wanda, thinking it was me. Rafael was just as untrustworthy as his older sisters. Sick of the way her ass felt in the mud, Xiomara stood up slowly, with all the clumsiness of a newborn doe.

Maybe Bambi wasn't actually clumsy. The thought forced itself into her head. *Maybe Bambi was just in a lot of pain.* What a stupid thing to think about at this moment, but it was all she could do to keep her mind off the immense fireworks-like pain that sparked in damn near every joint in her body. If something wasn't broken, it sure as fuck was strained, sprained, or fractured.

"Are you okay?"

Xiomara felt feral as she looked to Rafael. *Do I fucking* look *okay?* Her ex had died horribly in front of her and her cousin had beaten the dog shit out of her. No one was worried about how far they were taking this—they didn't have to care. Xiomara was her mother's daughter—which made her expendable.

"Unfortunately for you, I'm still alive."

Despite his face being shrouded in darkness, Rafael's nervousness came through in the way he shifted on his feet. "What do you mean—"

"What did you do to Mami's car?" Xiomara could no longer hold back. She sounded less like herself and more like a croaking frog. "Before

Mami's accident. You were trying to fix something, right? How did you mess that up?"

Rafael didn't speak. His silhouette froze at the accusation.

When lightning flashed, Xiomara caught sight of something glimmering from the corner of her eye. She turned away from Rafael, taking a moment to scan the area for a moment until she saw it—the half-submerged hammer. Whether it was because the darkness provided enough cover or because Wanda's demise provided enough distraction, Xiomara's relatives had completely missed the actual weapon used during their skirmish.

She turned away from it, hoping that Rafael hadn't seen it. *I need that hammer.* If he was going to have a gun, Xiomara wanted something just as sturdy to defend herself. She would just have to play it safe.

"Come inside. You know, when you're ready," Rafael said. There was an extended pause. His feet scuffled against the driest part of the ground and then slipped as he entered the home. Rafael cursed under his breath, but from then on, Xiomara was alone. She crouched quickly, wincing from the abrupt movement, and grabbed the hammer. She tucked it in the waistband of her jeans, sliding it horizontal so it didn't make too much of a shape, and tightened her cardigan around her.

When she turned around, she was suddenly faced with a bright light being held by Yaritza. The woman's silhouette had its arms crossed with a phone in hand and stood tall. Xiomara's heart pounded; had her cousin seen the hammer?

"You coming?" Yaritza asked. Her tone suggested she hadn't. She almost sounded bored.

"I thought you got attacked earlier," Xiomara said.

"You don't sound all that concerned."

"I'm not," she admitted. Yaritza made a sound like a breathy laugh, delighted to see her cousin with some bite in her. "Naomi went into Papi Ramon's room. I thought it was weird and followed her."

Xiomara knew she would. "You started poking around." She could guess what happened next. The demon attacked, protecting whatever it was

Yaritza stole. That was all the distraction Xiomara had needed to escape her mother's room.

Yaritza's light shook, nearly blinding Xiomara.

"What did it look like?" she asked.

"I didn't get a good look at it," Yaritza said. *Lied.* "But you should see what it did to Naomi."

Xiomara's heart plummeted. She clumsily shambled her way into the house, pushing past Yaritza and climbing the stairs. Papi Ramon's bedroom was closed. Before her hand could reach the knob, Xiomara's shoulder was gripped by a strong hand and she was dragged through the long dark hallway and into Rafael's old room. Cell phones with flashlights provided just enough light for her to see Marisa's scowling expression as she forced Xiomara into a seat. "*Sit.* Until we figure out what to do with you."

"Let go of me!" She struggled. "I need to see Naomi!"

"There's no need to be so rough." Rafael sighed, weary. "We need to calm down . . ."

"Don't tell us to calm down!" She stabbed a finger into the air. "With everything she's done, how can you still be on her side?"

"We don't know what happened between them!" Rafael waved her question off.

"My daughter . . ." Manuel finally spoke. The room stilled, having not heard Manuel say a word since yelling for someone to bring Xiomara inside. ". . . is dead."

He sat on the bed like he was still cradling Wanda, fingers splayed upward while down on his lap. Manuel didn't look up. "So I should decide what we do."

"Where's Naomi?" Xiomara asked. "What happened to her?"

Like always, Xiomara's question went unanswered.

"You should be more worried about yourself," Yaritza muttered, her haunted expression sharpened by the insufficient light. Xiomara gritted her teeth, arms folded over the hammer in her waistband. Part of her wanted to play it safe; the other part wanted to go out swinging.

"Why?" Xiomara scoffed. "Because *your dad* has the gun that he used to kill Wanda?"

The room had the stillness of an atomic bomb—and then, anarchy. "You did *what*—" Marisa shouted.

"That's a lie!" Rafael defended, waving his arms. "I didn't kill anyone! I didn't kill Wanda!"

Xiomara jumped to her feet. "Liar! I heard it in your tape! *I heard it!* Papi Ramon *said* you used his gun!" It might have been a leap to suggest that Rafael shot Wanda—but who else would even have knowledge of the weapon existing in Papi Ramon's home? In all the years Xiomara had visited, she'd never once heard mention of her grandfather owning a firearm. The thought alone solidified her gut feeling.

"There's a gun?" Naomi was at the doorway, a hand pressed to her cheek. No, not just a hand—a wad of paper towels was pressed to her cheek. Relief fell on Xiomara like a balm.

"You're okay . . ."

"I wouldn't say that," Naomi grumbled, crossing the room to Henry. Even injured, she was tasked with cleaning his wounds. If Naomi was at all concerned about hearing someone in the house had a gun, she didn't show it. "Do we all need to be in this little room? It's too hot to be all crowded like this."

"How is Henry doing?" Manuel asked. Xiomara could only see Naomi's figure swapping towels.

"Fine, if he beats this infection."

"An infection!" Marisa exclaimed. "So give him antibiotics—" she insisted.

"We don't have any antibiotics!" Naomi snapped. "Henry needs to see a *real* doctor—or an ambulance! If you can't magically bring an ambulance here, this is all I can do for him."

Once again, the room dropped into silence. The aunts stared at the uncles and vice versa. The cousins avoided looking at one another altogether.

Eventually, Marisa took a half step toward Xiomara and slapped her, clear across the temple. Xiomara felt a light crack in her neck as her head swam. Rafael immediately jumped between Xiomara and his sister.

"You better pray that Henry doesn't die next!" Marisa said.

"Stop!" Rafael forced her back. "You don't see how bad she's hurt?"

"That's *her* fault. Why are you defending her?"

Xiomara should have known this was going to happen. None of them were going to listen to her. They were all going to go in circles, blaming her for every misfortune of the night. She should've escaped when she had the chance.

The hammer pressed against her skin had warmed to her touch. How long would it take her whip it out and beat anyone who came close to her? It would force Rafael to expose himself as the true gunman, but after that, all bets were off. The family still didn't trust Xiomara. For all she knew, they could kill her anyway and make excuses for him. She needed another distraction.

Xiomara cleared her throat and said, "Think about it. Was Rafael alone when it happened?"

"We were all together," Marisa insisted, though Xiomara sensed it was a lie.

"Wanda was shot from behind and it hit her shoulder," she repeated. "The bullet didn't come out from the other side, so it probably traveled from an angle. The person who shot her was *upstairs*."

She was bullshitting. God, Xiomara was bullshitting so hard—she'd taken one course on forensic science and dropped out halfway through when it was taking her time away from her actual computer science major requirements. What the hell did she know about the bullet trajectory of a gun? Nothing, not a goddamn thing.

She just needed to sound like she *knew* what she was talking about, and with her background, at least one person would be liable to believe her. All she needed was one.

"Wouldn't we have heard a gunshot?" Yaritza asked, the one question that threw Xiomara for a loop, but she recovered fast.

"Not if you thought it was just part of the thunder." Xiomara held her cousin's stare. If she so much as blinked suspiciously, Yaritza would call her bluff. She stared unflinchingly, even as the flashlight gave her a headache.

Yaritza turned to the room. "Were we all together when Wanda went downstairs?"

"Yes," Aury answered first, hand coming up to scratch her nose. Xiomara wondered, was it just her imagination or was the motion a cover for lying? Unfortunately, she didn't have time to hedge her bets.

She made a quick calculation and decided to play into her injuries. Dropping her head on her lap, she let out a low, painful groan and snuck a hand under her cardigan.

"*I* didn't leave until after Manuel left." Marisa's alibi came out like a biting accusation. "And Manuel only went downstairs to get his daughter."

"And I stayed here with Henry until I heard all of you scream." Yaritza looked to Naomi, and the home aide cursed under her breath. "Where were you, Naomi?"

"Trying to stop bleeding," she answered.

Yaritza stepped in front of the door. "You were outside of this room for a while." Xiomara imagined it was to cut Naomi off if the woman decided to run.

Xiomara's fingers finally grazed the handle. She knew that if she wanted to fully grip it, she would need to stand. How fast could she pull it out?

"Ha!" Naomi laughed, closing the gap between her and Yaritza. "You mean when I went to find clean towels because the rest of you are too pussy to get them yourselves?"

Yaritza didn't budge. "You're cursing a lot for someone who's supposedly innocent."

"And you're getting on my last nerve for someone who can't fight."

Push her, Xiomara begged. All she needed was one push. She looked up and noticed Aury turned to her. Her aunt asked, "Xiomara, what are you doing?"

Now. Filled with adrenaline, Xiomara barely felt her nails digging into her skin when grabbing the hammer.

"She's got the gun!" Marisa screamed. She jumped onto Xiomara, forcing her to stumble back over the chair. They crashed onto the floor just as Xiomara wrenched the hammer free. Yaritza had already bolted out the door. Naomi pressed her back into the wall.

Xiomara swung wide, the claw end of the hammer catching onto Marisa's elbow. Her aunt's pitched scream shot through Xiomara's ears. She slammed a kick into Marisa's side, putting more distance between them.

A powerful blast sounded, sharpening all of Xiomara's pain at once. She curled into herself, half expecting another blast to come, half expecting to feel something leak out of her as a numbing darkness took over.

Neither came. All she heard was ragged breathing and the soft click of a gun.

Marisa gasped. "It was you? You . . . shot Wanda?"

"I didn't mean to!" Aury's voice cracked. "I didn't mean to—I—I was using the bathroom, and when I looked out the window, I saw Wanda fighting someone. I thought . . . I thought . . ."

She meant to kill me, Xiomara thought. Aury pointed the gun at her. It shook in her hands, filling Xiomara with more fear than if it had been Marisa holding it.

"Where did you get that?" Rafael asked sternly. "Where did you get that?!"

"It was in Papi's safe!" she blurted. "When the will said to remember his hiding places—I remembered he had one hidden, and I . . ."

Xiomara looked up at a crack in the ceiling where the bullet had gone in. Rafael approached Aury slowly, arm outstretched and only inches from his sister's shoulder.

"Aury." Rafael spoke calmly. "Aury, look at me. Put down the gun."

The bed squeaked as Manuel came to his feet.

"You killed my daughter . . . ?"

Aury spun around to face Manuel before she realized her mistake and put the gun back on Xiomara. Marisa ducked again, as though expecting the gun to go off again. But Manuel did not flinch. His pale face wore a glassy half-apocalyptic expression. Xiomara had never seen him so emotionally distraught.

"Manito . . ." Aury's voice broke. "I'm sorry. I'm so sorry. I didn't mean to. I thought it was her, okay? I couldn't see that well. I thought it was Xiomara." The barrel shook again in her direction; Xiomara leaned just enough to obscure the hammer in her hand behind her while Naomi attempted to sidestep out of the door. The floor whined, and Aury's head snapped back between the two of them.

"Stop!" she ordered. "Don't move. I'll shoot you, I really will." Her reddened eyes watered. Aury cried so much today that the mascara lines were diluted to nearly nothing.

Naomi slowly put her hands up. "Whoa, maybe we should all just calm down."

Rafael agreed. "Aury, put down the gun."

Aury's breath quickened. "Why? Don't you trust me?" Her head turned on a swivel, and she realized she was surrounded on all sides. Panic washed over Aury, and suddenly she was spinning, her head and gun pointing in the same direction. The abrupt movement pushed nearly everyone back. Except for Manuel.

He stepped forward. "You did it on purpose, didn't you?"

"No!" Aury yelled, turning to him. Manuel was close enough to feel the barrel against the flat of his chest. Both Marisa's and Rafael's jaws fell, and they froze. Xiomara looked to the door to her left. Could she get down the hall in time before a stray bullet caught her? Or should she bait Aury into wasting bullets?

Not without a casualty. Xiomara would have to figure out another way to deal with her.

"You were gloating earlier. About my church, and Henry. You said people like me deserved to die." Manuel took another step forward. Aury took one back.

"Manito, please . . ." She cried, arms shaking.

Xiomara's heart leaped into her throat. Just one more step and Aury was in arm's reach. She sent a look to Naomi and glanced at the door. *Get ready to run*, she hoped to communicate.

The home aide widened her eyes.

There was a very good chance that Aury was going to pull the trigger again. Xiomara's plan was to make sure that she could only do it one time. Tightening her uninjured fist around the base of the hammer, she prepared herself for the worst. While Aury begged Manuel to take a step back, Rafael caught sight of the hammer at Xiomara's side.

"Xiomara, don't!"

That warning was enough. Just as Aury spun to her niece, Xiomara's arm flew out in an arc.

The shot rang in her ears. Aury dropped to her knees, cradling her hand and screaming as she went down. She no longer held the gun.

Xiomara blinked, waiting to feel a warm puncture spread in her body. But just like before, there was none. Just the same aches and bruises she'd collected before.

"Let me see, let me see!" Marisa pulled at Aury's arm. She held up her crushed knuckles, fingers unable to straighten due to the pain alone.

Rafael wasn't at all concerned.

"Where's the gun?" he asked, frantically looking around the room.

Manuel had returned to the corner of the bed, catatonic. Marisa scanned the floor.

"I thought I heard it drop," she said, leaning far enough ahead to peek out of the door. "Is it in the hallway?"

"No," Naomi said, rising from door frame. She'd ducked but not made it out of the room. *Click.* The barrel reappeared in Naomi's hand, pointed straight at the family.

"I've got it," she said. And it did not look like she intended to leave or give it up anytime soon.

1:32 A.M.

The family collectively became a statue. A wave of alarms sounded in their heads as they watched Naomi take another step forward. Every single person leaned back.

"Hm?" she asked. "What's wrong?" The gun moved in a curve, pausing at each member of the family like points on a line, stopping just before she got to Xiomara. That puzzled her, but she watched as Naomi made eye contact with her family. Each time, they flinched at her sight, as if it were the first and only warning they would get before she pulled the trigger.

Xiomara wondered why Naomi wouldn't look at her.

"G-good job, Naomi!" she stammered, somehow finding the boldness to speak. She tried on a smile and laugh like a child trying a cigarette for the first time. Her confidence was about as real as the emperor's new clothes. "I can take the gun now." She tentatively held out her palm.

Naomi's lips curved upward, audacity solidifying in her eyes. "Go on, take it." She shook the gun. Marisa quickly stepped back and threw her hands up. "What's wrong? Don't you want the gun?" Naomi pursed her lips, in mock concern. Despite being ignored, Xiomara didn't think she was free to do as she pleased. The weapon was only ever a few degrees from being in her direction, and her wounds alone sang like they were going to drag her kicking and screaming into a dreamless sleep.

"Naomi, let's be serious." Rafael swallowed, inching toward her. Then she pointed the gun and he fell back.

"So why'd you do it?" Naomi asked. Rafael stilled, his face slackening into an expression Xiomara couldn't read. She watched his arms remain up and out, hands splayed in a defensive pose, while he kept his knees at an angle. Rafael looked ready to bolt.

"Do what?" He let out a breathy chuckle and swallowed. Naomi was not amused.

"You know what," she said. "But I'm sure your family doesn't. Do *you* want to confess your sin, or should I do it for you?"

Xiomara's eyebrows shot up. "The letter was you?"

Naomi didn't take her eyes off Rafael. "It was. But don't worry—I don't have a goddamn clue what your grandfather was on about with that demon business. That was as much a surprise to me as it was to you. But let's not get off track. Rafael?"

Though his lips parted and shook, Rafael would not speak.

"Oh no. The cowardly brother's a coward," Naomi remarked, deadpan. "You know what might help? If we all got a little *comfortable*." With just a simple look and a wave of her arm, Naomi corralled the family onto the bed, including Xiomara. They surrounded Henry on all sides, who made unpleasant groans when the bed shifted in a painful direction. Manuel avoided looking at Aury while she cried softly into her hand. Naomi's eyes swept over them, and because of the gun, every glance felt like it lingered a little too long. She looked at them like they wore targets, and adrenaline made every blink aggressive.

To her right, Marisa pressed her arm against Xiomara's, a subtle nudge meant to grab her attention, if only for half a second.

Xiomara looked and saw Marisa's eyes flutter to the home aide. *Do something*, her eyes seemed to say. The swelling from the beating Marisa had given her had barely gone down. Xiomara pushed her aunt's arm away.

Then Naomi took in a deep breath. "I've always known."

Xiomara studied her face. The heart-shaped face that belonged to Julia was shattered by the look in Naomi's eyes. The home aide swallowed, pushing down a feeling, a rising lump, and again, she breathed. Calmed. "I've always known you killed my mom," Naomi explained. "I don't know why exactly, but I think I can piece it together just by the way you look at me. You wanted her, but she didn't want you. And what drove you insane was she never told you why, huh? Just pretended like it was for the best that you didn't know.

"Until you found out." She reached an arm behind her back, Xiomara imagined she was going to produce a second gun from thin air. But she didn't.

Instead, she held another cassette tape. Naomi tossed it to them and watched it bounce off Manuel's chest onto his lap. Aury quickly plucked it, and turned it over—the label was torn right before the fraction *6/6*.

"Where did you find this?" Aury asked, as if forgetting who held the gun.

"Looks like none of you knew it." Naomi laughed. "I guess that's not a surprise. You Abreus do everything you can to die with your secrets. Play the tape," she said, tossing a look to Xiomara. "With the little *gift* your boyfriend got you."

"How did you know . . ."

Naomi blinked. "Who do you think told him to come?"

Xiomara realized it then—the moment Naomi asked Xiomara for her phone. She used it to contact Marcus. "Why would you do that?" she asked.

Naomi rolled her eyes, and again she ordered, "Play. It."

"It's downstairs. In the kitchen."

"Perfect. Yaritza? Did you hear that?" Naomi waited. No one replied. The house was made of silence. "I know you're there." The home aide raised her voice, slightly turning her head to the open doorway. "You've never known how to mind your business, and it's not like your ass can drive. I just need you to do me a favor."

If Yaritza was there at all, she was doing a great job staying quiet. Xiomara watched Naomi's stone expression. The woman was certain the loudmouth cousin was out there—and she was determined to bring her back to the group.

"How about this: if you bring the cassette player up here within, hm, twenty seconds? If you can do it that quickly, I *won't* shoot your father in the face."

The family gasped, each person extending a hand over Rafael, partially shielding him like any of them could stop a bullet. Their voices rose up in a soft crescendo, pleading with both words and alarmed noises.

"Naomi, please—" Aury begged.

Marisa's face went pale. "This isn't funny . . ."

"Am I laughing?" She called out to the hall, "You have fifteen seconds now. Fourteen. Thirteen." In the half second that stood between thirteen and twelve, footsteps came to life, clopping against the floor in quick and clumsy succession down the stairs. Naomi didn't stop counting. The family strained their ears to listen for movement on the first floor, mentally mapping Yaritza's journey to the kitchen and back.

"Five . . . four . . . three . . ."

Just a few feet away from the door, there was a loud slam. The family jolted and watched the door expectantly. Whatever happened, Yaritza finally blustered into the room just on the heels of "one." Her feet came down on the floor with such force that there was an audible *snap!* Xiomara looked down to see her cousin's kitten heel had broken and now dangled from her shoe in between steps. Yaritza stumbled as she held the cassette player at arm's length.

"Uh-uh." Naomi shook the gun the same way she shook her head. "Go sit with the rest of them. Aury, give Yaritza the tape. I want her to press play."

Yaritza's jaw flexed, but she obeyed nonetheless. Taking the tape from Aury, she clicked it into the recorder and raised the volume. Static immediately filled the air.

> "There are many things in my life that I regret. Many things I wish I had or hadn't done, not because I shouldn't have done them but because the consequences . . ."

Xiomara felt her heart slow and ache at the same time. Papi Ramon had never sounded so tired. No matter where she imagined him, whether in his room or in the study, she pictured him the same. Sunken eyes with crow's-feet and a parched throat. Softened bones and wrinkled skin folding over him like an oversized sweater.

She didn't understand why she could see him in such a state. Even lying in his coffin, Papi Ramon could have passed for a man ten years younger than he actually was.

Perhaps that's what it was. She'd looked past his exterior, dug through the superficial memories that painted Papi Ramon as a still-spry grandfather, bouncing her on his knees and tickling her imagination. That Papi Ramon was no longer with her. The only version of Papi Ramon that still existed was the one on this tape. His voice sounded like gravel, and he spoke like defeat was all he'd known in this life.

"I know you don't care about that. You're angry. But you have no right to be." The tone in his voice became so chilling, Xiomara wondered if this was the same person who'd doted on her. *"I had a decision to make. A tough one. And I made it. You're here for a reason. And that reason is to take everything. Just take it. Don't tell anyone I gave it to you—I have things set up in a way that it'll look like a charity donation. No one will know it was you. So please . . . please stay away."*

"Why should I?" Naomi mumbled, staring at the cassette player like she was contemplating shooting it. Xiomara leaned away as if to leave the splash zone, while her eyes traveled to her relatives. Their expressions ranged from distraught to incomprehensibly baffled.

Manuel suddenly found his voice. "What is he talking about?"

"Shh," Naomi responded. The tape continued.

"Stay away, and most importantly—" Papi Ramon was interrupted by an assault on his throat. He coughed violently and half gargled until he was calmed. *"Don't ever tell anyone you're my daughter."*

Rafael's jaw slackened as he paled at the audio recording.

Xiomara's head spun. She didn't want to believe it was him. That Papi Ramon had had a secret kid. She looked at the others—Rafael's jaw had slackened, and the shadows on his face heightened his shocked expression. The rest of the family circled a question that only Aury was brave enough to ask.

"Who is this for?"

Xiomara quickly did the math in her head. She and Naomi were the same age. Julia was . . . what, in her late thirties, early forties when she died?

How old was Papi Ramon?

Her brain short-circuited. Xiomara didn't want to do the math on *that*. It was obvious already. Papi Ramon was old, even twenty-one years ago. He had to have been in his fifties when he approached Julia.

Papi Ramon wouldn't do that. She refused to believe it. This tape was a lie. It had to be a lie, a fabrication made by the demon solely to fuck with her. Naomi might even be in on it. Xiomara could believe that. After all, she was just as much of a hostage as the rest of her family.

Xiomara felt a pressure rise over her shoulder. Aury leaned over, her chin nearly resting on her niece's head. She whispered, "Did Papi and—"

"No!" Marisa said, refusing the question before it solidified. "He wouldn't. Papi was a good man."

The home aide only stared, bored with the family's insistence. "You of all people should know Dominican men can't be trusted."

"Shut up!" Xiomara blurted, grabbing the player. "I can't hear it." She held it up to her ear, catching Papi Ramon's final words.

"... think about your mother and what she
would want for you. Goodbye, Naomi."

The tape stopped. The room felt like it had dropped several degrees. Naomi stared at the little square player with a blank expression that made the existence of the gun even more dangerous.

"You found out that Ramon and my mom used to be . . . involved." Naomi paused, the barrel of the gun aimed directly at Rafael. "And to say that it upset you would be an understatement."

"Th-th-that's not true!" Rafael shook his head. "I mean, I knew that Papi and Julia were close, but I swear, I didn't kill her."

Naomi continued, ignoring his pleas. "And then you rushed to cover up the whole situation by claiming it was a regular break-in. Did you think

I wouldn't notice that the TV was never taken? Just because you hide it for a week or two, doesn't mean it's automatically brand-new when you bring it back out."

The entire time Naomi spoke, her tone barely wavered from anything above spa day calm. The same calm Xiomara saw when she asked Naomi what would she do if her family had killed her mom. Well, it turned out, they had.

And Naomi was committed to revenge.

"You Abreus paid the police to look the other way. Not investigate too heavily. And then Ramon *generously* offered me a job. I had no one and nothing else, and he knew that—he knew I couldn't do anything to him if I needed him to survive." The home aide's eyes finally narrowed, lips tilting downward in a deep expression of casual distaste. As if she were simply staring at a pile of unwashed dishes, waiting for her to get to work.

As if she weren't holding a loaded gun.

Xiomara did not envy Rafael.

"Wait . . . so do you mean—" Aury began to ask.

"Do you need to hear it again?" Naomi picked up the fallen chair, gun still raised in the direction of the family. She moved like she wasn't concerned. Like turning away to reset the chair wouldn't give them enough time to get the drop on her. Her arm was steady, and her grip was strong. That alone made Xiomara remain planted on the old bedding.

"Yes, I am Ramon's kid, technically—not that he was all that great at hiding it. He was very sloppy at so many points. I don't think he's as smart as you want to believe he is. Do you know when I had that first suspicion?" Naomi asked. "That we were all related? I overheard Julia talking to Ramon around three years ago. It was in Spanish, but I could hear her nearly breaking through the barrier to Creole. That's how I knew that she was upset. She sounded like she was holding herself back."

Xiomara tried to remember it—a moment when Julia sounded strange or strained or even a little mad. Not a single memory was brought to the forefront of her mind. She watched Naomi carefully, trying to find a single opening to get the gun away from her. But unlike Marisa or Aury, Naomi was not someone who could be easily baited. She had endured too much to be caught lacking.

"And then, a few days later, my mother was dead." The home aide's shoulders came up in a half shrug. "A break-in. A bullet. Wrong place, wrong time. That's what Ramon told me. I'm sure that's what all of you would've told me if you had been at the funeral."

"We had a good reason for not coming—" Manuel tried, but Naomi shook her head and stopped him.

"Don't. Lying to me just makes me want to shoot you more." She gripped the gun. "The point is, a dead housekeeper is one thing. A dead housekeeper you had a kid with—*that* opens you up to a lot more scrutiny. And I'm pretty sure he had a reputation he wanted to maintain."

Aury was halfway to her feet before she caught herself. The gun was still there, a direct line to her chest. She sank back into bed. "He wouldn't do that," she said, more of a mumble than it was a proclamation. Her side was flush against Manuel, and he shifted half an inch away from her. He refused to look in her direction or acknowledge that she was there.

"He *did* do 'that.' This isn't an argument." Naomi dismissed her. "None of you get to pretend like you knew everything about him." She pitched her voice high and low as she mimicked the Abreus. "'He consulted me on the will' this or 'he begged me to stay with him' that. Or 'he trusts me the most because I'm godly,' right, Manuel?" She sent a jab at him then leaned back. "You all thought he was a good man, but he was just as terrible as the rest of you."

Me? Xiomara wanted to ask. *What did I do?* Her worst behavior included not speaking to Naomi for three years. That didn't warrant a bullet wound.

Naomi winced, as she pulled the paper towels off her face. The gash underneath it was gnarly. Blood caked the area, dripping over exposed flesh. Xiomara looked around for something to clean it with. All the cleanest towels were with Henry.

"Anyway, thanks for this." Naomi waved the gun. "I needed it to prove that my mom's death was an inside job. I don't give a shit about whatever money your dad was going to leave me—I earned enough money pretending to be Marisa's boyfriend for two years."

Marisa gasped audibly. Naomi gave a painful smirk. "It's a wonder how far AI has come, isn't it?" She made her way to the door, turning back at the last second for the final word.

"By the way, Yaritza." A cold look came over Naomi. "You were late."

They barely had the chance to register the bang of the gun before Rafael's nose collapsed into his face.

2:40 A.M.

There was screaming. The light thump of a body against the bed, immediately overshadowed by relatives violently throwing themselves onto it.

Marisa scrambled over Xiomara. Manuel formed a wall between the aunts and Rafael, hesitant to touch him. Xiomara looked over his shoulder—blood painted half of Yaritza's face, and she swiped at it in hysterics, throwing herself back until she dropped from the bed. She clawed her way up, bloodied hands leaving streaks in the sheets, and curled into her father's chest.

"Papi!" Her scream sounded like a chain saw. It tore through her vocal cords repeatedly while the older adults wailed in the background. All of it rattled Xiomara's head until she felt it in her joints.

"Welcome to the Dead Dad Club," Naomi said on her way out.

"Wait," Aury choked. "We can't touch the body. It's—it's a crime scene."

"Are you *serious* right now?" Manuel's eyes bugged out of his head.

"It's a crime scene!" Aury repeated. She blubbered as she tried to make sense. "I've seen it on shows! To know what happened, they have to—forensics needs to—"

"We all saw what happened!" Manuel argued.

"Stop yelling at me!"

Just outside the door, Xiomara thought she saw something flash by. It crashed onto the floor with a thud, grabbing everyone's attention in one go.

Xiomara ran to the door. Down the hall, Naomi was crumpled on the floor, groaning as she picked herself up. "Fucking . . . what?" She rubbed the back of her head, searching the floor for the gun. It was just beside her. Before Xiomara could think to dive for it, the home aide carefully picked it up.

"Xiomara, *move*," Naomi said, gesturing with the barrel of the gun.

"I don't think you want to do that."

Xiomara whirled around at that new voice, relief flooding her body. Mark walked leisurely to Xiomara and gave her a gentle smile. Which is when the relief left, because although his mouth was gentle, his eyes burned like a funeral pyre and he smelled like he'd bathed in charcoal.

Xiomara took a step back, spine hitting the door frame before she knew it was there. Mark chuckled with bemusement, and tipped his head into the room, carefully assessing the bodies, blood, and bullet holes.

"Looks like you've all had quite a time."

"Mark!" Manuel jumped to his feet and ran to his supposed savior. "Get out of here! Call the cops. That crazy girl—she killed my brother, and she has a gun!" Clinging to Mark's arms, he tried to push him toward the stairs. Manuel might as well have been pushing a wall. Still, the lawyer laughed at the attempt.

Xiomara swallowed, reaching a shaky hand to her uncle. "I don't think he's going to help."

"What?" Manuel glanced between Mark and his niece. The powerful smell of burning charcoal and rotten eggs swept the room, bubbling like an open wound. It forced Manuel to gag. He backed off, stumbling to the window and forcing it as wide as it would go. The wind did precious little to offer relief. He sank to the ground, while his sisters coughed into their elbows.

"Naomi?" Mark called. "Care to join us? And please, don't waste your bullets on me. You wouldn't like the repercussions."

"You . . . who are you?" Manuel stammered. "You're not Mark . . . What happened to Mark?"

"I'm not Mark in the way that you are not your shirt. The names I use are irrelevant. But you can call me what you've always known me as." His teeth flashed white. They were an ordinary set, slightly gray, like the before picture one would see at the dentist. He looked like he would be a dentist. "El bacà."

And yet, there was still that feeling—that unexplainable nagging intuition that this man was not what he looked like. It put her senses in disarray as she questioned what was real and what was imagined.

"No, but . . ." Marisa's eyes watered, unable to take the pungent smell without stinging. "Papi said it was someone in the family."

"He didn't say that." Xiomara's throat was so dry, she could hardly speak. Still, she forced saliva down and reached for her voice. "He didn't say it was someone in the family. He just said it was someone who was here . . ." Xiomara looked to Mark quickly, too afraid to make eye contact.

The demon smiled and waved. "Hello, nice to finally meet you. Well, nice for you to finally meet *me.* I've already met you." He stepped past Xiomara and wagged a circle in the air. The fallen chair immediately kicked up, jolting with the spry energy of a baby goat until it was back on all four legs. Mark sat comfortably, crossing an ankle over his knee. As if with the flip of a switch, the smell dissipated. The family gasped, filling their lungs with clean air.

"Naomi?" Mark called her again. "I won't say it again. Come. In." With the sharp turn in his voice, Naomi's body flew in, arms flapping behind her and slapping against the wall on her way in. She was dropped a few feet in front of the demon. Though quick to recollect herself, Naomi would not do anything more than glare at Mark. The gun floated in behind her. Mark plucked it from the air.

He studied the inner barrel, half-bored. "This was fun, but I'd like to collect my final payment."

"Payment for what . . . ?" Xiomara's voice came out like a croak. All the screaming she'd done was taking a toll on her. Mark looked to her with deepened interest.

"For you." He waved another finger, and Xiomara was thrust before him. "You remember now, don't you? The time you tried to fly."

Xiomara's head throbbed as she nodded. "I fell out the window. I died."

"You were *fine,*" Naomi spat.

"Yes, she was. Because of *me.*" Mark waved his hand. "Your father—*her* grandfather—already had a deal with me. It was the usual, of course: riches and fame and protection—you can only starve your family on a pastor's salary for so long before it becomes a problem. He traded his soul to fix it—and all of those riches and fame and protection would continue to be passed down through his family—*with me.*

"But then!" Mark gasped mockingly. "Little Xiomara had an accident. And suddenly he needed a new deal." He looked between Naomi and Xiomara. "A life for the youngest of his family."

"The youngest . . ." Aury repeated, looking to Rafael. "Wait, no, that would be Naomi!"

Marisa laughed. "It *is* Naomi! Take her! Take that bitch!"

"Oh, I can." Mark smiled. "But Naomi is the one who was given everything from your father—and that includes me. Which means—if she accepts—I am inclined to protect *her.*"

"What?" Manuel said. "Did it say that in the will?"

"It didn't have to." Mark shrugged and looked at the cassette tape player. "He said it himself—I pretty much trump any probate court, wouldn't you say?"

He ended with "One of you has to come with me. And the original deal was that he had twelve hours from his last message before I got to take my pick. Those twelve hours end in, oh . . ." Mark glanced at his watch. "Twenty minutes. So . . . how should we decide who lives and who dies?"

Naomi scoffed, the first sound she'd made since Mark's appearance. "If I accept, I'm rich and Xiomara dies because he forgot to 'pay' you for that? If I don't accept, *I* die and she keeps on living—is that it? Sounds like I'm getting the better deal here."

He tapped his nose in response. "You are! Until the natural end of your life, of course. Then you'll be meeting me again under less . . . pleasant circumstances."

Meaning damned. Xiomara could read between the lines.

"So how 'bout it? Who wants to keep the riches and give up heaven?" he asked, with the same cadence of a game show host.

"We don't get anything . . ." Marisa muttered, in stunned realization.

Mark laughed. "Your father loved you so much, he left you with nothing. Isn't that beautiful?"

"What if I make a deal with you?" Manuel asked. "Can you bring my daughter back?"

"For your life?" Mark gave a thoughtful nod. "A fair trade, but one thing at a time. I still haven't been paid for my last job yet, and I can't abide open invoices." He looked at the youngest women in the room. "Make your choice. You have"—he looked at his watch—"nineteen minutes."

Xiomara went over to Naomi. The home aide had squared her shoulders and glared at her. "I'm *not* giving up my life for you."

Xiomara nodded. Her throat was too dry to respond. And her body ached too much to want to live. And if Xiomara had been living her whole life on borrowed time, it was only right that she give that time back for someone else.

"You live." She forced the words out. "It's okay."

"Xiomara, no—" Marisa shouted. Mark snapped his fingers—zipping her lips for her. She screamed against her closed mouth and tried to force her lips apart with her fingernails. Mark laughed with irritation.

"I never liked that loud mouth on you." He shook his head and walked to Xiomara. "Look at you being noble. You really are your mother's daughter. How would you like to do it?"

"Gun, please." She held out her hand. Mark deposited it in her palm like it was nothing—like it was more of a stone than it was a weapon. She couldn't hurt him with it, and he knew it.

Xiomara turned her attention to the weight of the gun. She was surprised by how heavy it was. A sleek but traditional revolver. She slid her hand around the smooth curve of the handle. To mimic what she'd seen on TV, Xiomara pushed her thumb against the cylinder and heard it click outward. Her eyes widened at the number of bullets before shutting it again.

She slowly looked up to Naomi. The only question on her mind was, *Is it a sin to want to live?*

Naomi tensed, leaning away from Xiomara.

"Well?" Mark's smile grew wide and pointed. It was him. He was tempting her, just like Papi Ramon had said he would.

But for the first time ever, Xiomara didn't want to think about Papi

Ramon—the man who had foolishly set all this in motion. Instead, she thought about Josefina, who was robbed not just of life, but of happiness and joy and security. Her family had taken all that and more from Josefina—and someone had to pay.

"I'd like to pay the debt forward," Xiomara said, aiming the fully loaded gun at her older relatives. "You should have been nicer to my mom."

TRAGEDY STRIKES ABREU FAMILY OF THE A-B MILLENIUM SCHOLAR GROUP

Bizarre string of deaths follow the family's recent scandals that hit the news Friday night

Lilith Adams—Sunday, February 15, 2026

On Friday night, the once-beloved Abreu family were exposed for various scandals, earning the ire of the Latino community. By Saturday morning, all but one were dead. Officials say the Abreus had originally gathered to read the will of their recently deceased family patriarch, Ramon Abreu. Once their crimes came to light, they were concerned someone in the family was responsible, and turned on one another. The powerful storm that trapped them inside likely upped the tension and led the way to catastrophe. The struggle became violent. Though speculators cast suspicion on the sole survivor, Xiomara Castillo, an eyewitness account from the family's housekeeper clears her of any wrongdoing. The events unfortunately also claimed the life of Castillo's ex-boyfriend, Marcus Hart, who had rushed over upon hearing the danger she was facing.

The Abreus' spokesman, Mark McClaren, had this to say: "It was only by the grace of God that they survived the night."

AUTHOR'S NOTE

To write about Dominican intercommunity struggles, you have to grapple with anti-Haitian sentiments. Most other people find it strange that Dominicans would ever be so anti-Haitian considering that we share the same island with Haitians, and therefore the same history, but there is more to the concept of community than just proximity. Despite the fact that Haiti is responsible for so much progress enjoyed by Dominicans (progress such as revolting against slavery), Dominicans have often turned around and blamed Haitians for much of their misfortune. A popular example would be the Dominican dictator Rafael Trujillo, who was famously anti-Haitian despite having been born to a Haitian mother. Trujillo would go on to likening Haitians to animals and investing in his own brand of ethnic cleansing by massacring them, as well as any Dominican opponent who dared to stand in his way.

To repeat a popular adage among Black people: Not all skinfolk are kinfolk.

There are a couple of Easter eggs about Trujillo in this book—but I maintained a focus on the subtle notes of anti-Haitianism among the Abreu family. Many Dominicans today may not go as far as demanding the ethnic cleansing of a neighboring country, but they might suggest untrue or exaggerated facts about Haitians. They may still look down on them, hold poor opinions about Haitians, and continue to discriminate against them quietly. While you may think this is leagues better than openly committing genocide, you should know that this is still among the early stages of genocidal behavior. It is not a place to rest and absolve ourselves of reflective thought.

And in case it wasn't obvious as you were reading, Xiomara is not off the hook for her behavior. Though she treated Naomi much better than her other relatives, the power dynamic remains in place, and she makes little progress toward dismantling it.

After everything Naomi went through, wouldn't you agree that she deserves at least that?

ACKNOWLEDGMENTS

This book was so much fun to write, and for that, I have to thank many people. First, I'd like to thank my agent, Kristina Pérez, for hyping me up for this project. I often have a lot of different ideas swirling at one time, and it always helps to have another person keep me focused on the latest one. Special thanks goes to Dr. Robin Lauren Derby, a history professor at UCLA, who had studied Trujillo and was kind enough to answer my email and subsequent questions about Dominican perception of him during his run as a dictator. Though much of that conversation did not make its way into this book, it was illuminating nonetheless.

I'd also like to thank my editor, David Pomerico, who was very supportive as I delved deep into intercommunity Dominican struggles. I know it's a niche topic for so many people, but as a Dominican myself, it's integral to my understanding of who I am and what I care about. Great appreciation goes to Janet Rosenberg, my copyeditor, for catching all of my grammatical errors as well as continuity errors—the Abreu family is so large that it does take time to remember their actions and locations. Thank you to the cover artist and designer, Galine Tumasyan, and cover designer Julianna Lee, as your art is often what gets the book into the hands of curious readers. Thank you to the broader William Morrow team, who walked with me every step of the way and helped to strengthen this story.

Thank you to my mom, Ingrid Rodriguez, without whom I would not be alive or know what ingredients are used in sancocho. She also deserves credit for helping me spell the few the Spanish words that were in this novel—though I can speak Spanish conversationally, I am not the best at writing it.

And of course, thanks to my extended relatives, for providing an abundance of drama that inspired this novel. If you recognized yourself as a character in here and it upset you, well, I only have one thing to say to that:

You should have been nicer to my mom.

ABOUT THE AUTHOR

Vincent Tirado is a nonbinary Afro-Dominican Bronx native. They ventured out to Pennsylvania and Ohio to get their bachelor's degree in biology and master's degree in bioethics. Their debut YA novel, *Burn Down, Rise Up*, was the 2022 winner of the Pura Belpré Award and was a finalist for the 2022 Stoker Awards and 2023 Lammy Awards. Their sophomore YA novel, *We Don't Swim Here*, was called "a chilling ghost story" by *Publishers Weekly*. Their debut adult novel, *We Came to Welcome You*, was published in 2024.

ABOUT THE AUTHOR